GUARDIAN

GUARDIAN

A Young Adult Paranormal Romance novel

By Courtney Cole

Sometimes, the things that go bump in the night are real.

Lakehouse Press, Inc.

This book is an original publication of Lakehouse Press, Inc.

Cover Design by The Cover Lure (Matthew Phillips)

Library of Congress Cataloging-in-publication data

Cole, Courtney

GUARDIAN/Courtney   Cole/Lakehouse   Press Inc/Trade pbk ed

ISBN 13: 978-0692272923

ISNB 10: 0692272925

Printed in the United States of America

Foreward

It's been four years since I wrote this book. And even though my writing has changed and evolved since this book was originally published, *Guardian* will always hold a special place in my heart.

This book is the thing, the catharsis, that pulled me into writing full-time. It's the thing that saved me after my father died unexpectedly. It's the thing that kept me sane.

I don't write much Young Adult fiction nowadays. I tend to write New Adult Romance or Women's Contemporary Romance, but *this book* is what started it all for me. Because of that, when I acquired the rights back from the small press that originally published it, I knew I wanted to put it back out into the world.

In a way, this book is my beginning.
It started me down a path that has been exciting, life-changing and amazing. Every single day of my life, I'm thankful for where I'm at, and for how much I've learned.

I'm thankful that I have readers like you, I'm thankful that you want to read what I write.

Guardian is dedicated to my dad. He was a pastor, and while I'm sure he wouldn't exactly love the explicit nature of the books I tend to write nowadays (sorry, dad!), I know he'd approve of *Guardian*. He raised me to believe in Heaven and Hell, in angels and demons.

I love you, Dad.
Save me a place next to you in Heaven.

GUARDIAN

Chapter One

There is a place, on the edge of despair and grief, where normal life intrudes.

It's a cross-roads.

It's a place where you know you cannot stay, where you must go one way or the other. You can't remain in limbo.

I'm in that place today, my heart dripping as it thaws, as I stand on the edge of Lake Michigan.

I have my father in my hands.

What's left of him, anyway.

I run my thumbs back and forth over the cool metal, lingering on the sharp corners. The small black box has no label or engraved plaque to announce its purpose, so no one could possibly guess at the precious contents it holds within. I can scarcely believe it myself. It's too small to hold my dad. Yet, it does.

The last time my dad spoke to me was seven weeks and three days ago.

That chunk of time would be irrelevant to anyone else. Each second, minute and hour would blend into the next until weeks pass. But to a person who has lost someone significant, someone like me, time becomes a painful unit of measurement.

Seven weeks and three days since *it* happened.

Seven weeks and three days since I was just a normal girl with a normal family and a normal life.

But today, on the Seventh Week and Third Day, I'm very much different.

I'm a still a girl who has experienced loss and tragedy and fear.

But today, I am also a girl who is finally ready to say goodbye.

Not because of any virtuous trait on my part, but mostly because of the guilt.

It isn't fair to make my dad sit on a shelf in a metal box like a knick-knack collecting dust. He's more than that. He *deserves* more than that. So here we are.

"Whitney! Not yet!"

At the sound of my name, I turn to find my little sister bounding over the rippled sand dunes to get to me, her voice frantic and anxious. As she leaps over jagged rocks and sticks, I have to marvel once again at how tiny she is... all arms and legs with her long hair streaming in the wind behind her. Her hair is the exact color of the sand. Just like mine.

"Not yet!" she shouts again as she skids to a halt next to me, splashing into the frigid water. She doesn't even flinch, doesn't even comment on how cold the water was. And it is. Like melted ice.

Her dark eyes are stricken as she stares up at me, sad and afraid. A part of me, a tiny part, is resentful that I'm the one dealing with this... with her grief. It's a huge responsibility, one that I know I'm not ready for. I can barely manage my own.

"We can't do this alone," she beseeches me. "Mom has to be here or she's going to kill us."

She might. For real. With the way she's been lately, it's hard to know what she'll do... or if she'll even react at all.

My mother checked out of reality seven weeks and three days ago. She barely speaks, she barely eats. She doesn't even shower unless I tell her to. I'm not really sure if she has any true thought processes. She's a shell of her former self. We can't wait for her or we'll be waiting all year.

"It's ok, Ellie. She won't kill us." *Probably.* "She'll be happy that we took care of it." *Maybe.*

I grasp the plain little box with one hand and grab Ellie's sweaty hand with the other.

My heart pounds because this is too final. I think that's why I've been putting it off. At least with the box sitting on a shelf in the house, it felt like dad was still with us somehow. If I whispered something to him, I could pretend that he could still hear me.

But not after today.

Today, it will become final.

He'll become gone from us in every way.

We stand still for a moment, allowing the water to gently lap against our legs. Sea gulls scream overhead, circling in huge figure eight's, but I ignore them.

"Are you ready?" I look down at my sister.

Ellie stares back up with wide dark eyes and nods silently. Her face is entirely devoid of color, as pale as her white shorts. Even her lips are white and chalky. I squeeze her hand in encouragement and then hand her the box.

"Why don't you go first, Monster?" I use dad's nickname for her, hoping it will give her comfort. She flinches at the sound, at the feel of the metal box in her hands. "If you want to say something to him, now is the time. You can say anything at all. I know he'll hear you."

Ellie stares down at the box, every ounce of the sadness that she feels swimming in her eyes. She studies the horizon, the box, the water and the sea gulls before she finally looks at me again.

She whispers dejectedly, "I don't know what to say, Whittie."

My heart breaks into a trillion pieces and a lump forms in my throat that I can't seem to swallow. Watching Ellie's grief is almost worse than experiencing my own. She's too small to shoulder such wretched, debilitating pain. Two months ago, her biggest concern was not being able to hula-hoop.

"Just tell him whatever it is that you are thinking today, Ell. It's okay. No one's listening but you, me and daddy." I grasp her bony little shoulder encouragingly, trying to transfer some of my gritty resolve into her by osmosis.

"Okay." Ellie gulps and juts her pointy little chin out. "Daddy, I miss you. Every day. I wish that you hadn't tried to save that boy so that you didn't have to die. I wish…that you were still here with me."

As my sister speaks, my mind whirls back to the day when dad *did* try to save that boy- the stupid tourist who had ignored the red flag whipping in the wind and had gotten swept into a rip current. Red flags are a warning- a bright, obvious statement to anyone coming to the beach. *DO NOT SWIM* because the current is too strong. But the tourist had ignored it and now my father is dead.

"Was that okay, Whit?" Ellie's beseeching voice brings me back to the present, as she stares up at me with wet eyes. I kneel down and hug her gently, taking the box back and balancing it carefully on my knee.

"That was perfect, Ellie." My own voice breaks slightly.

Whoever said that grief gets better with time, that time heals all wounds, is a filthy liar.

I gaze down at the box, at the flat black paint, and try to think of the last words I want my father to hear. I close my eyes for a moment and pretend that he's standing right behind us, watching as we say our goodbyes.

He's smiling at us in encouragement. Picturing his chocolate brown eyes twinkling makes it easier.

"Dad, I don't know what we're going to do without you. We miss you every day."

My voice breaks again and I stop to get a hold of myself. The ice cold water numbs my legs from the knees down as I dig my feet into the silt. I wish my heart could numb so easily.

Ellie slips her tiny hand into my bigger one and squeezes lightly. I look down into her watery smile and then gaze out at the yawning breath of blue in front of us. It stretches from one side of my periphery to the other- as big as the ocean. It makes me feel small, and Ellie is even smaller.

It terrifies me.

"Dad, if you can hear me, can you watch over us? Please? Because mom can't right now and I don't know what to do."

Ellie sucks in her breath and stares at me, and I have to gloss that over. There's no reason to scare her. She has to think that I have everything under control, even if I don't.

"I love you, dad. We're going to be fine. I hope you are too, wherever you are. We'll love you forever."

We're not going to be fine.

Nothing is going to be fine ever again.

I inhale deeply as I push the lid of the box back, letting it fall back on its hinges. Ellie and I both peer inside.

All that's left of Peter Lane fills up a small clear plastic bag and looks like cigarette ashes. It's incomprehensible to me that my dad; a renowned archeologist, a doting father and loving husband, is tied up in a little clear baggie; like loose change or snack crackers or screws. The bag is so small and he'd been larger than life.

He was tall and handsome and had a lightening quick smile. He traveled a lot for his job, but he said good-night by webcam every single night that he was gone. He used funny accents to entertain Ellie and danced in the car at red lights to embarrass me. His eyes crinkled at the corners when he laughed. And even though he couldn't sing a lick, he sang in the shower at the top of his lungs... making our mom roll her eyes.

But he wouldn't be doing any of those things anymore. He wouldn't cheer for one more of my track meets or shoot baskets with me until dark. Not even one more time. He can't. Because he's in little baggie in my hands.

I shake my head, trying to shake the grief from my mind, as if that could possibly happen. I know I'll carry it with me every day of my life.

With shaking fingers and an even shakier breath, I open the top of the baggie and lift it carefully out of the box.

"We love you, dad," I whisper and then empty the contents into the wind.

Ellie and I watch the gray ashes glint in the sun and then drift down to settle on top of the clear water, floating like some sort of amoebic sludge with the current. We back up, out of the water, so that the ashes don't wash onto our legs. I know the current will eventually pull our dad further out into Lake Michigan, far beyond shore.

Just like it had on the day that it killed him.

Somehow, that seems fitting, too.

Ellie wraps her arms around my waist as we stand on the edge of the water for the longest time. The sun shines on our shoulders and the water laps against our toes. Anyone that observes us would assume that we're just enjoying a summer day at the beach. No one would guess that we just said goodbye to our father for the last time.

After a few minutes, Ellie looked up at me.

"Happy birthday, Whitney." Her voice is tiny, soft and uncertain. The knot in my throat clenches even tighter. My mom had forgotten and of course, my dad can't be here. But my baby sister had remembered my sixteenth birthday.

"Thank you," I murmur just as softly before I drop to my knees and hug her.

She smells like the sun, sand and little girl, all mixed up together. And she's strangling me with her tiny bird-like arms. Ellie is surprisingly strong when all of her strength is wrapped around my trachea.

She's not used to this side of me... the patient and loving sister. Before dad died, I was a typical teenager. I teased her, ignored her, pretended she didn't exist.

But that's all changed now, because I'm all she's got.

We take one last look at the water in front of us before we turn and began the hot climb over the sand dunes, walking toward our empty house and our hollow life. We leave our dad floating in the water, clinging to the edge of the shore.

Talk about irony.

Chapter Two

The air is fresh today, so I breathe it in, sucking it down into my lungs as we walk toward home.

In my opinion, the Leelanau Peninsula is the most beautiful place on earth and today is no exception. The air smells like ripe peaches, while the colors around me are vibrant and bright. On one side, I have the gorgeous panoramic view of Lake Michigan, on the other, the lush greenery of the state park.

Northport is a good place to live.

Ellie and I are quiet, immersed in our somber thoughts, as we cross the street from the marina. Our feet thump against the hot wooden boards of the pier, and I concentrate on that. On the noise.

Thump.

Thump.

Thump.

The steps synchronize with my heart and distract me from reality. I'll allow anything to do that, to distract me from reality, because my reality sucks right now.

Hard core.

But just when I'm really into it, into counting the beats and the steps, I feel someone watching me. Someone might as well be reaching out and stroking the back of my neck, lifting the hairs, because that's how strongly I feel their stare.

Turning ever so slightly, I find a tall dark-haired boy sitting with his legs dangling off a slip, next to a small boat. He has to be a tourist because I've never met him before. He sits all alone, deep in thought, and he's not watching me anymore.

His hair is longish and dark, almost black. Even though I can't really see his eyes from this distance, it seems like they're really dark too. His body is tall and slender and he's staring out at the water with a clouded, distracted expression; as though he's thinking about something else, something far removed from today.

Ellie trips over an uneven board, and slams her foot loudly against the boardwalk. I wince at the noise because it startles the boy from his thoughts, and he glances in our direction.

My direction.

He doesn't seem to even notice Ellie. His eyes immediately lock with mine.

I was right. His eyes are very dark.

They're large and serious.

And they're shooting daggers at me.

What the hell? We didn't mean to disturb him. I can't help it that my little sister isn't the most graceful thing on the face of the planet.

I smile apologetically and shrug my shoulders to say, *What can you do? Sisters.*

But he turns away abruptly, without another glance.

I'm beyond stunned, because ohmigod, how rude.

My cheeks burn and Ellie glances up at me.

"What's wrong, Whit?"

"Nothing," I mutter.

I hate the fact that I'm blushing and I hate the fact that I can't stop it. The heat of it spreads from my cheeks to my neck to my chest, and I desperately hope the boy doesn't look over at me again.

I don't want to give him the satisfaction of knowing he affected me.

Because I have every right to walk across this pier. It's a public place and he doesn't own it and he can't decide who gets to make noise and who doesn't.

This is *my* town, stupid tourist.

Just to spite him, I stomp as I walk, making extra noise. Childish? You bet. But I'm not in the mood for judgmental, condescending tourists. I know his type. He's probably from a big city and he came here with his parents for vacation and he thinks he's better than all of us 'small town lake hicks.'

Whatever.

I don't turn around, but I can literally feel his dark gaze burning into my back as I walk away. It scalds into my shoulders, tempting me to look.

Don't look back.

Don't look back.

With a Herculean show of will, I somehow manage not to look.

Ha. I win.

When we turn the corner, I'm out of his line of vision, without ever giving him the satisfaction of a reaction. I feel as though I've accomplished something and that makes me feel the tiniest bit better.

Until I see our house at the end of the street.

I can literally feel my steps falter as we approach, and even Ellie slows a bit, pulling my hand back as we unconsciously delay our return home.

Our sprawling Mediterranean-style house used to look happy. Sunshine practically burst from the windows like something from a shampoo commercial. Now it looks like a place where the Addams family might live. We might as well install a foghorn for a doorbell. It stands dark and gloomy, rising ominously from the horizon in front of us, obviously cloaked in sadness. It is somehow palpable in the air.

My feet rebel and stop moving on the threshold, as if they have a mind of their own. I force them to move and I open the door, dropping our beach bags directly inside.

"Mom, we're home!" I call out of habit, though I know she's not paying attention.

The only answer I receive is the shrill ring of our house phone echoing through the dark rooms. I briefly wonder how long it's been ringing as I rush to find the cordless handset. I find it buried in the couch cushions.

"Hello?" My voice is breathless.

"Maricel?" A harried male voice sounds surprised. The phone must've been ringing awhile, and this man was just waiting for voicemail.

"No, this is Whitney- her daughter."

"Oh, hi, Whitney. This is Dr. Evans. I'm just calling to check on your mom. How is she doing?"

My mom took a leave of absence after dad died because she's lucky enough to have partners in her Pediatric practice that can pick up the slack while she's out.

Dr. Evans is one of them. He's known me since I was in pigtails, which is how I know that he's growing impatient. I've heard it in his voice lately, when he's called to check on mom. He's very nice, but covering her patients in addition to his own must be wearing him out.

I paste on a smile.

"She's fine, Dr. Evans. She's doing so much better. It's been hard, for all of us, but we're adjusting. I'm sure she'll come back to work before long."

Lie, lie, lie.

I feel my ears burn as I lie through my teeth. There's no way she's returning to work any time soon. That would mean that she'd have to shower. And get dressed. And leave the house. And function. And I don't see any of that that happening.

Dr. Maricel Lane is a far cry from the stylish young physician that everyone in Northport knows.

They know the beautiful woman who leaves a subtle trail of Chanel no. 5 in her wake as she walks down the clinic hallways smiling at her little patients. They know the woman they don't hesitate to call if their kids run a high temperature in the night, or break an arm early in the morning. They know the patient and kind woman, the brilliant doctor with the radiant smile.

Right now, she's a woman who hasn't combed her hair in weeks.

With a sigh, I add, "She's really doing better."

Lie.

"That's wonderful!" Dr. Evans exclaims. "We've all been very worried about her. It's such a difficult thing to go through. You've all been in our prayers, Whitney."

As if that does us any good. I instantly feel bad for the snide thought. He means well. I know he does. But no one knows what it's like. No one understands.

I rush to sound pleasant, to make up for my silent rudeness.

"Thank you, Doctor. That's very kind of you. I'll make sure to tell her that you called."

"Thank you, Whitney. Have a good night."

I toss the phone back onto the couch and make my way into the kitchen, searching through the dark cherry cabinets for something to make for dinner. I'm not a great cook yet, but if I don't do it, we won't eat.

I dig some chicken out of the freezer and stick it in the microwave to defrost before wandering upstairs to check on mom. I'm hesitant, because looking for her is creepy sometimes. She moves through the house like a ghost, silent and eerie, and sometimes, I find her lingering in doorways, simply standing there staring at me.

Not saying a word.

It always gives me goose-bumps.

Luckily, that's not the case today.

She's in my dad's study, curled up in his oversized brown leather desk chair with her legs tucked under her and still in her nightgown. It's the same nightgown she's been wearing for three days straight.

Her honey-colored hair, just like mine and Ellie's, hasn't been combed and is tangled in the back. It's a far cry from the sleek French-twist that she usually wears to her clinic. She's absent-mindedly running her fingers lightly back and forth down the length of the mahogany desk, staring blankly at the closed window. I hesitate at the door.

"Mom?"

Her dull hollow eyes vaguely register my presence, as she looks at me fleetingly, without saying a word, and then returns her attention to the closed wall of windows. She's staring at it as though there's a movie playing there, but it's just a wall of closed blinds.

I don't understand it.

I don't understand *her*.

I know grief affects everyone differently. But *God*. Can't she see that she's not the only one grieving? Can't she see that we need her?

She doesn't seem to care.

Sometimes she speaks in short, stilted words. Sometimes she speaks about nonsensical things and sometimes, like today, she doesn't speak at all.

"Mom, we've got to let some light in here."

No response.

I cross the room to open the shades.

At this time of day, the sun is on the other side of the house, making dad's dark study even darker. It definitely needs light.

Mom squints as slats of light floods into the room.

She's probably been sitting in the dark all day. It's getting to the point where I really don't know what to do. But I definitely know what *not* to do.

I can't tell anyone.

To everyone outside of our home, I pretend that everything is fine – because to admit that it isn't, to say the words, would make it real. And that's just way too scary. I can't do that.

So, instead, I do the best I can to hold everything together. To pretend everything is normal.

I've been sorting through mom's mail, paying bills by signing her name, grocery shopping, and taking care of Ellie. I haven't liked it, in fact, I've hated it. But there's nothing else I can do. If I don't do it, everything will fall apart.

Everything.

"Mom, Ellie and I threw dad's ashes in the lake today. It wasn't fair to keep him on a shelf in the living room. He would've hated that. Are you mad?"

My mother stares at the wall harder, concentrating even more on the blank wall. And then she closes her eyes tightly, her lashes brushing her cheeks. A single tear escapes from the corner of one eye. I suck in a breath. It's an emotional reaction that I haven't seen from her yet.

"Are you mad?" I murmur. "Should we have waited for you?"

She doesn't answer. But after a moment, she gives a barely discernible shake of her head.

"I'm making some chicken. Why don't you take a bath while it cooks? Do you want me to start running the water for you?"

She nods silently, her eyes still closed, so I pad quietly down the hall to her bedroom and cross over thick carpet into her bathroom. Adobe colored tile envelope me and a thick white rug pokes up between my toes, making it seem like an upscale Southwestern spa.

Since mom was raised in Latin America, she absolutely hates winter, or anything even slightly resembling freezing precipitation. So each year, when the snow drifts in huge mounds around us and the ice covers everything in thick sheets, she threatens to move us all to Arizona. Or Venezuela, her homeland. But she hasn't... yet.

Despite my best intentions, I glance hesitantly toward my dad's sink. Everything is exactly the way he had left it. His razor, his toothbrush, his cologne. Just as if he's coming home from work tonight like usual and would be using it.

But he won't be. I swallow hard and unbidden, tears fill my eyes. I wipe them away impatiently. When am I going to stop crying? *God.*

A picture of my parents, taken from their last trip together, sits on the counter. They're laughing. Mom's looking up at dad, and he has his arm wrapped around her shoulders, pulling her up to him, kissing her forehead. The Mediterranean Sea sparkles in the sunlight behind them. I love that picture.

But those happy, carefree times are gone.

Long gone.

I quickly start mom's bath before I flee the bathroom without a backward glance.

"Ellie?" I call as I walk through the kitchen, "Where are you?"

"I'm here," she answers quietly from the long mahogany dining room table.

And sure enough, there she is, surrounded by workbooks as she works on her summer reading project without anyone even prompting her.

I flip the chicken over, start it up again, and go sit beside her.

She stares at her workbook, pushing her hair out of her face with grubby fingers. I gulp. That stupid lump is back in my throat, constricting my airway and making it hard to swallow. I swallow harder, trying to dislodge it by force.

"Are you ok?" I examine her as I speak. "I know today was hard. It was hard for me, too."

Ellie used to be a normal, laughing six-year old who had squealed when dad tickled her and had annoyed the crap out of me by getting into my stuff all of the time. She has morphed into a serious little old woman in a child's body who stares at me now with dark, solemn eyes. The sparkle in them is gone.

She's been having horrible nightmares, too. Dreams so dark that she dreads going to sleep. Every night before bed, she lines her stuffed animals up in a militant row on the side of her bed next to the wall. They have strict instructions to watch for anything scary. But they're only plush stuffed with cotton. They can't stop her nightmares.

She ends up in my bed at least five nights out of the week, although I can't stop her nightmares either. Sometimes she wakes me up and sometimes she doesn't; I just find her curled up beside me in the morning.

"I'm okay, Whittie."

She stares at me again, looking hopelessly small and vulnerable. I lean over and hug her tightly.

"You know that you can talk to me anytime, right?"

Ellie nods silently. "Why are you being so nice to me, Whit? You don't have to. You can just be normal."

That puts another lump in my throat. I've done a complete one-eighty since my father died, in every way. It's been a necessity, but hearing her small words make me ache to go back in time and be nicer to her, back when I didn't have to be.

"Well, obviously I'm not really your sister. I'm an alien in your sister's body. You'd better watch out for me."

I waggle my eyebrows dramatically together and cross my eyes, trying to make her laugh. She humors me with a giggle, but it's not reflected in her dark eyes. I sigh.

"It's ok, Ellie. I don't usually feel like laughing, either. But I promise, one day soon, we'll start feeling better."

Will we?

I feel wooden as I cut the chicken into strips and fry it before I toss it into salads.

Mom doesn't join us for dinner.

This isn't new. I usually make a plate for her and put it in the fridge, and the next day I find it in the sink with a couple of bites gone, the rest dried and caked to the plate.

She doesn't appear while we're cleaning the kitchen or while Ellie takes a bath, either.

So after I tuck Ellie into bed and arrange her stuffies in battle formation around her, I quietly peek in on mom. She's curled up on her bed now, a bed so large that she looks like a toddler curled up in the middle of it.

She apparently had taken the bath and she has a clean nightgown on, but she didn't wash her hair. It's still tangled and bone-dry. Her thick lashes rest against the dark circles under her eyes and I find myself hoping that she gets some sleep tonight. I pull a blanket up over her and quietly creep back out. She never opens her eyes.

Ellie and I share a bathroom, which means I have to clear out the rubber dolphin and floating plastic rings before I can run my own bubble bath, so that I can finally wash the grit from the beach off of me.

I pull my hair up into a pony-tail and then twist it up on top of my head so that it won't get wet. I've been trying to grow it out so that it would be long and glamorous for senior pictures in a couple of years, but that doesn't seem so important anymore. Right now, it falls just between my shoulder blades.

I've only just settled into the chin-deep water with a book when my phone vibrates on the counter. I glare at it in annoyance.

Like every other teenager on the face of the planet, it's usually attached to my hip and I like it that way. But right now, I know I won't be able to enjoy my bath until I see who texted me. With a sigh, I step from the peony-scented bubbles to grab my phone, finding my best friend's name displayed on the screen.

Holy cow!!! I'm downtown getting pizza- and Brady's here. Looks like they're back from vacation!!! Woo-Hoooo!

Delaney's emotions always show through loud and clear, good or bad, even in her text messages. I smile thinking of her mercurial moods. She's been all worked up lately because she hasn't seen Brady Parker around town for a couple of weeks. She's been terrified that he'd moved back to California, which would be a devastating state of affairs to every female in Northport.

Brady had transferred here two years ago and every girl in school- probably even the Jr. High girls- had lusted after him ever since…with good reason.

He's rather breathtaking.

Dark blonde hair, blue eyes, perfect brilliant smile. He's probably even a surfer. I don't usually go for fair-haired blue-eyed guys, but in his case, I could probably make an exception.

I text Delaney back.   *Great-you can rest easier tonight.*

I can almost see her roll her eyes as she reads it. She's never understood why I don't get as worked up about things as she does. I can't adequately explain to her that no one on earth gets as worked up as she does. Every cell in her body has drama queen DNA in it.

I shiver in the air-conditioning and decide to give up on the bath.

Throwing on my favorite pair of PJs, I grab a book and dive into the pink-sheeted sea of my bed instead.

Try as I might, though, all I seem to do is stare at the words on the page without comprehending them.

I should be riveted. I love vampire books. And werewolf books. Or basically any magical, unrealistic story-line. Anything to take me away from the reality that is my life.

But it isn't happening tonight. I'm restless, unfocused. Probably because we laid my dad to rest today, all alone, just Ellie and me. He's gone now and he's never coming back.

It's official.

With a sigh, I give up and snap the book closed before I turn off the light.

The sooner I go to sleep, the sooner it *won't* be my Sweet Sixteen birthday that I'm *not* celebrating with my parents, without a cake, a party or a new car. I feel even sorrier for myself because I know the elaborate plans that my mom had made a couple of months ago for a party. It was going to be a huge event, and my father would've been there.

But the day is here... and everything has changed.

No one is here but me, in my bedroom, alone.

Happy birthday to me.

I close my eyes and burrow into my pillow as I try to sleep, as I try to escape this life.

It's a life I never thought I'd have, a life I most certainly don't want.

I'm still feeling sorry for myself as the blackness of sleep finally overtakes me.

I don't know what time it is when I shoot straight upward like a rocket. Something had yanked me from the oblivion of sleep, something loud and shrill scraping my window.

My room is completely dark and I glance at my clock in confusion.

3:00 a.m.

As my heart pounds hard against my ribcage, I quickly scan every corner of the room.

In the last few hours, dark shadows had migrated onto my pink walls, but they're familiar, nothing out of the ordinary, although in the night, they seem twisted and scary.

I remain motionless as I allow the sleep-induced fog to clear from my brain.

As I sit, I feel common sense and logic slowly returning.

Of course nothing had touched my window because my bedroom is on the second floor. Nothing can reach it.

And there are no trees near enough to brush against it. It was just a dream.

It was only a dream.

I chant it silently to myself like a mantra as I consciously slow my breathing down, hoping that my racing pulse will soon follow. It was only a dream.

But just as I'm calming down, I hear it again.

A high-pitched shrill shriek, reminiscent of fingernails on a chalkboard, scraping down my window. I gasp and pull my feet up to my chest, which is when I notice the temperature.

I notice because I can see my breath.

Timidly, I blow a puff out again, watching the way my breath turns white in the air.

Holy crap. Oh my God.

What the hell?

The sound stops and stillness surrounds me once again, the silence so loud that it echoes in my ear.

Nothing moves around me, the shadows are perfectly still as they twist across my wall. They look like mangled fingers and arms and legs, but they don't move.

My legs are weak and shaking, but I know I have to move. I have to move off my bed because it feels like something is under it. Something terrifying.

With a leap, I bound across the room, my feet hitting the floor several feet away from the edge of my bed.

The floor is ice cold, as though it had been covered in a blanket of snow.

I'm trembling as I race to the far wall and check the thermostat. Because that's the only explanation. I must've bumped it earlier, I must've turned the AC way down.

But the luminous numbers stare at me in contradiction.

74 degrees.

It must be broken. *It has to be broken.*

My breath is coming in pants now, terrified, anxious pants.

My fear isn't logical. I know there's nothing here. I'm the only one in this room.

Or am I?

The air seems to push at me from all around, something dark, something heavy, something real. Something unseen.

My fingers shake, my legs tremble, and then all of a sudden, they can no longer support my weight. I go down like a pile of bricks, collapsing onto the floor. I lie still because I can't move, because something seems to sit on my chest, holding me down.

The shadows start to move, to slither across the walls, to reach and pull and dance.

I struggle to focus, to see what it is.

But all I can see are the numbers on the thermostat suddenly moving, rapidly counting down from 74 to 20.

Twenty degrees?

The air is frigid as I suck it in, as I try to pull the ice crystals into my mouth so I can breathe.

All of a sudden, there's a blackness in front of me. It hovers over me, a shapeless mass, sucking in the cells of the air, the atoms and the molecules. It's darker than the blackness of my room, blacker than the blackest black.

Something is here.

With me.

"Dad?" I whisper in a white puff. Because what else could it be?

I reach out a finger to touch it, and then I can't see anything else, because the darkness of it surrounds me, bleeding into everything else, even my vision. The shriek is back, screaming into my ears, bleeding into my brain.

Then there's nothing.

Chapter Three

I open my eyes to morning light.

With a gasp, I sit straight up in bed, finding that I'm safe and sound, tangled in my covers. My book is on my nightstand, my thermostat reads 74. My clock announces that it's nine a.m.

Everything is fine.

What the hell?

At three a.m, I'd been in a puddle on the floor by the window. Hadn't I? How did I get back in bed? What was the blackness that had shrouded my room?

Cautiously, I creep from my bed to the window, looking down.

The tops of the cherry trees rustle soothingly, tossing their sweet scent into the breeze. I open my window and take a deep breath.

Below me, my dad's hammock sways emptily between the trees. My mom's greenhouse stands quiet and still, covered in ivy. Everything is normal.

Leaning out, I examine the side of my house and my bedroom window, looking for evidence of damage. After something so loud had scraped it, surely it must be torn or scratched.

But no.

There's nothing there, not one mark.

Stunned, I sink back onto my heels on the floor, glancing about my room.

Everything is normal.

It didn't happen.

It was one hell of a realistic dream.

I'm such an idiot.

Blearily, I stare at the clock again. I'm an idiot who has to be in counseling in an hour. If I don't hurry up, I'm going to be late.

I take a quick shower, all the while lamenting the fact that I had gotten myself talked into counseling in the first place.

After my father had died, my school counselor, Mr. Blaine, had shown up on my doorstep.

You need to talk to someone, Whitney. It's important.

And even though I've never liked him, I agreed, just so that he would leave, so that I could curl up into a ball and cry in peace.

But now it's time to pay the piper. I have to actually go.

I get dressed, get Ellie dressed and dropped off at her friend's house for a play-date, and I stop in at the local coffee shop to get a latte on the way.

I deserve caffeine after the nightmares I had last night.

I'm very aware that every eye in the coffee house is focused on me. It's uncomfortable and it puts me on edge because I can practically hear their thoughts. I can see the same exact thing reflected on almost every face.

That's Whitney Lane- the girl whose dad just died in that horrible drowning. Should I say something?

Please don't, I beg silently as everyone continues to study me, so non-discreetly that it isn't even funny.

No one knows how to act around me anymore- they don't know whether to say something or not say something; whether they should ask how I'm doing...or not.   And of course, everyone knows exactly what happened.

Northport's a small town, where everyone knows everything about everybody.   It's tiresome.   But not as tiresome as the Mean Queens.

Courtney Williams and Brandy Delacour have been our token 'mean girls' from the time we were in kindergarten. I can clearly remember them arguing over whose daddy had the nicest car even back then. They're both snotty and superficial- and both are meaner than snakes.

As I wait in the mile long line, I overhear them whispering over their non-fat lattes from a nearby table.

"My mom told me that her mom doesn't even come out of the house anymore. She heard it from old Mrs. Levvins!" I can tell from Brandy's animated whisper that she's relishing the gossip.

I cringe and make a mental note not to take our elderly neighbor her newspaper anymore when it rains. If she wants to gossip about us, she can get her bluish bouffant wet from now on.

"Well," Courtney one-upped her smugly, not bothering to be as quiet, "I heard that Whitney can't even leave her little sister alone in the house with their mom... because she's afraid that Dr. Lane will hurt her!   She already tried to kill herself- my mom told me."

Oh my God.

The tops of my ears burn and I can't even think clearly.

Why do people spread such hateful gossip? Don't they have anything better to do?   I know Courtney is completely aware that I can hear her. I can tell from the vicious, overly-loud dramatic whisper that she's doing it on purpose.

Don't give her a reaction.

I take a deep breath.

Cleansing breath in, cleansing breath out.

The cheerful yoga instructor on my mom's DVDs always touts cleansing breaths. They actually seem to work because they give me something else to focus on.

Time seems to literally stop as I try to be nonchalant and act like I don't hear them.

Each of the five minutes that I stand in line stretch out painfully, but finally my turn at the counter comes and I hurriedly order an iced coffee and wait for them to make it.

It seems to take a hundred years, although it only takes a minute.

I grab it and hurry for the door to avoid Courtney and Brandy, who look like they're getting up to leave. In my haste to escape, I plow directly into a brick wall.

A brick wall dressed in a lime green t-shirt.

I peek up from under my eyelashes to find Brady Parker grinning down at me.

Perfect.

I had almost laid out the most beautiful boy in town. Color instantly floods my face and I feel dizzy with embarrassment.

"Oh God. Sorry, Brady. Really. I'm clumsy."

I try not to look at his face as my checks burn, but I can't help it. My eyes keep migrating in that direction with a will of their own. I find myself fixated on the dimple in his left cheek as my heart flutters wildly.

"No, you're not, Whit. You're just distracted." He smiles at me and I swallow hard and blink.

Blond, blue-eyed Brady Parker truly is breathtaking with his smile and his muscles and his charm. It's definitely an injustice to the rest of the males on earth that he'd been born so gorgeous.

"Do you need a hand?" He aims a flawless smile in my direction.

Wow. Beautiful *and* helpful.

At his question, Courtney's head whips around; even though already stepped out the door. I take a great bit of satisfaction in his question, and the fact that she hears it.

In the two years that Brady has been here, he hasn't shown the slightest bit of interest in Courtney, much to her disappointment and chagrin. It certainly hasn't been due to her lack of trying. She's tried, and she's been shut down. She's not used to that kind of rejection. It makes her even meaner.

"Um, no. I think I've got it," I say as I juggle my slippery coffee cup and my purse. The corners of his mouth twitch and he steps closer.

"It sort of looks like you need some help."

He opens the door for me and I'm about to thank him when he puts his hand lightly on my arm and leans his head in so that his mouth is right next to my ear. His warm breath grazes my cheek as mine halts.

"If you need anything, Whitney," he says quietly. "Even if it's just to talk... you can call me. I know what it's like." He smiles at me in a gentle, understanding way and continues walking out the door.

I can still feel exactly where his hand had been on my arm. I force myself to take a breath and then to take another one.

I know what it's like.

Of course he does. I don't know the details, but I'd heard that his brother drowned in a sailing accident right before they moved here. It's why they moved away from California.

I stand in place for a second, clutching my coffee, as I try to collect my thoughts.

"Whitney!" A loud nasal voice firmly breaks into my concentration.

I turn to see Mr. Blaine walking quickly toward me from a table in the corner.

Seriously? What are the odds?

I know Mr. Blaine means well, but I just don't know him very well, and truthfully, I don't want to change that status. He had just come to Northport shortly after my dad died, after our previous counselor, Mrs. Love, moved out of state with her husband.

To his credit, he's trying really hard to step into Mrs. Love's shoes, but it's hard to talk to someone you barely know.

I sigh and walk back toward him, to where he stands waiting for me. His pale, pasty skin is damp with a thin sheen of shiny sweat already, and I can see yellow stains under his arms. Nice.

"Whitney," he begins in an institutional voice, "Let's talk outside today… on a bench in the park. We don't have to go back to the school."

I nod and let him lead me to a nearby park overlooking the quaint main street. It's away from pedestrians, and fairly private. I should feel comfortable enough to talk to him here, but I don't.

I wait uncomfortably for him to start.

He stares at me. "You're signed up for Driver's Ed. Would you like for me to cancel it? You can take it at a later date, if you're not feeling up to it just yet."

I'd completely forgotten. My parents had insisted that I take it so that my car insurance isn't so high. And so that I'm as safe as I can be on the roads.

It had been especially important to my dad.

I swallow hard and shake my head. "No, I'll still take it. My dad wanted me to."

Mr. Blaine nods. "Okay. How are you doing?"

Every part of his body appears doughy and soft, but his dark blue eyes are piercing as they search my face. They're as sharp as a razor, which is in direct contrast with the rest of him. I hadn't noticed this about him before. The sharpness of his stare is unexpected and I don't know what he thought he would see. Weakness, maybe?

"I'm okay," I tell him. "It's getting a little better."

Lie.

He stares at me, like he's waiting for more, so I continue.

"I've been having some nightmares, but I think that's normal. Considering."

He nods quickly. "I would be surprised if you *weren't* having nightmares," he agrees. "It's perfectly normal. Just remind yourself, when you wake up, that you were just dreaming. It's all you can do."

He waits for more, but suddenly, I feel claustrophobic. I can't sit here and talk about it. I just can't. I stand up.

"I really have some other things I need to do today. Can we do this another time?"

"Sure. I'll be going through files in my office this summer. Feel free to stop in after Driver's Ed. You don't need to make an appointment."

He looks at me expectantly, waiting for me to agree. I nod. I'm always more agreeable when I'm discussing tomorrow (or next week) rather than today.

"But Whitney, make sure you do stop in. You've been through a tragedy. You can't handle it alone."

"I'm not alone," I start to say, but he's already walking away.

God, he's awkward.

With a sigh, I start walking home and notice Courtney and Brandy had abandoned their bench right outside of the cafe and are now further down the sidewalk- directly in my path.

They're probably lying in wait for me. Fabulous- this day just keeps getting better.

"Counseling go okay, Whitney?" Brandy asks as innocently as she can in her snarky voice.

I ignore her and walk past as they giggle together, wondering how many years a 16-year old could get for justifiable homicide. I don't know why they feel the need to be so mean. I've never done a thing to them. Except ponder homicide.

***

Icy water pounds against the shore, where I stand nervously watching a faceless dark head bob in the current. My dad is already swimming out to reach the boy with long, strong strokes oblivious to the fact that he's swimming towards death. I try to scream- to tell him to come back, but no sound escapes from my frozen lips and my legs are planted firmly in the sand. He just keeps swimming.

Nooooo, I try to scream. But no sound comes out.

Suddenly, dad is gone- replaced with Coast Guard boats and red and white Search and Rescue jet skis. Divers dive under repeatedly, coming up empty-handed, just as I know they will. I've lived this before and I can't change it now. And since I can't change it, I stand on the beach waiting in horror. Again. Because I know what happens next.

My dad's bloated, lifeless body washes up at my feet, rolling over so that his blank eyes are staring up at me.

I wake with a start to find Ellie standing directly over me.

Why is she here? Had I been screaming?

I can see that I'd kicked my flowery comforter off the bed, and my sheets are wound tightly around my hands like ropes. No wonder I couldn't feel my fingers.

I consciously force myself to loosen my vice-like grip. My hair is soaked in sweat. I can feel the dampness on my face, in my hairline and on my pillow. I don't usually sweat much, so this is new.

"Whitney, it's just a dream. Are you okay?"

Ellie's anxious dark eyes study my face, trying to find the reason for the terror hidden there. Her small hand feels for mine, soothingly. She understands nightmares. She doesn't know though, that tonight mine was based in reality. It was a memory.

"Go get your blankie and come crawl in bed with me."

She nods and creeps back off toward her bedroom.

I sit up and smooth my damp hair back away from my face. My hands are clammy, too.

Good grief, what's wrong with me? Normal people try to block out disturbing images, they don't replay them like a movie in their dreams.

I breathe deeply, trying to get rid of the horrible pictures in my head. It doesn't work. My dad's dead brown eyes haunt me.

I swing my legs over the side of my bed and sit for a second trying to collect myself. My heart still thumps like it's trying to escape. I need a drink or something to reboot my brain so that I have any hope at all of going back to sleep. I wait until Ellie climbs into my bed with her stuffed tiger and her blankie before I set off for the kitchen.

The stone tiles are hard and cold under my feet. The moon shines through the enormous windows lining the back wall of the breakfast nook as I grab a glass from the cupboard and fill it with ice water.

As the icy water touched my lips, my dream instantly flashes back to me.

I can practically feel the icy cold lake water pounding against my legs again.

It's almost like I have PTSD. I witnessed a horrific thing and I can't get past it. I have strange triggers and strange nightmares and I don't know if it's going to end.

But obviously, ice water isn't going to work. I dump my glass in the sink and walk into the living room instead.

My dad's giant saltwater aquarium casts a soft blue glow from the back corner of the room. He loved collecting new sea life to add to it. Once, he had a rare fish shipped all the way from Africa. Apparently, he'd been on a waiting list for an entire year for that one little fish.

Of course, he didn't tell mom about it during the course of that year... she found out when it arrived and she saw the invoice. That was an interesting night in the Lane household. The black and white striped Chrysurus Angel fish leisurely swims past me now, intent on swimming laps around the tank, oblivious to the fact that its benefactor is no longer here.

I slip past the bubbling tank toward the front door.

I don't know why, but I can practically hear the porch swing calling my name. I know that the soothing, rhythmic swing can help steer me to sleep. As I pull the door open, however, a screeching noise from the kitchen startles me, halting my footsteps.

Again?

My blood turns to ice in my veins as I listen, my fingers frozen on the door.

Something heavy and metallic scratches the tile, like fingernails on a chalkboard once again. I twist around and quickly scan my memory- trying to recall an object that would make that kind of noise in the kitchen, but come up blank.

Even though my legs are frozen in terror, I summon every ounce of my courage and quietly creep back to the kitchen, peeking around the kitchen doorway.

There's nothing there.

Everything is in place.

Everything on the granite counters is as it should be. Canisters housing sugar and flour stand undisturbed. The cordless phone lays motionlessly on the counter next to the stove where I had placed it after talking to Delaney at dinner. The rugs are uncrumpled on the floor in their normal places.

Nothing is out of place here.

But I had definitely heard something in this room.

I scan the room again. It's still the same. Not a single thing is disturbed.

The window over the sink is closed. The dishwasher isn't running. There's no source for any kind of noise.

Good Lord. Am I going crazy, like my mother?

Because my fight or flight instinct has definitely been triggered, as if there's a threat lurking nearby. I want to run, far away from here, as far as I can go.

But there's no reason. Nothing is here.

I feel just like I did last night... only I'm not dreaming now.

I gulp hard.

Please God, don't let me go crazy. Please.   I shake my head and walk as normally as I can out onto the porch. There's nothing here. I don't need to creep. Although I do look over my shoulder twice before I open the front door.

As I settle back into the cushions of the swing, I begin to feel more peaceful.

My mom and I used to sit out here... snapping fresh peas for dinner, talking about nothing or drinking tea. It's a safe, happy place for me to be. The rhythmic rocking does its job, just as I knew it would. My eyes start to get heavy and I allow them to close.

"Whitney?"

My eyes pop wide open at the sound of a low male voice.

Brady Parker is standing on the top step of my porch, looking just as impossibly glorious in the moonlight as he does in the sun. I sit up quickly.

Am I dreaming?

"Brady? What are you doing here? It's like... really late." I know it's after midnight.

My front lawn is illuminated with the violet hues of night, as the stars twinkle mutely from behind the low-hanging cloud cover.

"I know," Brady sighs as he walks toward me. "I couldn't sleep, so I went for a walk to get some fresh air and saw you walk out of your house."

He stops in front of me, looking down at me observantly, his blue eyes sparkling.

"It appears that you have the same insomnia problem. Can I sit with you?"

My heart stills for a beat, before resuming at double-time pace, thudding lightly against my ribcage. Brady Parker is on my porch. His masculine scent wafts lightly toward me in the breeze and I take a deep breath, inhaling it, fighting the urge to hyperventilate.

"Of course- please, sit."

He sits down and as he settles in, he pulls me back against him as though we had sat in such a way a million times before. It feels that comfortable as I rest my head naturally in the crook of his shoulder. I feel my nerves still and I wonder what I had been so nervous about in the first place.

Just as I'm about to remark about how comfortable I feel with him, he tilts my face back with his finger... and lowers his lips to mine. He hesitates a fraction of an inch away, staring into my eyes. Need fills me up in a way I've never experienced before and I feel as though I might die if he doesn't kiss me.

"Kiss me," I whisper.

"Do you want me to?" he asks softly, waiting for permission. I nod.

Of course I do.

I lean up to meet him and his lips consume me. My head starts spinning. His mouth is hot against mine and the porch feels as though it's a different place, a hazy dream-like place where moonbeams are the only reality.

This is a dream, I realize.

But then it doesn't matter because his arms wrap around me and his hands are everywhere... running lightly down my arms, over my back and across my hips. I arch against him, completely uninhibited, whispering his name. It feels so unbelievably good to be in his strong embrace, to feel just for a second that everything is fine...to feel like I'm normal.

"Whitney," he murmurs against my ear as he nuzzles my neck lightly.

His lips feel like raw silk, and cause goose bumps to form everywhere on my body. "I've wanted you ever since I saw you the very first time. Is that bad?" I'm molded against his body and I melt even further into him.

Nothing feels bad at this moment.

I'm feeling something other than grief for the first time in weeks. And that feels very right to me.

I've been waiting for this. For the grief to pass, to feel alive, to feel good, to feel safe and sound and normal.

Everything around me swirls and melts together. I can't think straight, but I don't let that bother me. Right now is a time for feeling, for experiencing. Not for thinking.

My body seems to know what to do without my brain having to tell it. My back arches against Brady again, inherently trying to get closer. He pulls me to him, then gently twists us around so that he comes down on top of me. His hands are gentle but his mouth is rough as he kisses me hard on the neck. I like it.

He smiles in the moonlight and I close my eyes.

When I open them again, the porch is filled with sunlight.

I blink. I'm still on the porch-swing. I look around. Everything is normal. And very bright. I'm alone, except for the neighbor's cat sitting in the corner licking her paws.

Brady's gone.

Because he was never here in the first place. It was a dream. An elaborate, very real dream. I remind myself, just as Mr. Blaine had advised, that I was dreaming.

Everything is okay because it wasn't real.

The details of it are fading quickly, but it had been a lovely dream. Perfect, in fact. I felt good—really, really good for the first time in almost two months.

I'm a little astonished at my behavior- even if it had only been in my head. I'm not usually so impetuous- even in my dreams. But even so, I feel a strange sense of loss that the wonderful familiarity in Brady's smile had only been a figment of my imagination, because at the time, it was so freaking real.

The dreams are getting more and more realistic, to the point that I can't tell them from reality.

Because you're going crazy.

I ignore the niggling whisper in my brain.

I'm not going crazy. I can't be.

I jog up the stairs and turn on the shower, brushing my teeth as I wait for the water to get warm. I'm stiff and sore from sleeping on the wooden porch swing and I spit out my toothpaste so that I can stretch.

As I do, I glance in the mirror and freeze.

There's a bruise on my neck.

A purplish-red splotch stretches into the curve of my neck where my neck meets my shoulder.

My fingers shake as I touch it, as I trace the edges.

It can't be.

I can't have a hickey because Brady was never here.

It was a dream.

I must've bruised it on the wood of the swing as I slept.

I fight to believe that. I *have* to believe that because it's the only explanation, because I was alone on the porch last night.

You can't give yourself a hickey on the neck.

It's impossible.

But it's entirely possible that I'm crazy.

Chapter Four

An hour later, I find myself folded into a school desk and sitting next to Delaney, waiting for Mr. Divine to arrive and start teaching us the mechanics of driving.

It's funny—a couple of months ago, I'd been so excited when I turned in my registration forms. Now, I couldn't care less that I'm here or even that in a few weeks I'd have my driver's license.

I bounce my foot against the side of my chair.

I feel like I have better things to do than be here in this hot room, cooped up in a classroom in June. I could be at home, trying to figure out what's going on with me.

Besides, the air in the room is already stale, even though it's bright and early. It has the distinct odor of a place that's crammed full of too many bodies, some of which don't believe in regular bathing.

Beside me, Delaney is busy mutilating a candy bar.

"Why don't you put it out of its misery?" I ask, laughing at her. She picks at it again gingerly and precisely, like she's dissecting a frog in Biology.

"You mock," she says, lifting one perfectly sculpted eyebrow. She's been addicted to the tweezers since eighth grade and uses them diligently every morning. I always tell her that she's going to run out of eyebrows.

"Of course I do- I've never known anyone but you who picks the peanut butter out of a peanut butter cup. What's the point in that? Why don't you just get a different kind of candy bar—or maybe even something a little healthier for breakfast?"

She rolls her eyes. "You don't get it, Whit."

"Apparently," I shake my head, but she's not paying attention.

Instead, her eyes are frozen to the side of my neck and her mouth is hanging open in a perfect O.

"What the...what?" she breathes. "Who did that? You're holding out on me! Ohmigod!"

She drops her breakfast and practically bounds over her chair to examine my bruise. I try to protest, but it's not working. She pulls my hair back and has her face buried in my neck within a second.

"It's a bruise from sleeping on the porch swing last night. My neck was against the chain." *I think.*

She stares at me dubiously.

"For real?"

I nod. "When I have my first kiss, you'll be the first to know. And if things progress to a hickey stage, well you'll definitely know about that."

She relaxes, pacified now. "That's true. You haven't even kissed anyone yet. You're such a child, Whit."

She shrugs her shoulders, trying to act sophisticated, but it only makes me laugh. "As if. You've only kissed one person, and that was during Spin the Bottle."

She stares at me drolly, but her reply is cut short when the classroom door opens. I glance up, expecting to see Mr. Divine, but Brady walks in instead, surrounded by three other football players.

The football team tends to stick together, even in the off-season. Drew Hayden brings up the rear like an overgrown blonde moose. Like many of the kids in Northport, I've him since kindergarten. In fact, I threw up all over him once after afternoon snack that year.

Good times.

He grins and waves at me now as they all take seats in the back. Brady also smiles at me- the normal, dazzling Brady Parker smile. Not the one from my dreams, the one laced with the familiarity of a lover.

Gah. That crazy-sexy-perfect dream that is getting me worked up again just thinking about it. So I stop thinking about it and watching them, too, but I hear them rough-housing while they wait. Heaven forbid they just sit quietly and wait like the rest of us.

Football guys. I mentally roll my eyes.

Pretty soon crumpled up balls of paper are flying past me and hitting the back of other unfortunate heads- slightly nerdy boys who made the mistake of sitting on the front row. I turn around and glare at them. I hate bullies.

"What?" Justin demands. "Do you have a problem, Whitney?"

After Brady moved here, Justin Graber had quickly become his closest friend.

I don't know how Brady can even stand being around him—he's loud-mouthed, arrogant and annoying- and has been since grade school. He has ears that are too big for his head, his face gets too red at the slightest amount of exertion and he wears his letter jacket, dripping with football awards, everywhere he goes until it gets ridiculously warm outside. He's the epitome of obnoxious.

He's staring at me now with an agitated sneer on his red face. He's never liked me and I don't know why, but that's ok. The feeling is definitely mutual.

"Knock it off, Graber," Brady grins as he punches his arm, which of course triggers a punching contest, which of course ends up being a good-natured wrestling match on the floor with desks getting shoved out of the way.

I'll never understand football guys.

I shake my head and turn back around in my chair. Thankfully, Mr. Divine hurries in and starts class. As his dull monotone voice stretches from one hour to the next, Delaney kills time by passing me notes, old-school style, complete with doodled pictures in the margins.

She thinks she's being incredibly crafty, but in reality, she's blatantly obvious. As her long pale arm stretches to drop her latest missive onto the center of my desk, Mr. Divine appears out of nowhere, intercepting her pass.

"What do we have here, ladies?" His stern tone is disapproving.

I cringe. Mr. Divine isn't known for his leniency or sense of humor. I only hope that this note didn't say anything insulting about him, like her last one. It had read: "Check out Mr. D's hair. So bad! It's got to be a toupee- or a really bad dye-job." And then she'd drawn a picture of Mr. Divine with two hairs on top of his head, combed over, while he held tightly onto his crotch.

I hold my breath. Is it possible to get detention in the summertime?

"Let's take a look…if it's important enough to interrupt class, then it's important enough to share with everyone."

Please, please God- don't let it be horrible.

I glance at Delaney and she has the classic deer in the headlights look frozen on her face. Not a good sign.

"Hmm. Interesting." Mr. Divine raises his eyebrows as he peers over the edge of the note at me, then looks at the rest of the class as he crumples it up in his hand.

"Mr. Parker, apparently you've been staring at Whitney throughout the course of class today. Please keep your attention on me so that you might actually learn something."

Oh my God. It's worse than I ever imagined.

My cheeks explode into flame as Mr. Divine stalks back to the front of the class and starts a movie about accidents. I keep my eyes fixed straight in front of me while the whole class giggles.

I want to curl up and die under my chair. I glance over at Laney and she gives me her best "I'm sorry" face. I'll have to kill her later. For now, I keep my eyes glued on the excruciatingly dated movie showcasing horrible accidents caused by negligent driving. It's an effective way to tune out the tittering class.

As I observe the twisted metal of a circa 1985 Ford Escort after a drunk-driving incident, I distinctly feel someone staring at me. I turn my head as casually as I can and glance behind me.

Brady's blue eyes are fixed firmly upon me.

Ohmigod. Delaney had actually been right!

When my startled eyes meet his, he smiles gently, exactly as he had in my dream. The familiar, soft smile of a boyfriend.

My stomach turns to jello and my heart starts racing. Why the heck is he staring at me like that? He barely knows me.

But as he stares at me with his friendly, warm smile, I find myself feeling better.

My embarrassment slips from me and I shrug my best *What can you do?* shrug, smiling back before I turn back around in my seat. We hadn't exchanged a single word, but the simple interaction leaves my palms clammy and my heart racing. I can't help it. He's beautiful. And he likes me. That much is apparent.

Three long hours later, Mr. Divine releases us and we all charge for the door like someone opened a flood-gate. Delaney turns to me in the hallway.

"Hey, do you want to pick Mini-Me up from her play-date and come over for lunch?"

"Sure. It'll give me an opportunity to kill you."

Because I owe Delaney a long excruciatingly painful death. I briefly wonder how much work pulling out her fingernails one by one would entail.

"Miss Lane?" Mr. Blaine's nasal voice comes from behind me. Again. The man seemed to have a radar for when he could catch me. I groan silently.

"Whitney, are you available to meet with me today for a few minutes?"

He looks like he just rolled out of bed. The only neat thing about him is his sparse hair. He's bald on top, but the sides are cut short and neatly combed. I mentally give him props for not attempting the comb-over thing.

I quickly try to come up with a viable excuse but nothing comes to mind. I helplessly glance at Delaney, so she pipes up- probably trying to get back into my good graces.

"We sort-of already had lunch plans, Mr. Blaine." He pierces her with his blue eyes.

"Well, Miss Harris, I think that Whitney's session with me is slightly more important than your 'sort-of' lunch plans."

Yikes.

My 'session?' I don't need to have a *session* with anybody! I sigh though and turn to Delaney. It's quite obvious he's going to be persistent. If I don't just get it over with, he'll corner me somewhere else. And that's definitely something I don't look forward to.

"Lane, we'll have to take a raincheck. Thanks for the invite, though. I'll text you later. You know, like a normal person." I can't help referencing the note-passing incident and she smiles sheepishly before she heads out.

I stared at her retreating back wistfully, wishing I was going too. Mr. Blaine turns to me.

"Whitney, why don't you go ahead and take a seat in my office. I have to take care of something and I'll be right in." He stiffly walks away, leaving me to wonder once again how I get myself into these situations.

Ten minutes later, I'm still waiting impatiently in his office, staring at the pale green walls. I bounce my foot again, a nervous habit that I've had ever since I was a kid. Everyone always teases me about it. I can consciously stop when someone points it out, but it never takes long for my foot to start bouncing again on its own accord, particularly when I'm nervous.

I'm not nervous now, per se, but I do just want to get it over with.

When you think of a guidance counselor, you kind of assume that they'll be comforting and helpful. Something about Mr. Blaine put me on edge. But then again, he doesn't seem to be that comfortable around teenagers, either. I wonder, then, why he chose to be a high school counselor?

I can hear someone whistling tunelessly as the door opens and he finally comes in, bringing with him the smell of stale Old Spice which almost, but not quite, masks the subtle smell of body odor. He sits down at his desk and folds his pale, doughy hands, looking over them at me.

"How are you feeling today, Whitney?"

So, I guess we're jumping right into it, then.

"I'm fine, Mr. Blaine. I'm a little stressed out, but that's it. I actually can't stay long- I have to pick up my little sister."

"That's interesting," he answers quietly. "Because that's the very thing I want to talk to you about today. I have someone else who is going to join us if you don't mind."

Without waiting for my permission, he gets up and goes to the door, motioning someone to come inside.

A woman enters, small and well-dressed, with her dark hair cut into a sleek bob. Something about her is familiar.

"Whitney, this is Mrs. Getlin, the elementary school principal."

I'm confused as I stare at her, as she extends her small hand and I shake it. She'd come after I left grade school, so I've never official met her. "It's nice to meet you." I say slowly. "But I don't understand…"

"How is everything at home?" Mr. Blaine interrupts me, his sharp blue eyes trained on my face again.

"Everything is fine. It's been… hard. But we're adjusting, like I told you yesterday. We're going to be okay."

"I called Mrs. Getlin yesterday, after we spoke, and she told me that Ellie was having a very difficult time before school ended." This catches my attention and I gaze at him with my brow wrinkled. My hands grow damp.

"Why would you be interested in Ellie? You're a high school counselor."

I'm pretty sure that he's overstepping some sort of boundary here. Ellie isn't his concern. I look over at Mrs. Getlin. She's watching me with a sympathetic expression. Ugh. I hate that.

"My dad died right before school let out," I point out to her, ignoring Mr. Blaine. "Of course Ellie was having a hard time. It was a shock on all three of us. It's normal for us to struggle."

She nods kindly. "Of course it is, Whitney. I think Mr. Blaine just wants you to know that you're not alone. We're all here to support you if you need it."

I glance over at him, and he smiles in what I'm sure he means to be a reassuring way.

"Whitney, a counselor that is good at their job keeps their ears to the ground to find out what is going on. Teenagers aren't always forthcoming about their feelings or things that are going on with them. Don't you find that to be the case?" He looks at me, but doesn't wait for me to respond before he continues.

"I've heard that your family has been having a really hard time these past several weeks. That your mother, in particular, has been struggling. I want you to know that you can talk to me about that." Again he stares at me. His probing blue eyes are unsettling and not comforting in the least. I really miss Mrs. Love.

"My mother lost her husband a couple months ago. Of course she's having a difficult time. Anyone would. She took some time off work to recuperate and she is just spending it around the house. Ellie is also having a hard time, but we are adjusting. *Like I said.*" My voice gets infinitely sharper with my last sentence. "I don't know what you're getting at or what this is about, but if you're trying to help, it's not working. All you're doing is stressing me out even more."

I stare him directly in the eye now, defiantly wanting to stare him down. Something about the way he's framing this conversation is putting me on guard, although I'm not sure why.

He stares back at me, his pudgy hands still folded.

"Whitney, do you have any relatives that you could go stay with while your mom gets her strength back? Maybe, a grandparent? I understand that your mother's parents are out of the country... perhaps there is someone else?"

It suddenly becomes clear what his purpose is. If I'd gotten more sleep last night, I would've have understood it sooner. No wonder I'd been subconsciously nervous.

"My mom is fine. We don't need to leave her and go stay with someone else. Ellie and I are both clean and dressed and fed every day. Do I need to have my mom call someone?" My voice is glacially cold. I stare at him unflinchingly over his stupid pale clasped hands.

Something shifts in his demeanor and he suddenly smiles, although his smile is vaguely reminiscent of jagged piranha teeth. No, there's nothing at all comforting about this man. He had definitely chosen the wrong profession.

"No, there is no need for your mother to call. I'm glad that everything is fine. Mrs. Getlin and I just wanted to check in with you. If anything changes, please know that you can come to either of us at any time to talk." He finally unfolds his hands and shuffles some papers around on his desk. Apparently I've been dismissed.

"Yeah, I'll remember that. Thanks."

I'm out of his office like a shot. I flee through the empty halls, and out of habit head straight for my locker from last year, sliding to the floor and sitting with my head leaned back against the cool metal. If only I *could* ask my mom to call the school.

Eight weeks ago, if I'd gone home from school and relayed the conversation that I had just had to my mom, she would've been on the phone within three seconds, calling the principal, the superintendent and probably even the mayor all at once and talking them blue in the face and then some.

I knew though, that if I were to return home right this instant, my mom would be listlessly sitting in a chair, staring out the window. She can't call anyone, even if I asked her to. I doubt she would notice if an entire army of Guatemalan Black Howler monkeys took up residence in our house.

I replay the conversation with Mr. Blaine again in my head. What exactly can he do? Can he actually call someone and have Ellie and I taken out of our house until mom gets better? Good Lord. What grounds would he need to do that?

I have very limited options regarding people that I can turn to for advice.

My dad doesn't have any family left. He was an only child and his parents had died before I was born. My mom's parents live in Venezuela. My grandpa's family has owned a home near Maracaibo for generations. I ponder whether I should call them. I know my grandma would come if I asked, but my mother would kill me. Well, she would eventually- when she starts caring about things again.

But still.

Maybe it *would* be best to run everything across someone who wasn't immersed in all of this craziness. I'll call Grandma first thing in the morning. She'll know what to do.

I feel two pounds lighter after making that decision. And better yet, I still have extra time to kill before I pick up Ellie. I know exactly how I'll pass the time. I yank my phone out of my pocket, text Delaney and ask her to meet me at Barb's Bakery downtown and head in that direction.

There are very few things in life that a freshly baked Danish dripping with chocolate icing can't fix.

As I pass Northport Harbor, I stare at the boats that are neatly lined up and bobbing gently in their slips. It won't be long before we can go sunfish sailing. I've been sailing them since I was ten or so. My dad had picked my first one up at a garage sale for $200 after I had caught the sailing bug from my friends and I had been sailing every summer since. I wasn't sure how I felt about being out on the lake this year after everything that had happened, but the idea of being out on the open lake with the wind in my face is definitely calling to me. I can't help it.

I'd gotten my current sunfish for my 13th birthday...the *No Problem*. Her 14 ft. hull is glistening mother-of-pearl and her sail is brightly striped- green, white and blue. There's room for two, so I'll take Ellie with me this summer. It'll do us both good.

Someone brushes against my arm and I step aside to let them pass.

I'm in no hurry. I'll get there when I get there, even though I know Delaney's probably already there. More than likely, she's picking out the center of her Danish, too. The girl is strange. And she's my best friend so I can say that.

When I realize that no one steps around me, I turn around and find that there's no one there. Not on the sidewalk and not up or down the street.

Goosebumps raise up on my neck.

I could swear that someone bumped my arm.

I can actually still feel the exact place they touched me. I rub at it, and then I rub at my goose-bumps. Clearly, I'd been mistaken.

I pull open the bakery door, and with relief, find that Delany is already here. Normalcy. Thank God. I head straight for her table without looking back.

She's not poking at her Danish as I had expected. She's sucking the cream out.

I stare at her, watching as she holds up the entire long cylinder and noisily sucks until she's sure that all of the decadent goo is gone before she places the shell back onto her plate. Only then does she delicately cut it into bites with silverware like a normal person.

Her porcelain skin and green eyes look beautiful in contrast with her long red hair. I wonder if I should tell her that she has a big dollop of cream in it.

"You're an enigma, Laney." I lean over and wipe the cream out with a napkin.

She smiles widely. "But you love me."

I shake my head again, something I seemed to do a lot around her, and take the roll that she hands me. She knows what I like... the chocolate long johns with the custard middle.

Of course I love her. She knows me better than anyone.

And I love this quaint little bake shop with its little tables and gauzy curtains, too. I've been coming here with my mom ever since I was a baby. Since she was forever on a diet, she would reward any and all good behavior with a sweet roll from Barb's. It's a family tradition now.

Delaney finishes chewing her last bite of sweet roll and delicately wipes at her mouth with a napkin, like a perfect lady. She seems to have forgotten that she was sucking the entire thing like a straw two second ago. She primly places it back down on her lap before she folds her arms on the table and stares at me over her soda glass.

"So, what's going on with Brady?" I knew that she would come back to this. She's like a dog with a bone. "He was staring at you like his eyes were super-glued on you this morning. Something's going on, and you're holding out on me."

She glares, but there's no way I'm going to tell her about my strange, erotic dream. She'd never let me forget it. She'd think it was some sort of sign.

"There's nothing going on, I'm not holding out on you, but I *am* going to kill you. For humiliating me this morning. Should I do it in here or outside where there will be less mess?"

The entire conversation with Mr. Blaine had deflected my agitation with her for a little bit- but it's back now in full-force.

"Cop-out!" She sings the words as she licks the glaze off of her fingers. "It wasn't my fault that Divine was right behind us. I didn't know. Besides, Brady didn't seem to mind. He kept staring at you even after Divine read the note."

She's right and I have to admit that I find it curious.

In fact, every time I think of it, a little thrill courses through me and my stomach does back-flips. A part of me feels guilty about that. I'm not supposed to be interested in Brady Parker right now. And I'm definitely not supposed to be having sexy dreams about him.

I'm supposed to be grieving. My dad just died a minute ago- what kind of daughter am I, anyway?

"I can't think about that right now." I mutter.

"Yes, you can. It's okay, Whitney." Delaney stares at me from across the small table, with a serious expression on her usually carefree face. I watch her play with the multi-colored string bracelets circling her slender pale wrist. I'd made one of them for her. "It's okay for you to

miss your dad and still do normal things. My mom said
so."

"Your *mom* said so? Since when do you discuss me
with your mother? And your mom is a lawyer, not a
psychologist, so she doesn't know, anyway."

"Yes, she does. Right after your dad died, she told me
that I needed to make sure that you still did normal things.
She said that she could easily see you letting yourself get
caught up in grief- and doing what was right, but forgetting
about yourself. For once, my mom was right."

Delaney and her mom tend to butt heads a lot-mostly
because they're just alike, from their red hair to their red-
hot tempers. In fact, they sort of fight like cats and dogs.
You would think that *they're* Venezuelan, but they aren't.
They're Irish- somewhere down the line, anyway.

"You're a good sister and a good daughter, Whit. But
it's okay if you think of yourself sometimes, too. You need
to." She tosses her long hair over her shoulder. "And you
might as well think about Brady while you're at it." She
grins at me mischievously as she sips her soda. She glances
out the window and surprise lit up her lovely features.

"Oh my God. Speak of the devil! This is a sign,
Whit."

With a sigh, because she thinks *everything* is a sign, I
follow her gaze to find Brady crossing the street directly in
front of Barb's. The amber strands of his hair pick up the
golden light from the sun and I find myself remembering
how he had looked last night in the moonlight. It might not
have been real, but I can't stop thinking about it.

I idly wonder what he's doing here. He could be
shopping-- but he doesn't have anything in his hands.
Whatever he's doing, he must feel us staring at him,
because he looks up and meets my gaze. He grins broadly
and my breath catches in my throat.

A smile like that should be illegal. He waves and casually continues on his way, walking out of the window frame and out of my line of sight.

I lean forward ever so slightly to see if I could catch another glimpse, thunking my forehead on the window in the process. Luckily, he doesn't notice. He passes from my field of vision.

"Go," Delaney tells me firmly, picking up my purse and shoving it at me. "Hurry up, or you're going to miss him."

I protest, trying to sit back down, but she kicks my chair out of the way.

"*Go*," she tells me again. "Seriously. Take one minute for yourself. He's into you. Big time. Just go say hi."

I don't know why, but I do as she says. I push away from the table and hurry out the door. I look up and down the street, but Brady is nowhere to be seen.

Disappointment wells up in me, and I hadn't even realized how much I'd like to see him. How much I'd like to talk to him, to hear him say my name in that familiar way.

"Hey, Whitney."

Yeah, just like *that.*

With butterflies in my stomach, I turn around to find him stepping away from a tree. He'd been leaning on it. *Had he been waiting for me?*

No way.

"So, class was crazy this morning, huh?" he asks, his voice quiet but sort of flirty. I know exactly what he's referring to and my cheeks flush.

"Yeah, uh, about that. I'm sorry. Delaney was just bored and entertaining herself..."

Brady grins, interrupting me. "It's okay. Because I *was* staring at you."

I almost swallow my tongue.

"You were?"

I already know he was. I saw him. But to hear him admit it so openly... he wants me to know. *He's flirting with me.*

He nods. "Of course. How could I not?"

I stare at him dumbly, and I hope to hell that I look halfway decent in this moment. I fight the urge to smooth my hair.

He smiles again. "You'll be there tomorrow, right?"

I nod. "Yeah."

"Good." Brady smiles one more time, then walks away. I watch him for a minute, at the way his broad shoulders sway, at the way the muscles in his biceps move. And then I realize that I'm almost late picking Ellie up.

Reluctantly, I turn away and head toward home.

But it feels like I'm floating the entire way.

Chapter Five

"Grandma, I can't put her on. She doesn't know that I'm calling you. She'd be furious."

Well, she would be if she could comprehend or care what I was talking about. And that's doubtful.

I speak in a low conspiratorial tone, whispering as I glance around me.

As much as I hope my mom will snap out of it, I hope that today is not the day. Well, at least not this morning, anyway. I don't want her to catch me discussing her with my grandma- she really would kill me. Even though the probability is slim, I keep a watchful eye on the dining room door. Ellie's in her room getting dressed- so even she doesn't know that I was calling. This is a completely covert operation.

"I don't know what to do." I can hear the helplessness in my own voice. I sound more like a little girl than the capable teenager that I am. That's bad. I try again.

"I don't know long it's normal to act the way she is acting. She doesn't want to shower, she barely eats, she barely sleeps. My counselor from school was asking all sorts of questions, and he suggested that someone should come stay here with us. I promise, Grandma, we don't need someone to take care of us. Ellie and I are fine, but I am worried about mom. She doesn't seem.... right. I don't know what to do. And I definitely don't want someone to try and take us out of our home."

It's the most I feel comfortable telling her, without feeling utterly disloyal to my mother. I'm not going to explain that mom will sometimes go days without speaking to us, because *if* she sleeps, she sleeps during the day like a vampire. I'm not going to tell my grandmother that I'd woken up last night to find mom standing in my bedroom doorway with the strangest expression on her face, like she was angry, and that she had turned and walked wordlessly away when she noticed that I was looking at her.

No, Grandma doesn't need to know that. I wouldn't be able to put the troublesome part into words anyway- the ferocious expression that had been on her face.

It was like she was furious.

At me.

Grandma Ava is instantly concerned, but to my relief, she respects my opinion that Ellie and I don't need to be taken care of. After she makes sure that we're getting enough to eat, her initial reaction is that it's only been a couple of months, a handful of weeks, really.

Her familiar, strong voice soothes me through the phone.

"Whitney, your mom is a strong woman. All of the women in our family are! But we're passionate- about life and everything in it. Because of that, we tend to feel emotions very strongly." She states this proudly, like a badge of honor.

"Let's just give your mom a chance to work through this on her own- to figure out how she's going to handle it. She loved your dad more than life itself, so of course she's going to be devastated now. It's natural. Everyone grieves in their own way. I promise you, no one is going to try and take you from your home. That's ludicrous."

I bite my lip. I can't decide whether to try and better verbalize my concerns.

On the one hand, I knew that Grandma Ava's right. My mom had loved my dad more than everything in the world rolled up together. Just as I had told Mr. Blaine, anyone would be devastated. But on the other hand, I know in my heart that her behavior isn't normal. She isn't going down a path that's going to end well.

The expression on her face when she'd glared at me in the night from my doorway lingers in my memory. No, it definitely wasn't normal.

My grandma clucks and bemoans and says all of the dramatic things that you'd expect from a Latina grandmother. I imagine her on the other end of the phone waving her hands around, then wringing them, as she speaks to me half the time and relays our conversation to Grandpa Vin the other half. He's always a solemn voice of reason and I suddenly hear his deep voice speaking from behind Grandma.

"Tell Whitney to give Maricel a couple more weeks. Tell her to be patient and take care of her mama. If things don't change, though, you tell her to call us and we'll be on the next plane. She's not alone. Tell her that I love her."

A knot forms in my throat. I love him, too. He's tall, strong and calm, so much like my dad. Everyone always says that girls marry someone like their dad… and my mom certainly had. Grandma relays his message, clucks some more, gives me her love a hundred times before hanging up.

Well, that's that.

I feel a bit bad about not giving them the entire scope of mom's downward spiral, but I do feel so much better knowing that they're poised and ready to climb aboard the nearest 747 and fly here to fix everything the minute that I call and ask.

In fact, I feel a giant weight lift off my shoulders.

I hadn't realized how much all of this responsibility had been weighing on me, until my grandparents had taken some of it just by being willing to share it. And if my grandparents think that this is a normal part of the grieving process, then maybe it is. I choose to forget that I hadn't completely explained everything. Those were just details, anyway.

I grab a banana from the kitchen and eat it on the way to my room. Mr. Divine had told us that we were learning to change a tire today, so I'd need my strength. I'm not really a physical labor type person- not if it involves grease or tools, anyway.

At first, I try and look glamorous, but I end up simply pulling on a pair of clean shorts, a blue tank top and yanking a brush through my hair. I'm girl-next-door pretty. I'll never be glamorous. I sigh at my reflection and give up. I'm only going to Driver's Ed, anyway.

With Brady Parker.

I stifle the little voice and peek in my mom before we leave.

She's sleeping, which is good. I'm not sure what time she'd actually drifted off to sleep. She wasn't in her bed- she was in dad's office, curled up in his chair, her head resting on his desk. She's wearing one of his sweaters over her nightgown and has a bunch of his things spread out around her.

I wish that she'd sleep at night, rather than act like a vampire, but I guess at least she's sleeping. For the first couple weeks, she barely slept at all.

I decide to quit thinking about it for the moment. Worrying about it constantly isn't going to help. I drop

Ellie off at Alexis's house and thank Alexis's mom, before I head to Driver's Ed.

Learning how to change a tire doesn't seem like completely useless information and so I pay close attention as Mr. Divine shows us how to jack up the car, loosen lug nuts, take the tire off and then put it back on.

I've never done anything mechanical on a car, so I'm instantly nervous, and so of course, because it's a law of nature, I'm called on second, right after Drew.

Perfect.

Of course, because it's Drew, he tightened the lugs nuts inhumanly tight. I glare at his gigantic ham fists as I tug on the lug wrench.

I struggle with it unsuccessfully for several minutes, before giving up. I look up at Mr. Divine helplessly. I don't want to be the girly-girl in class, and I don't want to ask for help, but there's no way that these lugs are coming off.

The morning sun is actually starting to get hot as it shines down on the concrete pavement of the parking lot and I can smell the grease from the wheel. I'd rather be anywhere other than here right now and I'm actually starting to get a little dizzy.

I'm just getting ready to bite the bullet and ask for help when Drew takes a step forward.

"Here, Whit. I'll help. I'm sorry, I didn't mean to get them so tight. My fault!"

But Mr. Divine holds up his hand.

"No, no. She can get it. There will probably be a time in your life when you are stuck on a highway without anyone to help you. And many mechanics use an air-wrench to tighten lugs. In those cases, they're much tighter than these. It's helpful to know what to do. Whitney, carefully use your foot to apply pressure." He demonstrates in the air as he speaks.

Carefully is obviously the key word here.

Unfortunately, I've always had balance issues, which are compounded today because I'm feeling dizzy. So when I try to *carefully* do what he demonstrated, I lose my balance and fall backward. In the process, I somehow turn the lever that handles the hydraulics for the jack.

The car comes crashing down, rocking vicariously in place as it slams loudly onto the ground.

Instant embarrassment floods through me in the form of red splotches spreading onto my cheeks and chest. Glancing around at my classmates, their reactions range from shocked to wildly amused. Over the roar in my ears, I can hear Justin wise-cracking from the back. I can't even look at Brady. Luckily though, there's no need for concern- no one was near enough to get smashed under the car. I try to concentrate on my breathing so that I can calm down. No one was hurt- it's okay.

"This, ladies and gentlemen, is an example of how *not* to do it. Thank you for the demonstration, Miss Lane. Let's try it again- and this time, let's leave the jack in an elevated position while we change the tire, hmm?"

Humiliating. My cheeks are on fire.

I doggedly make a second attempt, and this time everyone makes a big show of backing up and giving me wide birth as I work, just in case I mess up again. Everyone but Brady. He stands in front of everyone, staring at me intently, offering me a smile of encouragement.

It makes me even more nervous.

With quite a bit of very careful tugging, I'm able to get the lug nuts off this time and manage to change the tire without further incident. My hands shake the entire time.

Oh, well. It doesn't help to stress about it. Besides, how many people can say that they've dropped a car?

I gratefully take my place back within the group as Justin takes his turn. He smirks at me after he accomplishes it in two minutes flat with no issues. I look away. He's a jerk and he wouldn't have had such an easy time if he'd gone after Drew. I make a mental note to not follow Drew in anything of this nature again. I like him, but he really is a giant moose. He has no idea how strong he really is.

As we finally finish up and walk back through the school to get to the classroom, I realize that my hands are covered in grime and grit, probably because it took me twice as long with my turn as everyone else. I also have grease smeared on my shorts- and I can only pray it's not on my face, too. I grab Delaney's arm.

"Hey, I've got to go wash up. You can go on ahead if you want."

"Sure. I'll grab your purse for you and wait on the benches outside."

We part at the main T in the hallway. The smell of school- floor wax, stale air and various forms of paper- waft over me as I walk.

As I pass the massive, glass panels of the trophy cases, I'm startled to hear angry voices hissing just inside the big metal doors of the gym.

The hallway is deserted- not even a janitor. My curiosity piqued, I decide to take a short-cut through the gym instead of going the long way around. I don't really need to save time- the nosy side of me just wants to see who was arguing so heatedly. I don't recognize the hushed whispers and they're definitely not joking around.

As I pass through the doors, I stop short.

The voices are gone. It's completely silent.

There's no one in the gymnasium. The gym floor is empty, the bleachers are deserted. It's a ghost town in here.

I'm alone.   And I'm hearing voices. This can't be good.   I can't even blame this on a dream, because I'm very clearly awake. The grease on my shorts can attest to that.

This is real.

I'm really imagining crazy things.

But the crazy things don't stop, because out of the corner of my eye, I suddenly catch a glimpse of blue.

I whirl around, but the only things there are stacks and stacks of folded tan bleachers.

But I know what I saw.

The blue had been in motion, a blur on the edge of my periphery. It hadn't made any noise, but there had been movement right next to me. I'm sure of it.

Aren't I?

I step inside the door and sink to the dirty gym floor, still scanning the room suspiciously.

Brightly colored championship pennants hang motionlessly from the ceiling. The huge digital scoreboard is dim and dark.   The only noise in this room is the persistent ticking of the wall clock behind me.

There are no voices.

No one is here.

Is it possible that my emotions are causing me to see and hear things? I'm suddenly dizzy again, and I rest my chin on my knees, hugging my legs.

"Whitney?" Brady's voice echoes from across the gym. "Are you alright? What's wrong?"

He emerges from the boys locker room door and crosses over to me, wearing a black t-shirt that stretches tightly across his chest.   He must've had the same idea as me about washing his hands because he smells like soap.

"Are you okay?" he asks again, sliding down to sit beside me. Great. This is just what I need... Brady Parker witnessing my nervous breakdown. "Is this about the car?"

"Um, no. I'm fine." I'd actually already forgotten about the car. I look up at him through my lashes, which I'm startled to realize are wet. I'm crying and didn't even realize it.

My emotions are out of control.

"You're not fine, and this isn't about the car, is it?" Brady puts put his arm around my shoulders and pulls me close to him.

I'd been mistaken- only his hands smell like soap.

The rest of him smells like cedar and musk. I fade into the warmth of his body, resting my head on his shoulder. I've never been an overly huggy person, but I suddenly realize how much I've been needing a hug.

At the same exact time, I realize that I'm getting snot on his shirt. I wipe at my nose with the back of my hand. He lowers his head so that his eyes are level with mine.

"Whitney, you probably know this, but my brother died a couple of years ago. I remember every detail of it like it was yesterday. I thought I shouldn't cry, because I was supposed to be a man, but I wanted to cry every minute. Bryant knew me like no one else did. And I didn't get to say good bye to him that day, because I didn't realize I'd never see him again. I thought it was an ordinary day. Just like you did. When I heard what happened to your dad, I felt an instant connection to you, because I know exactly what you feel like. Is that weird?"

Tears start running down my face all over again as I shake my head. Great. I'm a human faucet.

"I haven't talked about it much with anyone here, even though I know people are curious. Sometimes it makes it worse to talk about it- have you noticed that?" I nod silently. "But sometimes, it makes it better. You'll eventually notice that, too. It just takes awhile longer for that part."

Everything he's saying is exactly right.

Losing his brother must have matured him, because he sounds so much older than his years, so much older than the other boys in school. In fact, I know grown men who don't communicate as well as he does. They wouldn't have known to offer the comfort that he's offering, but he knows. He knows what I need, because it'd been what he needed two years ago.

I know what it's like.

Remembering his words make me cry harder.

Because sometimes, when a person is so sad, you just crave the knowledge that someone else has been there, that they came through it and so you will too.

You crave physical contact- the warmth of someone else near you or someone else's arm around you. It breaks through the numbness.

Brady being here right now is just what I need.

I sag against him, staring at the wooden planks of the gym floor, enjoying the warmth from his body and his masculine scent. We sit that way for a few minutes, as he lets me regain my composure- a perfect gentleman. After a few silent minutes, he speaks again.

"Okay, so I haven't seen you out much lately. I think you need a distraction…something to keep your mind off of things. What do you think about a movie?"

He has no idea how much I needed a distraction, but I don't elaborate for him.

I find myself wanting to go out with him-especially after my dream the other night.

I haven't been able to stop thinking about him ever since.

But I can't. Literally.

"I can't. I mean, I wish I could, but I have to take care of my little sister. My mom…isn't well right now."

"You know what? That's fine. No problem. How about this—I'll come over to your house. You can just hang out, right?"

He looks at me imploringly, waiting for me to come up with an excuse. I surprise myself when I don't.

"Okay. Sure. That would be great." It's not like my mom is going to notice.

"Great. I'll call you."

He stands up and I immediately feel the absence of warmth on my shoulders where his arm had been.

I watch his lips as he speaks to me, and I feel the ridiculous urge to step forward and kiss him. Heightened emotions seem to do strange things to me. I tear my eyes from his lips and zoom out again on his face.

"I'll talk to you later, Brady….thanks." I say softly.

He smiles at me, and then gets up and walks out.

I find that my knees were weak. Until this moment, I'd always thought that the phrase "weak in the knees" was just a literary phrase. But no, it's an actual physical reaction.

I pull my phone out and text Delaney.

OMG- just talked to Brady! I'll catch up to you later.

I'll call her later and discuss the details, but for the moment, I just want to relish them alone for a while. I need to try to make sense out of what had just happened before I can explain to someone else. I ignore the way my phone buzzes in my pocket with Delaney's questions. I'll answer them later.

Right now, Ellie's still at Alexis's house, so I head out into the sun, into the opposite direction from where my best friend was waiting for me.

The Northport Market is practically deserted as I enter it. As I walk through the door, I suddenly have the strange sensation that someone is hovering right by my elbow. I quickly look, but there's no one there.

Again.

My stomach sinks because my craziness is getting out of hand.

I seriously have to get a hold of myself.

With a gulp, I make a bee-line to the fresh floral section at the back of the store. I try to zip in and back out again without bumping into anyone that I know, but I should've known that would be futile effort. In a town the size of Northport, you can't go anywhere without running into someone you know- because you literally know everyone.

"Whitney, dear. How are you doing?"

Miranda Eli had zeroed in on me from the end of the aisle and had broken her neck to get to me.

She's now grasping my arm with her glistening crimson nails in a motherly way. I know I'm not going anywhere. She means well, but she's a busy-body. I know that anything I say here will be shared with everyone on Miranda Eli's speed dial.

There's a movement from behind her and a tall dark-headed boy moves into focus.

With a jolt, I realize it's the boy from the pier.

His dark eyes contain a slightly condescending stare in them as he stands next to her. He looks to be about my age. His glare unnerves me and I try to focus on what Miranda is saying.

"I'm fine, Miranda. How are you? How's your mom?"

I utilize a newly learned talent of redirecting conversation back onto the other person. It works 98% of the time because people almost always like to talk about themselves and their own problems.

Except for me. I'm definitely part of the 2% minority.

It's clear, though, that Mrs. Eli is not and ten minutes later, we're still in the same spot, discussing her elderly mother's aversion to her new nursing home.

"I just don't understand it," she says. "I do all of her laundry personally and visit her every day at lunchtime. I see her now more than ever!"

She's absorbed in our one-sided conversation, but I am not. As I try to avoid the uncomfortable stare of this new boy and Miranda's ramblings, I daydream myself back into the gymnasium with Brady's arm wrapped comfortingly around my shoulders.

"Whitney?"

I snap to attention. Clearly this isn't the first time she's said my name. She's now phrasing it as a question.

"Whitney, I want to introduce my newest swimmer. This is Carter Kelly. He and his family just moved here from Chicago. He's going to be on my swim team next year."

Of course, that made sense. Miranda coaches the city swim team in Traverse City. Northport isn't big enough to have its own team.

I inwardly groan. I'd absolutely nailed it. He's from a big city.

I hold out my hand politely and smile what I hope is a passable "Welcome to Northport" smile. I should be a bigger person. Besides, this is my town. If he doesn't like it or the people in it, he can go right back to Chicago and breathe the smog.

"It's nice to meet you, Carter. I hope you'll like it here." I keep my voice perfectly pleasant.

"It's nice to meet you, too." But his dark eyes tell me that he doesn't mean it. I can't help but wonder why. I hadn't done anything to him. We've only just met- I haven't had time to do anything yet. Is this going to be another Justin Gerber situation?

I let my eyes do a quick casual appraisal. He definitely looks like a swimmer- tall and lean. His eyes and hair are dark brown and his jaw is square with a cleft in his chin. His lips look soft and are perfectly shaped. He has the brooding good looks of a starving artist.

Well, to be honest, I've never actually seen a starving artist but I imagine that one would look like Carter Kelly. He must be a pretty good swimmer, too, in order to make the team in Traverse City. They'd won State last year. I'm just about to ask him what grade he'll be in when he speaks.

"I don't mean to be rude, Miranda, but we're going to be late for practice if we don't hurry." My eyes flash up to meet his and he doesn't look like he much cares if he sounds rude.

He just looks impatient. He's staring at me again, as if I had imposed on his Gatorade run with his coach, making both of them late. As if! I could've done without this little catch-up session.

"It was nice to see you, Miranda. Nice to meet you, Carter!"

I force a smile and duck back to the floral section without another glance. If I don't hurry up and get out of here, I'm not going to have time to get out to the bluffs before I have to pick up Ellie.

Luckily, the cashier isn't in a talkative mood today, so I'm able to pay for my things quickly and make my escape before I see anyone else I know.

As I walk toward Grand Traverse Bay, the sun sweeps across the treetops like a golden paintbrush. The air smells fresh and clean and as I take a deep breath I'm reminded of why tourists love it here. We really are surrounded by beauty. Just being around it makes me feel good. Whereas just the other day when I was here I had felt hopeless and hateful and bleak; today I feel like there's a chance that I can start feeling normal again, like maybe someday things would be okay.

I want to sit on the beach and be alone with my thoughts, to dissect everything that had just happened at the school... every word that had come out of Brady's mouth, every smile, every gesture, every touch, including his arm around my shoulder. Had he just been trying to comfort me or had he also wanted to be near me?

As I cross the wide street to enter Leelanau State Park, I suddenly have the odd feeling that I'm not alone.

Again.

You've got to be kidding me. Before I even turn around, I know what I'll find.

Absolutely nothing.

Nothing is there.

Even the beach is empty. My frustration is really starting to well up even though I try to curb it. I'm getting really tired of being paranoid and I'm *so over* feeling crazy.

I walk directly up to where the water gently laps against the beach and toss the flowers out as far as I can... my offering to my dad. With the absence of a real grave, this is the best I can do for him.

I watch as the flowers float and then as a couple of them sink from their own weight.

The lake is calm today, and the water is still and blue. I turn and climb back up the dunes so that I can enjoy the view from an elevated vantage point.

I sit with my elbows on my knees and stare out at the water, enjoying the sun on my shoulders and the lake breeze. The sand is slightly damp, but the sun had warmed it up and it feels really good to sit on it. I stretch my legs out, and as I turn my head, I catch a quick blur out of the corner of my eye. Just like in the gym.

I look and there's nothing there. Just sand and tall grass.

But then it happens again a few scant seconds later.

I'm not crazy.

There's definitely a brief, undefined movement from my right side. It's there for a second and then gone. My heart starts pounding with something.... a premonition? An instinct?

I stand up and look over the tall waving grass that had obstructed my clear view.

There's something there now.

A boy dressed in blue.

I suck in my breath and examine him.

He appears to be about my age, or maybe a couple of years older, and he's standing on the sand. He hadn't been there two seconds earlier. I'm sure of that. The reason I'm very sure of that is that there are no footprints leading to where he's standing.

It's as though he'd been set down in that exact place.

All thoughts of anything else that had happened prior in the day disappear from my head, as a strange feeling constricts my chest. I look up and down the length of the beach. There's no one else with him.

I suddenly remember to breathe and my eyes fly back to him.

He's staring right at me, his gaze concentrated and unmoving.

I stare back. He doesn't flinch and he doesn't look away as a normal person would.

His eyes bore straight into mine.

He's suddenly closer, although he didn't appear to have moved.

His eyes never leave mine. Then before I can even register it, he's even closer- no more than 20 feet away. I still hadn't seen him move. He was simply first in one spot, and now he's in another.

I hadn't even blinked, so I know his legs didn't move.

A strange conviction washes over me- unlike anything I've ever felt before.

This boy isn't here sightseeing, hiking or swimming. He hasn't bumped into me by chance.

He's here for me.

I feel it. It's a ridiculous thought and I feel foolish thinking it, but it doesn't make it any less true.

The waves continue to gently lap at the shore and the sun still shines down on my shoulders... but these are insignificant details in the fading backdrop of a stage. I barely notice them.

I'm preoccupied with the overwhelming physical pull that I feel toward this stranger. It starts in my chest and radiates outward, upward and downward.

Every surface of my body urges me toward where he's standing, like the gravitational pull of the tides. He's definitely here for me. I know it. But at the same time, I realize that I'm not afraid and I take a step forward.

Chapter Six

"Who are you?" I ask softly, unable to take my eyes from him.

I'm not scared. I probably should be, but I only feel expectant, like I should already know the answer but just don't remember it. It's like when you forget something and it lingers on the tip of your tongue, so close but just out of recall.

He doesn't seem threatening, so I take a step toward him.

"I know you." I still feel the strange magnetic pull to him but I resist it, standing with my feet planted instead, while I wait for him to answer me. It's odd how hard it is to resist. "How do I know you?"

He looks at me with brilliant aquamarine eyes, as clear and beautiful as a tropical ocean in the sunlight. I've never seen eyes that color before, and I realize with a start that they're the exact shade of the Mediterranean that sparkles in the picture that I love of my parents.

His brown hair curls against the nape of his neck and his bangs sweep easily across his forehead. His slender arms host lean muscle, nothing flashy, nothing showy. He shifts forward again, and as he moves, I get the same feeling again in the pit of my stomach, stronger this time...like Déjà Ju.

At the same time, I know for certain that I've never actually seen him before because I would remember that.

Even still, I *know* him.

"I'm confused," I hear myself whisper softly, but I didn't mean to make a sound. The uncertain words had spilled out without my permission.

My common sense finally kicks in and I back up-away from this curiosity. Away from *him*- because I know in my heart that something isn't normal here. Just like my dreams haven't been normal and all of the things I think I've seen lately. *None of it is normal.*

He advances as I retreat; his eyes shimmering oddly in the sun, rippling like someone dropped a rock in a pool of water. My breath freezes in my throat.

"What are you?"

"Don't be afraid, Whitney. I won't hurt you." His voice is soothingly deep and masculine, maybe a little too much so for his boyish body- and he holds up his hands. His fingers are long and I can see unexpected strength there.

He knows my name and I know his voice.

It touches something deep within me and I stop moving.

He smiles and it's like the sun and the moon and the stars and all other possible sources of natural light are radiating from him. His teeth are white and brilliant and his face brightens the entire beach around us.

There's no denying that he's beautiful, but it's more than that. Being next to him touches something inside of me, like a guitarist strumming a chord.

He's familiar, like home.

"Who are you?" I demand. "How do you know my name?"

My head is swimming. The past several days of feeling crazy for seeing things that aren't there and hearing noises that have no source have culminated in a frustration that I can't help but direct at him.

I somehow know he's the key here.

I can feel it.

A stranger that I know, but have never met.

I throw my hair back out of my face, even though the wind keeps blowing it right back in.

"Please?" I add, in a more polite and somewhat pleading tone. "What's your name?"

Aside from my frustration, I still feel strangely calm. I should be terrified. My heart should be in my throat. I should be running away as fast as I can.

But none of these things are true. I'm eerily calm as I face this strange boy head-on.

He gracefully sits on the bluff and stretches his legs out in front of him, gesturing for me to sit with him. I notice that his feet are now making footprints.

I hesitate, resisting the strange magnetism that draws me to him.

"Please?" he adds, copying my polite tone from a second ago. I carefully perch in the sand, a few feet away from him and watch his face intently while he speaks.

"My name is Samuel. Is that a good place to start?" He places a slight emphasis on the last syllable of his name, pronouncing it 'Samu-el'.

He smiles patiently again, as though he's talking to a child.

The beauty of his smile captures my attention. I've never seen anything like it- not in a movie, not anywhere. Even Brady's 100-watt Hollywood smile dims in comparison... yet strangely, I don't feel any sexual attraction radiating between us.

It was as though I'm sitting next to the most magnificent painting in the Sistine Chapel, beautiful and breathtaking, but not a flesh and blood man. All I feel is a comfortable familiarity.

"Samuel *what*? Do you live here, in Northport? Why do I feel like I know you?"

I'm intimidated by him... and by the strangeness of the situation, but I can't stop the questions from spilling out.

He smiles again and I swear the earth stills on its axis. I literally feel as though everything around me stops. He seems so patient, as though he has nothing but time and nothing better to do than spend his time with me.

"Samuel is my only name. No, I don't live in Northport, but I do spend most of my time here. You've never seen me before, that is true, but I'm sure you feel as though you know me. Don't you?" He cocks his head and waits...gauging my reaction.

What's he waiting for? For me to realize something? Recognize him? I'll have to disappoint him. I'm not able to connect the dots.

"Why are you speaking in riddles? You have to have a last name!" Frustration makes me agitated and I leap to my feet. "Forget it. You're insane."

I skid down the sand dune, but before I've taken three steps, Samuel stops me.

I'm literally stopped in my tracks, by something physically halting my movement, but he hasn't touched me. He stands three feet away.

My stomach drops into my feet.

What is going on?

"Please sit with me again. I have your answers. I'm sorry. I'm not being kind and you've been through a lot. You certainly don't need added stress."

I feel shell-shocked as I sink back to the sand.

He knows about my dad.

"How do you know I've been through a lot?" I ask quietly.

"I know everything there is to know about you, Whitney. I've known you since before you were born."

He sits next to me and watches my face for a reaction before he continues. I'm too frozen to move, too stunned.

"That's impossible," I whisper. But he's already shaking his head.

"It's entirely possible. Shall I prove it?"

He doesn't wait for me to answer before he continues.

"Your middle name is Diane, which is a family name. You have a compulsion to keep the volume of your radio turned to eight, although you don't know why. You like to sleep with your feet hanging out of the blankets although a small part of you, deep down, is afraid that something will grab your feet. You love your sister, but sometimes you desperately wish that you didn't have to take care of her and that makes you feel guilty. Your favorite cartoon as a child was Scooby-Doo and you've wanted a Great Dane ever since, which you would name Sampson. You love to play basketball, but you don't really like watching it. Should I go on?" He raises an eyebrow and I feel all the breath whoosh out of me.

He knows me.

I can't deny that. There's no joking here, no sarcasm, no metaphors or similes. I know in this instant that he's serious. And I somehow innately know that he's not crazy....and neither am I.

"*What are you?*" I breathe, staring directly into his startling beryl eyes.

"I'm your guardian." He says it quietly, without preamble or explanation.

"My…guardian." I repeat, watching his face, trying to read it, to interpret something there, something to help me understand… because my brain isn't getting it.

"You mean… like an *angel*?" The wheels in my brain are spinning and I'm desperately trying to keep up-like a mouse running on a wheel that's way too big. "Angels aren't real."

"Aren't they? Why is that? Because you've never seen one?" Samuel raises one perfect eyebrow again, smiling slightly. "You've never seen me, because you weren't supposed to see me. Humans very rarely see their guardians, although it isn't unheard of. And yes, you all have one." He seems to know that it was going to be my next question and answers it with a smile before I can ask. He studies me calmly from his perch on the bluff.

I pause. Because how do you respond to something like this?

"What do you guard me from?"

"From things you can't see. From things you wouldn't want to see. I guard you from mundane earthly things. I protect you from harm and from things that aren't in your plan. You're never alone, Whitney. Not even in the end."

In the end. My plan. I'm never alone.

Several things swirl together in my head but the one thing I can't help but concentrate on is *I protect you from harm*. I'm sitting here on the bluffs with what is apparently my guardian angel and the only thing I can think of is my dad.

"If everyone has a guardian that protects them from harm, then why did my dad drown?" I demand. "Why did his *guardian* stand aside and let him die? That doesn't make any sense."

Just talking about my dad's accident make emotion well up in my chest and spew hotly down my cheeks as tears until Samuel reaches over and wipes them away. I don't shy away. I hadn't even realized until this moment that he'd moved closer to me.

He's gentle now, quiet.

"You see death as the worst possible thing that can happen to someone. It's not, Whitney. You view it differently than I do because I know what waits for you on the other side of life. Death is not the end, it is just a different beginning."

"I don't understand," I whisper, desperately wishing that I did. That I could wrap my mind around this entire crazy situation. "Am I dreaming again?"

I must be. I fell asleep on the warm sand and I'm dreaming.

Samuel shakes his head. "No, you're not dreaming. Your dad's guardian stood aside and let him die that morning. Those were his orders. And I stood behind you on the beach and watched as you waited for the rescuers to find him. Because those were *my* orders. We do what we are told to do- every day, every hour, every minute. You'll see your dad again, Whitney. Life doesn't end with death, I promise you. Every human has a plan; everything here is connected in ways that you can't begin to understand."

He's looking at me sympathetically, because he knows that I can't grasp what he's saying- that even if I were capable, I wouldn't want to.

"What I *understand* is…. My dad is gone and I miss him. I miss the way my life used to be. If there is a God who plans everything out, why did He have to take him now- why couldn't He have waited? Doesn't he know that I need my dad? That my life has fallen apart?"

I beseech him with wet eyes, my lashes clumped together and tears dripping down my nose, falling onto my shirt. I feel like Ellie, but I can't help it. The pain never seems to get any less significant and talking about it only makes it worse- even though I'm supposedly talking with an angel. And I'm not entirely convinced of that last point. It's still entirely possible that I might be crazy.

"I can't answer that because I don't know. We're not given those details. We're only told what we need to know. Angels have many strengths, but we're limited, too. We're not 'all-knowing'. Things are revealed to us as we need to know them and not before. And we can't be in more than one place at a time." He shrugs lightly, apparently unconcerned with his perceived shortcomings.

"You poor thing, it must be rough to be so limited." I say sarcastically, but then stop myself from saying more. It's probably safe to assume that you should watch your P's and Q's around an angel.

"Why do I get to see you? I mean, if humans rarely see their guardians, why are you showing yourself to me— why are you telling me? How old are you?" I can't seem to stop with the rush of questions. They're like an endless data stream as I try to fit the puzzle pieces together in my mind.

"I'm revealing myself to you because those were my orders. I don't know why- but I know that it'll work out like it's supposed to. Trust me, it always does." He smiles again. "I chose to look like a teenager- someone your age- because I thought it would make you more comfortable. I can appear in any form I wish."

For some reason, out of all the information he's handed to me this afternoon, this last bit makes me the most uneasy.

What is he really?

"What do you really look like? Am I allowed to know?" I'm almost hesitant to ask, because I'm hesitant to know. But at the same time, if he's with me all of the time, and it sounds like that's the case, then I need to see exactly what he is.

He looks at me again. He has a strange way of examining me, as though he's looking straight through my eyes, into my deepest thoughts. He stares at me for a moment longer and then stands up.

"Are you certain? I'll show you, if you like."

I consider, re-consider and then nod. I close my eyes briefly and open them again, ready for the transformation to begin.

But it's already done.

Samuel is seven foot tall. His sinewy muscles bulge like an Ironman Triathlon champion's. The soft knit fabric of his blue shirt clings to his chest where I can see the indentions of a highly muscled abdomen. Enormous wings are folded behind him- but they don't resemble the angel wings that live in my imagination. I'd always pictured them as snow white and downy soft, like those of a baby bird, perhaps.

There's nothing diminutive about Samuel's wings… they're gray and enormous– and probably have a wingspan of 20 feet or more. And I can tell just by looking that they're strong. There are no downy soft feathers present here. These feathers look like a strange leather-hybrid; the actual material is definitely not of this earth. I don't know what it is, but it's definitely not fluffy and soft.

His hair is dark, but it's straight as an arrow and shoulder length, parted in the middle. His skin is bronzed and glistening, his cheekbones chiseled like an ancient Roman sculpture. In fact, he looks like an enormous gladiator. He exudes strength. It's literally palpable in the air around him. His teeth are blindingly white.

But his eyes are what struck me the most…with fear.

They're black as pitch.

Absolutely blacker than the blackest, moonless night.

No pupil, no iris, no white. Just solid inky black.

Samuel is perhaps the single-most frightening thing I've ever seen.   And he's not a creature from a horror movie or a mythical bogey-man.

He's real. And he's standing in front of me with black eyes.

Chapter Seven

"Change back, please." I whisper, closing my eyes. I reopen them a moment later, and Samuel the boy is sitting next to me again; safe and beautiful.

"Are you all right?" he asks gently.

"Your eyes…" my voice trails off. I don't want to offend him. *Can* you offend an angel?

"I'm sure you've heard the saying, 'the eyes are the windows to the soul'?" he asks me, as his eyes, now shimmering and turquoise, are trained on my face.

"Yes," I murmur.

"I don't have one."

I gasp and my eyes never leave his. I can feel my hands shaking in my lap. He's soulless?

"Why does that upset you?" he asks in a gentle voice. "I don't need one. You have a soul for a reason—to carry the essence of who you are to Heaven after you die. I'm a heavenly creature already, so I have no need."

He must realize that it's a lot for my earthly brain to take in because he backpedals a bit.

"Whitney, things are not what they seem to you. Here on earth, you see things as you believe that they are, but you don't have the whole picture. You see with a very narrow-sighted lens. And that's the way it's meant to be. But someday, you'll truly be able to see, and you'll realize then that there is so much more to everything than you ever dreamed possible."

"Why do you have to be so scary- I mean, in your real form?" I look up at him hesitantly, hoping again that I didn't offend him. Apparently, angels have really thick skin, because he doesn't even hesitate.

"It's a human misconception that angels are sweet little cherubs. I've seen the pictures of the little chubby angel babies flying around the clouds kissing with their little scarves wrapped around their waists. It's laughable, really.

"In real life, angels are deadly warriors, Whitney, because we have to be. We can't be sweet and harmless. We can't be innocent because we fight evil. That is what we were created to do. We fight evil of the caliber of which you have never seen, not even in your scariest horror movies, because your human minds can't begin to fathom it."

Chills run down my spine.

"What do you mean, 'evil like I have never seen?'" I ask. "Everywhere I look; there are stories about murders, child abuse, drugs…. That's evil. I see it every day, every time I turn on the news. I am fully aware of what is around me."

"You're right," Samuel agrees. "But that's a different kind of evil. That evil is man-made and we can't interfere in that, unless it threatens to interfere in your individual plan. The evil that I fight- and the evil that I protect you from- is of the supernatural nature." He shifts gears as he realizes that I'm following.

"You and your friends have gone to see countless vampire movies… and you calmed your fears by telling yourself 'they aren't real.' And you were right. Vampires aren't. Werewolves aren't. But the abilities that your movies portray them to have... inhuman strength, the ability to influence humans, super-human speed... those abilities exist in us. And we don't all use them for good."

I suck in my breath, staring at him, waiting.

"Whitney, do you remember hearing about a war in Heaven? About Lucifer being cast down from Heaven to live on Earth?" I nod, because I do vaguely remember hearing that in church. We aren't overly religious, but we do go sometimes- and he knows that.

"Well, other angels were cast down with him. Fallen angels have the same abilities as I do, but they aren't the same as me- they have the worst intentions possible. And that's just the tip of the supernatural iceberg. Lucifer has an army of demons at his fingertips to do his bidding-anything that he wishes."

I'm stunned and cold and scared and Samuel stares down at me.

"Humans like to make movies and write books about demons, but they tend to treat them like scary movies...as entertainment. Society has evolved to a point where people tend to believe that they aren't real. In fact, that's Lucifer's greatest accomplishment. But they're just as real as you and me, and they're all around you- more evil than you can imagine.

"I guard you from that. I protect you from bumps in the night- the bumps that you can't see, but that I can. This is the evil that I fight – the evil that I protect you from."

He watches my face carefully as he speaks. I hope that my face doesn't betray my fear, or the chills running down my spine.

"The reason that you feel that you know me, Whitney, is because you do. I was in the room when you were born and took your first breath. I stood watch beside your crib every day after that. I watched as your mom crept into your room five times a night to make sure that you were still breathing. I watched you learn to walk. I was there when you broke your arm when you were eight. I was right beside you when your dad died. I sat on your bed that night as you cried yourself to sleep. I know you and you know me. Even though you never saw me with your eyes, you knew me with your soul. That's why you felt it there, like a memory, as soon as you saw me."

His comforting voice silences any reservations that I have. I can't argue with that. I *did* feel it- as soon as I saw him- in the very innermost depths of my ...soul. It feels silly to think of it in such a dramatic way. But it's the truth.

My soul recognized him when my eyes did not.

"Why did you let me break my arm? Aren't you supposed to protect me from harm?"

"How did you break your arm, Whitney?" Again with the patient voice.

"You were watching—I know you already know. I fell when I was ice-skating."

"That's right. You fell while you were ice-skating. How did you fall?" He politely inquires.

"I don't know. It happened so fast and I was only eight. I never saw what I tripped on. Delaney didn't either." I shake my head. I remember part of that day like it was yesterday- because breaking my arm was so painful, but the details of what actually happened are blurry.

"Allow me to elaborate for you." I stare at him in awe. It's incredible to listen to someone else talk about your life with more detail than you know yourself.

"It was very close to spring," he continues, "and even though it was really too late in the season to ice-skate, you badgered your mother until she gave you permission to skate 'just one last time'. She thought it was still cold enough to be safe. She was wrong. You eventually began skating toward thin ice. Very thin ice- but you didn't see it because it didn't look thin.

"You would have fallen through- and your friend, Delaney, wouldn't have been able to pull you out and she wouldn't have been able to get help in time. I grabbed your arm, spinning you backward to safety. You fell, of course, when I spun you around, and you skidded across the lake. Your arm broke where I grabbed it, not from the fall, like your mother logically thought."

"I would have drowned." My words are a statement, not a question.

I'm stunned. I can't help but imagine my eight-year old body breaking through the ice and flailing in the dark, ice-cold water until I stopped thrashing and drifted to the bottom, trapped helplessly under the ice. The thought makes me shudder.

"You would've drowned." Samuel is matter-of-fact, without a trace of arrogance or pride.
"But it wasn't your time. I pulled you back, but I broke your arm. I'm sorry for that. You cried for hours that night from the pain. I remember that you cried so much on Muffy that her fur was stuck together for a week." His mention of my old childhood cat makes me smile. He knows so much about me.

"Thank you. For breaking my arm." I smile. He smiles back, and I swear that my chest vibrates with the brilliance of it. "Thank you for protecting me. I wish I would have known…"

"You're most welcome. But you don't need to thank me. It's my job. It's what I do. And I'm really good at it." He grins and I finally detect a bit of smugness. "I did a much better job this morning. Not a single broken bone!"

I stare blankly at him.

"I pushed you out of the way. The jack was going to fall from all of your tugging. I pulled you backward before you could use your foot -but I'm guessing that you felt like you were just losing your balance, correct? You kicked the jack- releasing the hydraulics and the car safely crashed down. No harm done- except to your pride."

"I didn't even feel you touch me. I didn't feel a thing." I feel my mouth hanging open and consciously close it.

"That's the way it usually is. I can't tell you how many times I have stepped in like that."

I'm having a hard time absorbing everything and shake my head. I need to talk about something else. I have a million questions to ask.

I zero in on his blue shirt. It's the exact shade of blue I've been seeing out of the corner of my eye. I feel a puzzle piece drop into place.

"Were you in the gym earlier?" I ask hesitantly.

"Yes."

"Why? Who were you arguing with?"

"I can't share that with you. I'm sorry." And he does look sorry.

Why can he help in one situation but not in another, and why can he reveal himself but not explain everything? My mind might explode. I decide against asking him to clarify the rules. I have a feeling I wouldn't understand anyway.

"All right.... can you tell me more about you instead? About angels, I mean?   You're not what I would have thought. Do you ever die? How old are you? Are you with me every minute?"

I can't stop myself, my curiosity is overwhelming. He knows everything about me and I don't know anything about him. It hardly seems fair.

He laughs and the sound of it is contagious. It makes me want to laugh too.

"How do you do that?" I ask incredulously.

"What?" I can tell from his face that he honestly doesn't know what I mean.

"When you laugh, I feel happy myself... I mean, like really happy. When you smile, it seems like everything is beautiful all around me. Like every light in the universe is coming from your body, but I'm still able to look at you. How do you do that?" I can't stop myself from staring.

"Oh, that." He's blasé. I guess I can understand that. He's used to walking around like that. "I'm a heavenly creature, Whitney, so I have a piece of that inside me. It's hard to explain to someone who hasn't seen it."

"Try." I implore. There's a Heaven. And a God. I'm fascinated, intrigued... and relieved. A part of me, deep down, has always secretly doubted the existence of both.

Samuel is endlessly patient. "Heaven is everything that is right and good and beautiful. Every time a human eventually sees it, they finally grasp that they should never have been afraid to die in the first place. They realize that they should have been waiting for it, not dreading it. Your human mind cannot possibly comprehend the beauty of it, because it's not simply a physical beauty. The beauty is within everything. It wraps itself under, around and through everything like a ribbon. Does that help?" He looks at me expectantly, clearly expecting me to get it now.

"Not really. But we can come back to it another time. How old are you?"

"Time isn't the same for me, as it is for you, Wh"— but I interrupt him.

"Can you not give me that kind of explanation, please? It's too frustrating. Explain it in a way that I'll understand." My request accidentally comes out as more of a demand.

"Okay, Miss Bossy, I've existed since the beginning of time. I'm millions of years old."

I gasp again. I have never gasped so many times in one day before today.

"Will you ever die?" I'm proud that my voice doesn't shake.

"No. I'm not human, Whitney. I'm not like you. I was never born- I was created, to be exactly what I am. I'll never die, I'll never change. My emotions aren't the same as yours. I have them, of course, but mine are different. For example, I don't feel fear. I've never once known what it feels like to be afraid." He stops and looks at me, waiting for me to absorb what he said. I nod mutely, mulling over his words.

Surprisingly, I realize that I don't want to ask any more questions. I'm too overwhelmed by everything already.

"My brain hurts," I tell him softly. He smiles.

"I'm sure. But it's just as well. You've got to go, or you'll be late picking up Ellie."

Before I can even blink, he's gone. He's not visible on the beach or the bluffs... and no footprints lead anywhere.

I'm stunned, frozen, as I spin in a circle, but then I hear his voice.

"Go. Or you'll be late. You'll see me later."

His voice comes from nowhere. And everywhere. I still can't see him.

I numbly rush from the bluffs and head across town, my mind blown by the realization that Samuel exists. I have a guardian angel.

But most importantly, I'm not crazy.

Chapter Eight

R U going 2 tell me what is going on???

Three question marks, which means Delaney's fit to be tied. Probably screwed to the ceiling.

As I lie with my feet propped up in dad's hammock, I notice that there are three missed calls from Delaney, as well, but I never heard my phone ring. I check to make sure that I hadn't accidentally turned it to vibrate only, but that isn't the case. The ringer is set for 'loud'.

I turn my thoughts back to Delaney. She's asking about Brady because she has no idea that something so earthshattering had happened to me mere moments ago.

She has no idea about Samuel.

I can't decide if I should tell her about what happened on the bluffs or not. It's one thing that I had questioned my own sanity. I don't want other people to start.

After a brief moment of contemplation, I decide to keep quiet about it while I ponder everything myself. It's not exactly something you can work into conversation. It's something you have to see for yourself to believe.

When I'd returned home from the bluffs, Samuel was nowhere to be found.

I don't what I expected… whether I thought he'd be waiting for me in the living room reading a newspaper or what. But he definitely wasn't. I'd done a quick walk-through of the house and he wasn't anywhere. I felt like an idiot standing in the middle of my room and whispering his name, and even stupider when he hadn't appeared.

It's all just so....mind-blowing.

For the past several weeks, I've been feeling so alone, so sad and miserable because I thought my dad was just gone and emptiness had replaced him.

But if there really is a God and a Heaven... then it means that my dad is still somewhere.

He's not just scattered on the bottom of the lake. A feeling of comfort washes over me. Maybe everything really is going to be okay.

But I do have one lingering question. Something that Samuel couldn't answer, but that niggles in my mind.

Why was he allowed to reveal himself to me? To what end? He even said himself that it's a bit unusual. So why now? And why me?

I'm saved from torturing myself with it though, because Delaney gives up on texting and tries to call again. My phone rings noisily in my lap, and strangely, the ringer works just fine now.

I pick it up and wait for the onslaught of questions from the examining panel otherwise known as my best friend. She should consider being a journalist... she covers the "What, Where, When, Why and How" questions quicker than humanly possible, omitting only the "Who," because she already knows that one.

It's actually a welcome distraction. I describe my little episode with Brady with as much detail as I can while she chatters like a parakeet on speed on the other end. I can barely answer one question before she's on to the next; pondering, supposing and predicting.

She's just deciding upon a future course of action for me when I notice what appears to be the top of my mom's head bobbing along the top of the fence. I recognize the tangled blonde hair. I quickly murmur to Laney that I'd have to talk to her later and go investigate.

I push open the gate to the yard and peer down the sidewalk.

Sure enough, mom is strolling the length of the sidewalk barefoot and in her nightgown. She's looking around in wonder, like a two year old observing a rainbow. I push through the gate and rush over to her, crushing fallen cherry blossoms under my feet as I run.

"Aren't the trees pretty, Whitney?" Mom chirps, staring absentmindedly up at the cherry trees, which truly are gorgeous.

I'm surprised to hear her speak because she hasn't said a word in weeks. She doesn't seem surprised to see me, although she doesn't appear to be expecting me, either. She just absorbs my sudden presence as though I've been here all along.

She doesn't seem to notice, or care, that she's in her nightgown outdoors with her hair standing up everywhere. Her skin is china doll white and her slight smattering of freckles are drastically visible against the paleness of her skin. It suddenly occurs to me that she hasn't seen the sun in almost two months.

This is so not like my mother. She always looks healthy, she always looks perfectly put together. Seeing her like this is just....stunning. And not in a good way.

I grasp her elbow gently and try to steer her back toward the house.

"Mom, why don't we go back inside and get some clothes on? Don't you think that would be a good idea?"

I recognize the patronizing tone in my own voice and instantly pray that she doesn't. I shouldn't have worried. She doesn't even notice that I'd spoken. She squats down by the edge of the sidewalk to examine a working ant hill. I make a mental note to look for some ant killer in dad's shed.

"Mom, you're going to get ants on your feet. They're red--they'll bite."

She pokes her finger at the ants, suddenly drawing the letter 'M' through the sand of their hill- apparently, she's going to write her name, Maricel. A couple ants begin a trail, beginning on her wrist and continuing up her arm.

"Mom!" I brush at the ants and tug her upwards. "Let's go inside!!"

Out of the corner of my eye, I see Mr. Masapollo start down the sidewalk for his evening walk with his enormous Saint Bernard, Mutson. Oh, Lord. I don't need this right now.

I yank her arm harder and she cooperates this time.

She has red ants crawling up her ankles and up one of her arms. I know enough not to track them into the house, so I drag her through the back yard to her little ivy-covered greenhouse and grab a garden hose. I turn it on and spray her down, all in the name of washing off the ants. I have to admit, though, dousing her gives me more than a little bit of grim satisfaction.

But even with the icy water spraying on her and her wet nightgown now clinging to her legs, she still appears unfazed.

Instead, she just looks around her curiously, as though she has no clue where she is.

She loves this greenhouse. Dad built it for her for her birthday several years ago- and she loves puttering around out here every minute of her spare time. She used to say it kept her sane with her otherwise crazy life. But she looks at it now like she's never seen it before.

"This is a nice place, Whitney. What do you call it?" She looks at me with wide, child-like eyes.

"I call it *your green house*," I answer through gritted teeth.

She's clearly getting worse instead of better. I don't know how these things normally go, but I'm pretty sure that we shouldn't be descending further down the mountain of insanity- we should be climbing upwards toward reason by now.

Of course, this is coming from the girl who just met her guardian angel.

I swallow hard.

Ellie chooses this moment to seek me out, and finds mom and me standing in the middle of the defunct greenhouse with mom's nightgown dripping on the ground and the hose in my hand.

Ellie's eyes widen, but she doesn't question me.

She simply says, "Whit, the timer went off on the oven." She continues to stare, but doesn't ask a single question.

"Thanks, Monster. Could you possibly run in and start a hot bath for mom? We'll be right in and I'll dish dinner up."

I'm starting to feel a little guilty about the ice-water that I had just hosed down mom with. She's shivering, even though she's oblivious.

Ellie obediently turns and goes back into the house, not glancing behind her even once. It's pretty bad when a six-year old knows that things are too weird to ask questions about.

I haul mom back to the house and up to her bathroom. She doesn't offer any resistance.

I practically dunk her in the bathtub... her hair smells like old bacon grease. Disgusting.

I doubt that she's washed it in weeks. Possibly even seven weeks.

She sits limply in the tub and lets me wash her and towel her off before I head downstairs to pull dinner out of the oven.

Ellie and I eat in silence. I get the feeling that she doesn't want to know what's wrong with mom any more than I want to tell her.

My phone buzzes against the wood of the table and I pick it up, expecting to see Delaney's name. I don't.

Would tonight be a good night to come over?

Brady.

Ohmigod. My stomach still flutters over him, even after the weirdness of today. Maybe even more so, because at least my infatuation with him is something familiar to focus on, it's something definitely real.

But regrettably, after my mom's stunt with the ants earlier, I just can't have anyone over.

Not today.

Sighing, I answer him back.

I wish, but I can't tonight.

He answers within a minute.

Raincheck?

I smile. *Absolutely.*

It's because of Brady and the butterflies that he puts in my stomach, that I'm able to calmly clean up after dinner, without collapsing into a nervous breakdown over the circumstances of the day. I just focus on Brady's smile and the fact that he likes me, and everything else fades away...even Samuel, because there is no sign of him now.

When I'm wiping the kitchen counters, Ellie turns to me.

"I forgot, Whitney. Alexis wants to know if I can come over for a sleepover next week." She actually looks hopeful, which is encouraging. She hasn't shown much of an interest in anything lately.

"Sure. Just have her mom call me and let me know when... and give her my cell phone number, okay?"

The last thing I need is for someone to call the house. Mom hasn't been answering the phone as of yet, but with her recent strange behavior- who knows what she might do? She could answer the phone and start singing the Battle Hymn of the Republic.

I'm actually so unsettled by my mom's behavior earlier, that I don't want to encourage her to come downstairs with Ellie. Instead, I make a tray and carry it up to her room.

The problem is, she's not there.

I push open the door to the bathroom and find her curled up on the bathroom floor, stark naked, with her towel covering like a blanket.

She's sound asleep.

You've got to be kidding me. She won't sleep at night in her bed, but she'll curl up on the bathroom rug like a cat? Shaking my head, I bend over to rouse her. She can't stay on the floor naked. *This, ladies and gentlemen, is why I can't have Brady Parker over to my house.*

Even though I want to pull my hair out and then hers, I grit my teeth and help her with her nightgown before getting her settled into her bed. She barely even opens her eyes.

As I walk around her bed, I notice her closet door ajar. Moving to close it, I see a large box shoved into the back corner.

It's odd, because I've never noticed it before. And I've been in and out of my mom's closet a hundred times in the past two months. Her closet it perfectly organized in color-coded fashion. This box is definitely out of place.

Bending down to investigate, I see the label is covered in Hebrew writing.

Ah. This makes sense. It must be dad's things from his last dig site in Israel.

I ruffle through it—papers, books, an old dirty spoon of some sort, a small flat marble disc with an ugly looking eye on it, several pottery jars and a little bowl made from the same clay material.

I handle them carefully since I know they must be extremely old. In fact, I should really be wearing gloves. I pick each item up, re-wrap them carefully and replace them in the box.

But as I turn the last item over in my hands, the cold disc, I feel unsettled.

A weird feeling floats down around me, raising the hair on my neck. I almost feel like I did the other night, when I dreamed about the black presence in my bedroom. A weight seems to hover around me, pressing against me.

I stare down at the marble, at the strange eye that seems to stare back up at me. Why would anyone carve an eye on a marble disc? It's just flat out creepy.

And then I see my breath.

It's only now that I realize that this closet has gotten incredibly cold. Unnaturally cold.

With a start, I whirl around, expecting to find something…dark behind me. But I'm alone.

You're never alone, Whitney.

Samuel's words come back to me, only this time, they don't give me comfort. The feeling around me right now isn't the safe feeling that Samuel brought with him.

It feels wrong. Scary.

Evil.

I swallow and hurriedly replace the disc in the box and shove it back into the closet. I'm being ridiculous. There's nothing evil here.

But then Samuel's words fill my head again. *I protect you from bumps in the night- the bumps that you can't see, but that I can. This is the evil that I fight – the evil that I protect you from.*

I swallow hard and back away from the closet, away from the dark feeling that surrounds me.

"Samuel?" I whisper nervously, hoping that he'll appear, hoping that he can reassure me.

But nothing happens. I remain alone.

Crap.

In a hurry to get out of the room, I rush over to my mom. I bend to pull her covers up, since she'd already kicked them off, and her eyes pop open. I startle, and yank away, but she grasps my arm hard, her fingernails sinking into my flesh.

"It's not what it seems," she half-whispers, half-hisses. Her fingers are ice cold.

"What's not?" I ask uncertainly, staring into her eyes. They're wide-open, but empty. Like there's nothing behind them. My fingers start to shake. I wait for her answer, but there isn't one forthcoming. Instead, she closes her eyes again.

"Mom?" My whisper is small in the quiet room.

She doesn't answer.

I can't get out of the room fast enough. I scramble for the door, and close it with a click behind me before I hurry down the hall.

As I go, something bothers me, something in the back of my brain. I can't put my finger on it until I hit the bottom stair.

The date on the label indicated that it arrived the week after dad died, from someone named Josef Amir. Mom was pretty preoccupied with other things during that time… like grieving, so she'd just left the artifacts in her closet.

They should really be at the University, where my dad had worked as a professor when he wasn't out in the field. They always examined any artifacts that came from archeological digs- and then they kept some in their libraries, but sent most to museums- after they had been catalogued, examined and photographed from every possible angle.

Besides the fact that it's the right thing to do, I really just want them out of the house. They freak me out for some reason.

It's not what it seems.

My mom's hiss still makes the hair raise on the back of my neck when I think about it. *What's* not what it seems?

And why am I giving my completely crazy mother's words a second thought? She was poking at red ants earlier, for God's sake.

With a sigh, I head for my father's study. Mr. Amir must be one of my dad's colleagues from Israel- and he was obviously involved with the dig. He'd know exactly what to do with the artifacts. It only takes me a minute to locate his name in my dad's inbox.

Dad had received an email from him two months ago, shortly before he died. It doesn't mention the artifacts, it just says that he needs to speak with him soon. Interesting. I wonder if he even knows my dad is dead?

I quickly type an email.

Dear Mr. Amir,

My name is Whitney Lane.   I'm Peter Lane's daughter.   I'm writing to let you know, in case you didn't know, that my father has unfortunately been killed in an accident.   I did, however, find a box of Israeli artifacts in our home. If you could advise me what to do with them, or how to return them to you, I would appreciate it.

Best wishes,

Whitney Lane

I'm just closing the lid to my father's laptop when Samuel suddenly appears next to me, perching on the desk like some gigantic bird. Startled, I shove back in my chair, almost knocking it over.

"Hey! You can't just *do* that! You scared me to death!" I push my hair behind my ear with a shaking hand. "I've asked for you a couple of times tonight. You can't just ignore me, then appear out of nowhere."

My heart is still thumping. But unless I'm seeing things, at least I knew he's real.

I reach out a shaking hand and poke his shoulder.

He looks at me, mystified.   But my curiosity is satisfied.   My imagination isn't good enough to trick myself into imagining a tangible flesh and blood body. Well, not when I'm awake.

My dream about Brady comes back to me, causing redness to flare into my cheeks.

"I'm sorry," Samuel murmurs.   "I forget sometimes that you experience fear."

"Oh, right," I mumble. "Because you don't."

God, that must be nice.

Something else *nice* is the air surrounding me when Samuel is near.

It feels thick with a strange, safe feeling. I realize that I've felt it before, many times, before I'd even known

Samuel existed. Now that I know the truth, it's easy to identify.

It's invisible strength.

"I *am* sorry," he murmurs. "I only wanted to tell you that you're not crazy."

He leaps lightly off the desk and turns to face me. His eyes shimmer with movement and I find myself wondering what causes them to do that. I'll ask him later because I'm so not able to absorb any other weirdness today.

"How did you know that I thought I was crazy?"

"My powerfully accurate mind reading abilities."

I look at him doubtfully. Seriously?

He smiles and once again, it radiates through my chest. "Fine. I've gotten very good and observing you. I could see that you were doubting your sanity. Don't. I'm real."

"Samuel..." My voice trails off softly. I'm not sure how this whole guardian-human relationship is supposed to work. What exactly can he share with me? "Were you with me earlier, when I was in my mom's closet?"

He shakes his head. "No. I was needed somewhere else. Why?"

Because it felt dangerous. Evil. Terrifying. Things that you aren't. I should've known he wasn't there. But then who was?

You're never alone, Whitney.

I shake my head. "I just had a weird feeling. I can't explain it."

Samuel studies me, his hand on his knee.

"What's going on with my mom?"

It's his turn to shake his head. "Unfortunately, you can ask me anything, but I won't always have the answers. I don't know anything about your mom. Or what is wrong with her."

"Does she have a guardian?"

Samuel nods. "Yes, she does."

"So, when she does these things... like wandering out of the house in her nightgown.... What does her guardian do? Stand aside and do nothing?"

"No. He follows her and protects her from everything that isn't in her plan. I wish I could offer you advice, but I don't have anything to base it on. This situation is unusual, Whitney. Something is coming... something big. I just don't know what. All I know is this: We need to be ready for it."

A chill runs down my back at his ominous tone. Then the hair on my neck stands up at his next statement.

"Nothing is what it seems, Whitney."

I'm stunned as I stare at him, as he utters the same thing my mother did.

He raises an eyebrow. "What's wrong?"

"You...uh... my mother said the same thing a little bit ago."

He's interested in this, I can tell. I can practically see him filing my words away. "Well, it's good advice. I can't always tell you everything I know, Whitney, and there *are* things you don't know. Just know this, I'll do everything I can to keep you safe."

I stare at him.

"Until you're ordered not to."

He stares back and doesn't answer, and I know I'm right.

That so does not make me feel better.

Chapter Nine

By morning, I'm starting to calm down again.

I've come to the realization that I can't control whatever happens. Last night, I didn't dream, so that's good. I didn't wake up and find my mother glaring at me, so that's good too. What I'm going to have to do at this point is just trust that Samuel has my best interest at heart. I'm going to try and continue with life as usual, and just focus on keeping my head above water.

Water.

All of a sudden, something occurs to me that causes me such instant panic that I drop my spatula and grip the edge of the counter hard enough to turn my knuckles white.

Ellie doesn't know how to swim.

Our father drowned in the lake. How in the world have I not signed Ellie up for swim lessons? There's no way I'm taking her out on the *No Problem* with me this summer, or anywhere near the lake, actually, until she can swim.

I immediately pick up the phone and call Miranda Eli.

Her voice is entirely too cheerful for this early in the morning and I find myself wondering if she'd gone through an entire pot of coffee by herself. But I'm able to get the information that I need and I enroll Ellie in swim classes online with my mom's credit card.

Mom's just lucky that I'm a responsible kid... someone else might have a field day with their parent's credit card. I'm only buying the necessities.

Turns out, it's going to work out perfectly. I'm getting my driver's license on Thursday, and Ellie's swim lessons will start that same day. I'll drive her to the aquatic center in Traverse City twice a week for the rest of the summer.

But that's ok. Obviously- especially now, Ellie needs to know how to swim. Miranda's doing me a huge favor by letting Ellie start after the class already begun.

As I let the scrambled eggs cool for a minute, I dart into dad's study to see if Josef Amir answered my email yet.

He hasn't. I try to console myself with the fact that he might be out in the field, so it could take him a while to get back to me. But that's not really a consolation. For some reason, the mere idea of that box of weird stuff sitting in my house puts me on edge. That cold feeling around it.... Ugh. I shiver unconsciously, even now.

"Whatcha doin', Whit?" Delaney leans in the doorway, watching me curiously, distracting me from my uneasiness.

"That's a better question for you, Laney." I smile and get up, walking out of the study. I'm not surprised by her sudden appearance, though. She and I come and go as we please in each other's houses. She trails after me into the kitchen, eyeing the eggs.

"Did you make enough for me?" Without waiting for an answer, she grabs a plate from the cabinet and a coke from the fridge. She's definitely comfortable here.

"So…. What in the world are you doing out so early?"

Another thing about Delaney- she's always late. She hates to get out of bed and she arrives for everything at the last minute. She always just assumes that nothing will start without her. The fact that she's up and around an hour before Driver's Ed is unheard of.

"I just thought I'd stop by and walk to our last day of class with you. Is that okay? I haven't been here in forever. You've been coming to my house instead." That's true. I *have* been making a point of that, for good reason. I don't want anyone, even my best friend, to see how bad mom's really gotten.

"Also, I wanted to borrow your hot pink tank top. It'd look way better with these shorts."

"Ah, the truth comes out," I smile at her anyway. "It's going to clash with your hair but okay."

She doesn't seem concerned about the color scheme and pushes back from the table. "I can go up and get it while you guys finish if you want."

She runs up the stairs. Ellie and I have time to finish our eggs and bagels before she comes back down, not only wearing my pink shirt, but also a pair of my white capris. She feels *very* comfortable in my house. I have to admit... the pink doesn't look bad at all with her hair.

I ignore her gloating expression as we drop Ellie off at Alexis's house and swing by the coffee shop on our way to the school. Anything to delay class... because we have to take our driving tests today. I don't know a single person who enjoys parallel parking.

As we push open the door of the coffee shop, the bell over the door tinkles our arrival. The first thing I notice is Brady. He's at the counter ordering. When he turns around and sees us, his face visibly lights up.

"Whitney! Oh, and hey Delaney! What do you guys want? I'm buying."

Delaney elbows me in the ribs before she saunters ahead to place her order. I trail behind, suddenly feeling shy.

I've been analyzing every detail of my encounter with Brady in my head. Now that he's standing right in front of me, buying me a coffee, I'm awkward. It's much easier to pretend I'm charming when he's a memory. Real-life Brady is even more beautiful and intimidating than Memory Brady.

You've got more important things to stress about, I try and tell myself. But my heart doesn't listen, because it continues to flutter in my chest.

"Whit? What would you like?" He looks at me expectantly. His cologne smells really masculine and distracts me for a second.

"Oh, um... just an iced coffee. Regular, extra ice," I murmurs. "Thanks, Brady, but you don't need to buy our breakfast." Behind him, Delaney's making all sorts of gestures... I interpret them to mean, *What are you doing, idiot? Talk to him!*

I turn my back on her. I can hear her audibly sigh.

Brady cocks and eyebrow. "This is your breakfast? That's no good. You're gonna be starving after class. We should get some lunch together."

"We'd love to," Delaney smiles engagingly up at him. She apparently has decided not to mention that we'd already eaten at home. Clearly, Brady had been talking to me, but equally as clearly, Delaney isn't about to miss an opportunity to put her plans for me into action. She grins at me triumphantly, then turns to face Brady.

"How about the Sandwich Hut? We can eat by the beach?"

"Sounds good." He smiles and my mind snaps to attention. Whatever else is going on in my life, I'm having lunch with Brady Parker. It's surreal.

"Is that okay with you?" I ask him. I don't want him to get bull-dozed by Delaney just because he's too polite to say no.

"Absolutely." He lightly touches my elbow, sort of guiding me toward the door, and I like it. It seems protective, somehow.

When we step onto the sidewalk, he removes his hand and I immediately feel the absence of it. My stomach turns flip-flops again. What is it about him that sets my skin on fire? Every single nerve ending is tingling like it's been soaked in peppermint oil.

Since Brady is walking next to me, the trip to school seems to take five seconds. Every time he bumps me, or his hand nudges mine, electricity shoots through my body.

But too soon, the school doors loom in front of me, large and depressing. Brady opens them for me, and my heart melts.

A gentleman.

Gah.

Delaney waggles her red eyebrows behind his back and I roll my eyes. She's going to take credit for this somehow, I know it. But it doesn't matter. All that matters in this moment is getting through this last day of driver's ed.

Mr. Divine splits us up into pairs for the driving test. Luckily, I'm paired with Laney. If I'm going to mess up, it needs to be her that sees it. I can't stomach the thought of Brady watching me strike out.

Luck strikes a second time when he calls our names first. Since I have to do it, I might as well do it first.

Laney practically leaps into the back seat, ensuring that I have to go before she does. I glare at her and she sticks her tongue out. With a sigh, I position myself in the driver's seat, adjusting the seats and mirrors, and I notice my hands are shaking.

Mr. Divine notices too. His lips twitch. "Just relax, Miss Lane. I won't bite."

I wasn't worried about *him*. I'm worried about *me*. Ramming the car in front of me, or rolling our car, or completely looking like an idiot as I attempt to parallel park.

Just as I think I'm going to throw up, my nerves suddenly calm. Peace descends over me in a wave.

With a start, I glance at the empty seat beside Delaney. If I didn't know better, I'd think that Samuel was here. I feel the same strange feeling in the air, the calming, strong feeling.

But he's not. It's just Divine, Delaney and me.

I pull the car slowly out of the parking space and ease it into the road. I hear the gravel crunch and I give it a bit more gas.

I glance in the rearview mirror as I turn, and am startled to see Samuel lounging comfortably on half of the backseat. Startled, I twist around to look, but he's not there.

"What?" Delaney demands. "Is my mascara smeared?"

"No, you're fine," I say uncertainly, because when I look in the mirror again, Samuel is there. In the mirror.

He winks.

Good Lord.

"Calm down, Whit. You're going to do fine." Laney offers me assurance from the backseat, completely unaware that there's a hulking angel sprawled out next to her.

Doesn't she notice the change in the air?

I glance in my mirror again and he grins at me. I might kill him. But that won't do any good.   Angels can't die.

"You'll be fine, Whitney," Mr. Divine tells me again. "I have an emergency brake over here that I can use if I have to."

I can't help but roll my eyes. You drop a car one time and everyone loses faith in your abilities.

For the next fifteen minutes, I manage to keep it under the speed limit, I use my blinkers and it only takes me two attempts to parallel park.

"Beat that, Laney," I crow, as I turn back into traffic.

She rolls her eyes, but Mr. Divine pipes up. "You're doing a great job." His voice has a distinct note of surprise in it that I choose to ignore. "Go ahead and take this next exit and then turn left."

I feel an enormous sense of relief. My turn's almost over and I'd done a next to perfect job. One less thing to worry about.

As directed, I pull onto the exit ramp behind a large construction truck, doing exactly the speed limit posted. Unfortunately, my diligence to the rules of the road doesn't do me much good because the tailgate of the truck bounces open and a roll of wire fencing flies out.

Laney screams as the roll of wire flies straight toward our windshield.

It seems to happen in slow-motion, but then it becomes a non-event.

It doesn't hit the windshield, instead it seems to fly over the top of our car, bouncing off behind us.

My driver's education hadn't prepared me for this. There's no chapter in our book entitled "How to avoid unexpected construction implements."

I try not to panic and lightly brake as I pull off to the side of the road. My instinct had been to slam on the brakes and swerve hard, but I managed to ignore it. It's crazy how sometimes your instincts are exactly the opposite of what you should do.

Adrenaline makes my pulse thunder through my veins as the truck continues on its way- not even stopping as a couple of cinderblocks also tumble from its bed, landing in the middle of the road.

Put your flashers on," Mr. Divine instructs. He gets out, looks to make sure the exit ramp is clear and then removes the cinderblocks from the middle of the road.

I glance in the mirror. Samuel's not in the backseat anymore. I suddenly know that my ability to control the situation hadn't been my own. He'd done something to help.

"Holy cow, Whit! I'm so impressed! You didn't freak out or anything!" Laney gushes from the backseat, but her praise is interrupted when Mr. Divine gets back into the car.

"Whitney, you've successfully passed your driving test. I'm extremely proud of the way you handled that situation. A good driver keeps their head in a stressful situation, which is exactly what you did. Excellent job!" Well, at least he's right about that. No matter what Samuel physically did to help me, I did manage to stay calm, so at least *that* much is my accomplishment.

Delaney and I change places so that she can do her test, which is completely uneventful. Twenty minutes later, we both have written approval to get our licenses.

Brady and Justin get called next, and Delaney and I look at each other.

"Want to wait at the Hut?" Delany asks cheerfully. "We can get a coke. I'm dying of thirst."

I nod because I'm determined to pretend that having lunch with Brady is perfectly normal and I'm not freaking out, and so we start out for the beach.

As we walk down the boardwalk, I happen to notice a dark head sitting on the end of the pier. Without even studying it harder, I know exactly who it is. I recognize the long lean legs dangling over the edge.

Carter Kelly.

I don't give him the satisfaction of giving him a second glance. I know he'd only glare at me anyway. So, instead, I throw myself into conversation with Laney, steering her away from Carter, because I know that if she sees him, she'd be all over him instantly. Because he's new. And new means 'challenging' in Delaney's book.

I just can't do it today. I'm so not into boys who hate me when I haven't even done anything.

So I make sure she sits with her back to him at the Hut. We order cokes as we wait and I close my eyes, soaking in the sunshine on my shoulders.

With my eyes closed, I catch part of a conversation from the table next to me. I immediately recognize the voices. Two girls, Haley and Manda, from school. They're on Miranda's swim team.

"I don't know what made him freeze up," Manda whispers. "He's supposed to be really good. Like, he won the 100 *and* 200 meter freestyle at state last year. I saw him compete, and he's like a machine. Or he *was*. I don't know what's wrong with him now."

Haley answers her, in a voice just short of awe. "I know. I couldn't believe it. Miranda says he'll bounce back."

They continue to speculate and gossip, and I'm sort of stunned. They have to be talking about Carter. So he froze up in front of everyone, apparently? That must've been a huge blow to his obviously arrogant ego.

I glance over at him again, against my will, and I almost soften, just a bit, at the expression on his face.

He's staring out at the water and he seems vulnerable, somehow. Like his guard is down. I can't explain it. All I know is that he's silent and still.

And just as I start to look away, he turns his face and meets my gaze. His stare is like black fire. It ignites a trail between the two of us, freezing me into place.

My cheeks erupt into flame and he doesn't look away. He doesn't scowl or glare, he just stares, then very deliberately, very purposefully, he turns away.

Just like that.

What the hell?

"Hey girls."

Brady comes out of nowhere, appearing by my elbow. I startle and glance up at him, then find myself startled again.

God, he's gorgeous. God, his eyes are so freaking blue. God, I feel like I could fall into them.

"Hey," I answer weakly, turning away from dark-eyed Carter so that I can fall into blue-eyed Brady.

Without hesitation, Delaney pushes out the chair next to me for Brady, and he takes it.

Gah.

"So how'd your tests go?" he asks casually after we order. Delaney promptly launches into a diatribe, explaining how I'd maneuvered around the construction implements. I find myself blushing hard beneath Brady's appreciative blue gaze.

He seems sufficiently impressed. "Geez, Whit. I'll never believe another word that anyone tells me about women drivers," he teases.

I can't help grinning at him, even if he *is* indirectly insulting women as a whole. The warm feeling I get in my chest when he speaks is totally worth it.

"Well, feel free to believe every word, as long as they are speaking the truth, that women are clearly superior," I zing right back at him.

This light-hearted banter in the sun feels good. Maybe my life really is going to get back to normal. Maybe nothing bad is going to happen, after all. Maybe Samuel is wrong.

Because guardian angels have to be wrong sometimes, right?

Everything feels perfectly right as Brady slides his arm around my back on my chair. I feel his warmth through my shirt, my skin soaks it up. I swallow hard.

When our check arrives, he snatches it up and won't let us pay.

"No way, ladies. I invited you. I pay. That's the way it works, right?" He drops some cash on the table. "What plans do you have for the afternoon? Do you want to hang out and watch a movie or something?" He's oh-so-casual and it makes my heart pound.

Delaney answers before I do. "Of course we would! Why don't we go over to Whit's house? She has to pick up her little sister first, but they have a huge T.V. in their basement."

Brady looks at me. "Is that cool?"

I nod. Of course it is. As long as my mother stays in her room.

We push our chairs into the table and walk over the sand, beneath the pier. As we pass under, I catch sight of Carter's legs, still swinging in the breeze. He's still here.

And as we walk along the beach to reach the sidewalk, I can't help but glance over my shoulder.

Because he's watching me.

He stares into my eyes now, then his lips curve into a smirk.

Heat spreads through my chest, even though I have no clue what he's smirking about. He's the one sitting alone on the beach. Not me. I'm the one surrounded by friends.

Coldly, I turn away, and don't look back.

But even though I'm walking next to Brady Parker, the most gorgeous guy in Northport, I can't help but remain very conscious of the fact that Carter Kelly is still staring at me. I can feel it long after we've crossed the street and faded out of his sight.

Chapter Ten

After we pick up Ellie, we walk along the flower-lined sidewalk toward my house. Before I know it, Brady grabs my hand and all thoughts of Carter disappear.

Brady Parker is holding my hand.

As I would've expected, his hand is perfect. Not hot and sweaty, not icy cold. It's just right and he grasps my fingers lightly. Miss Matchmaker herself stares at me with satisfaction from behind Brady. She wriggles her eyebrows again. I know she's going to take credit for this, but I don't care. Brady Parker is holding my hand, and I'm going to enjoy the moment.

Ellie chooses this very moment to turn around from where she's skipping ahead of us. She stares at Brady, then narrows her eyes.

"Are you Whitney's boyfriend?"

I'm dying inside. Literally dying. If I could claw open a hole in the sidewalk, I would so do it. But Brady only smiles.

"I'm Brady. And has anyone ever told you that you're as pretty as your sister?"

Ellie is, of course, immediately charmed and practically preens before my eyes. The rest of the short trip to our house, she keeps him engaged in a conversation about sea turtles.

Apparently, she and Alexis had been watching the Discovery channel and had learned that sea turtles eat jellyfish, which both girls found repulsive and interesting at the same time. She shares the news with Brady to which he shows the appropriate amount of disgust. She smiles in satisfaction.

"I like your boyfriend, Whittie."

God.

My cheeks burn, but Brady just chuckles as we enter the cool darkness of my house.

I nervously glance around but mom is nowhere in sight.

Thank you, God.

I internally cross my fingers, because I just know that if she makes a spectacle in front of Brady, he'll run as far from me as he can. And I wouldn't blame him.

Ellie decides that she wants to continue watching the Discovery Channel upstairs, so I lead Brady and Delaney to the basement, to our fully stocked family room. We have everything down here… my dad had made sure of it. An 80" inch flat screen, surround sound, a pool table, even air hockey. We literally have hundreds of movies.

Brady looks around and lets out a low whistle.

"Holy cow, Whit. Your family doesn't mess around."

This had been my dad's man cave and I haven't been down here since he died. But of course, I don't say that.

Instead, I show Brady to the tall cabinet that houses the movie collection and leave him with the task of choosing one while Laney and I go back upstairs to get some sodas.

She look sat me strangely since there's a mini-fridge fully stocked with sodas downstairs in the wet bar, but I don't care. I just need to get her alone for a minute.

"You aren't planning anything, are you?" I ask her suspiciously as I load her arms with icy cokes from the fridge.

"Of course not!" She pastes an innocent look on her lovely face. "What would I possibly be planning?"

I almost feel dizzy from anxiety. I have to consciously calm myself down. There's nothing to be nervous about. He's a boy and I'm a girl and we're going to watch a movie. Period.

I tell her that very thing as I grab a big bowl and dump some pretzels in it. We'd just eaten, but it seems like boys are always hungry. Delaney rolls her eyes.

"Okay, okay. Calm down. I have no idea what you're talking about, anyway. I won't leave you. I promise."

When we return to the basement, we find that Brady already chose a movie, a comedy, and is popping it into the player. I pause, appraising the situation.

He's sitting on the long end of the sectional. There's clearly room next to him for me. Or I could sit on the short end by myself, or in a recliner, which is across the room from him. Laney quickly takes that option off the table by choosing it for herself.

I can feel her gloating with her eyes.

"Here, Whit," Brady pats the seat next to him. "I hope this movie is okay?"

I stifle my nerves and sit next to him. Of course I should sit next to him. Sitting on the other end of the sofa would be weird. And I'm not weird.

But I *am* nervous. I sit the pretzels on the big ottoman in front of us and settle into the couch next to him. He un-pauses the movie and propped his legs up, getting comfortable.

"Are you cold?" he asks softly.

Without waiting for my response, he pulls a soft chenille blanket from off the back of the couch. He quickly wrap sit around me and then leans back next to me. He lays his arm along the back and I sink back into his arm.

It's so comfortable that I could just curl up and go to sleep.   He smells the same as he did the other day- masculine. My heart skips a beat. Everything about him screams testosterone and masculinity. I decide that must be what's wreaking havoc on my nerve endings. That... and the memory of that dang dream.

I suddenly remember Samuel and wonder if he's here, watching. I don't feel his presence. But then I feel silly, because of course he's here. His job is to watch me.   I make a mental note to discuss with him how he handles the whole observation thing when things get private.   For instance, I don't want to feel like Samuel's hovering right over us when Brady's arm is wrapped around me or if he holds my hand. I don't need to be any more self-conscious than I already am.

I glance over at Brady.

His pale yellow t-shirt is stretched tightly across his chest. I can easily see the prominent muscles that exist in bulk there. In fact, I can practically identify the individual striations.

The heady feeling of being so close is intoxicating enough to make my head spin. I quickly decide that I need to return my attention to the movie before I hyperventilate.

I focused on the screen. It's the same today as it's been the other six times I've seen it- funny and lighthearted. Perfect for today. I let myself become absorbed.

Halfway through, Laney jumps up and announces that she's going upstairs to the bathroom.

"Can you pause it? I don't want to use the one down here... I don't want you to listen to me pee!" She darts off toward the staircase.

Brady and I stare at each other, then start laughing.

"She's... something." He smiles. He reaches over with his free hand and grabs mine, drawing little circles with his thumb on the back of my hand. It should feel soothing, but instead it just makes it difficult for me to concentrate. I shake my head to clear it.

"Um, yeah. She is- she's always been that way, too. Ever since I can remember."

I smile back and hesitate as I notice that Brady's brilliant blue eyes are fixated on my mouth. I'm silent and so is he, and then he gently dips his head to brush his mouth against mine.

I stop breathing.

My first freaking kiss.

"I've wanted to do that ever since I saw you for the first time. Was it okay?"

He's staring into my eyes now- which I discover when I open my own.

It's almost exactly what he said in my dream. I freeze for a minute before relaxing again.

Coincidence.

"It's nice," I whisper. "Let's do it again."

He smiles against my lips, as he obliges.

His lips are warm and perfect, with just the right amount of gentle pressure against my own. My heart pounds in my chest as he gently caresses my back. My first kiss was absolutely perfect.

I can't wait to tell Delaney. She's been teasing me for so long about this, even calling me Sister Whitney sometimes. But I couldn't help it. There was no one that I wanted to kiss. Until now.

Our lips part and I move back to stare at his face. He's watching me with a gentle, sweet expression, and he tastes like spearmint. I'm just about to jokingly tell him that I like his gum, when Delaney's terrified scream pierces the air.

Startled, I jump up, getting tangled in the blanket covering me. Brady steadies my arm as we untangle the blanket and my legs. Delaney shrieks my name, and I lunge up the stairs two at a time with Brady right behind me.

I find Laney and my mom facing each other in mom's bathroom.

My mother is covered in blood.

Chapter Eleven

"What the..." I rush over and grab my mom, holding her away from me while I do a quick head to toe appraisal.

She has long angry scratches on her arms and chest, deep enough to bleed. There are no other signs of trauma. Everything else seems intact, except that there were bloody M's drawn everywhere around us...on the floor, on the counter, on the mirrors.

Brady lingers in the doorway, quietly taking the situation in.

"Laney- what happened?" I try to keep my voice calm, but it's proving difficult, especially with Ellie standing fearfully in the doorway peering around Brady's waist.

"Ellie, it's okay. You can go back to your room. I'll take care of this. It's all right." She backs quietly away without argument.

Laney looks at me helplessly. "I don't know what happened. I was just coming out of your bathroom when your mom came up and grabbed me. She wouldn't answer me when I talked to her and just kept pulling me until we got in here. Then blood started dripping down her arms..." Delaney's voice breaks and her wide green eyes fly from mom's injured arms to my face.

"Mom?" I look at her quizzically. "What happened? Why did you do this?" She calmly looks around the room before she answers.

"I don't know, Whitney." And honestly, it doesn't seem like she cares. Delaney's startled eyes wait for my reaction. Brady seems to be intently waiting, too.

"Okay. It doesn't look too bad. I mean, I don't think I need to take her to the doctor. I'm going to clean up her scratches and get a better look to make sure and then I think I should probably call my grandma."

"Grandma Ava? Oh, tell her hello from me, will you, Whitney?" Mom asks in a sing-song voice while she plays in the blood on her arm. She's drawing 'M''s again.

What. The. Hell. I'm astounded to the point that I'm motionless.

"Whit?" Delaney's voice is hesitant. "I know you don't like him, but maybe you should call Mr. Blaine. Maybe he'll know what to do."

Yeah, that was what I'm afraid of. He'd know exactly what to do. He'd start calling people and before I know it, Mom would be in padded restraints in a mental facility and Ellie and I would be in foster care or something.

Not happening.

"Um, I don't think so. My grandma Ava said to call her if it didn't get better and they'd come right away. They'll know what to do." My voice is deceptively confident as I steer my mom to the sink. There's blood all over the front of her nightgown where she'd wiped her arms. Besides the fact that it's going to be ruined, it also makes her look like an assault victim.

"Whitney, how long has she been like this?" Brady speaks from the door, his voice low and serious. I watch in horror as blood begins to trickle around mom's ankles, as well.   Her nightgown sticks to her as big reddish-pink splotches bleed through the fabric.

She'd scratched her legs, too.

"Um… Since the day after my dad died, but it wasn't this bad. She's gotten worse."

I push up her nightgown to assess the wounds on her legs, as Brady discreetly looks the other direction. I fight tears and can't bring myself to look at his face. I can't see the judgment that I know I'll find. Yes, my mom is crazy. I know. But I don't want to see that realization in his eyes.

"Why didn't you tell me?"

Delaney's voice is hurt as she gathers up the bloody towels that I'd just used. She watches me douse the scratches with anti-bacterial spray and bandage my mother as best I can. My mom doesn't even flinch from the sting of the spray.

"I was afraid you'd tell your mom and she'd call someone. I kept thinking that mom would get better any minute. I still keep thinking that. I don't know what is normal when someone is grieving and what isn't…"

"Whit, this isn't normal."

Delaney's eyes scan the bathroom. There's blood all over the sinks and even the walls. It looks like mom had done the scratching in here. The counters are smudged with her blood. Even the mirrors have fingerprints and M's on them. She's clearly obsessed with her name.

"I know." I acknowledge softly as I finish bandaging my mother. I help her into her room, sit her into her chair and hand her a magazine. I doubt she'll even look at it. Right now, she's staring listlessly out the window.

"I'm going to call my grandma right now. They'll come."

"Do you want me to call my mom?" Laney's voice is gentle, but I definitely don't want her to call her mother. I have the feeling that the more people that know, the worse it'll become- like a snowball rolling down a hill. It's already bad enough as it is.

"Thanks, anyway—but I think we'll be fine. I'm sure my grandparents will come right away. Probably tomorrow."

Delaney seems uncertain. "

Really, Laney. Please don't call your mom. I've got so much stress right now... I can't take one more thing. I promise, it'll be fine."

"Okay. I won't. But you have to promise to call me if something else happens and you need me. I mean- if *anything* happens. I can't believe you didn't tell me this."

She's hurt and I do feel guilty. I haven't kept a single thing from Delaney since we were in the first grade—we both had a crush on the same boy. I didn't tell her for the longest time that I had a crush on him, too. When I finally told her, she didn't talk to me for a week. Not because of the crush, but because I had kept it from her.

"Deal." I give her a quick hug. "Thanks, Lane. You really are the best... although you got blood on my shirt." She rolls her eyes at me.

"How about... I go change my shirt and then I'll keep an eye on your mom while you call your grandma?" I nod and she flits from the room like a red-headed sparrow.

I can't put it off any longer, so I muster the courage to look at Brady. He's watching me intently. He steps forward and puts his arm around my shoulders.

"Have you been dealing with this alone?" he asks softly. I don't trust my voice, so I just nod. He pulls me to his chest and I can feel his breath on my hair.

"Why didn't you tell someone? This is too much to deal with by yourself!"

There's no judgment in his voice as I had feared. There's only sympathy. He brushes the back of my neck softly with his fingers.

"Do you know what my dad does?" he asks with a slight amount of hesitation in his voice.

"No." I have even more hesitation in mine. What does his dad have to do with anything?

"He's a psychiatrist. I think we should call him. I promise you it'll be okay."

His voice is low and soothing, but I back away, startled. I feel like a cornered animal. I had no idea that his dad was a shrink. I know full well that my mom needs one, but I can't control the instant overwhelming sense of panic that I feel.

I don't want him to call his dad. I'm afraid of what might happen.

"They'll take us away," I whisper. I can't stand the thought of Ellie being separated from me. We're together- we're on the same team. I take care of her. The thought of her in a different household with strangers leaves me breathless and shaking.

Brady stares into my eyes.

"They won't. I promise. I give you my word that I'll get my dad to think of something else." His voice is solemn and protective, and I realize that I trust him. I find myself nodding.

"Okay," I softly agree. I know he's right. My mom needs help on a scale much larger than I can offer her.

"But I want to call my grandma first."

I pull out my phone and dial her number with shaking fingers. She answers on the second ring and I quickly recount the events of the past few days, ending with this latest bloody incident. I then listen abashedly while my grandma rails at me for not calling sooner. She hangs up and I look at Brady.

"She's going to check with the airlines and call me back."

Brady nods at me and pulls out his phone. I leave to find Ellie because I can't stay and listen to his conversation with his dad. I just can't.

I find my sister quietly playing with the dolls in her room.

She's busy being a normal, mentally-healthy mommy to her little plastic babies. Something her own mother is currently not.

My throat constricts. I walk softly in and sit on the edge of her bed. The image of her face, paralyzed with fear as she took in the bloody scene from the doorway earlier, runs through my mind like it's on a loop.

"Ellie, I don't want you to worry about mom, okay? She's going to be fine. She's just under a lot of stress and her brain has kind of gone into hibernation to protect itself." That's the best way I can think of to explain it to a six-year old. She knows what hibernation means- they had learned about bears in school.

She looks up from her dolls. "Is she ever going to get better?"

"Of course she is! One of these days, she'll be back to her normal self." I grip the footboard of her bed for support. I feel faint as I lie. It's a lie, because I have no way of knowing if it's the truth.

"Do you promise?" Big brown eyes stare at me expectantly.

"Of course I do," I utter without hesitation. My voice doesn't betray my uncertainty. My white knuckles, on the other hand, do.

Ellie nods, looking at her doll instead of me. I hug her and turn for the door. Before I even take three steps, she jumps up and throws her skinny arms around my waist.

"Thank you, Whitney!"

"For what, Monster?"

"For taking care of everything."

I gulp hard. I hadn't done a very good job. The crimson scratches on mom's body attest to that. The emotional scars that are sure to be imprinted permanently on Ellie's psyche probably could, too. But I obligingly say, "You're welcome, Ellie-Bellie," before I leave her to her dolls.

I leave her door cracked, just in case I need to hear anything because I'm paranoid now.

I'm anxiously waiting for the phone to ring, when the doorbell rings instead.

Peering through the door, I find an older version of Brady standing on my front porch. It has to be his dad, Dr. Parker. He's not wearing a white coat or anything, though. In fact, he's wearing shorts, a polo and brown loafers. Very normal looking and dad-like. Not how I picture a shrink.

I open the door.

"Dr. Parker?" My voice is a question. Of course it's him, I just can't imagine how he'd gotten here so fast.

"Hi, Whitney. My son Brady just called and said that you needed me here- that it's an emergency. Luckily, I have the day off today." Which explains the speedy response and the casual attire. I swing the door wide open.

"Please come in. Thank you for coming. I'm not even sure what to tell you we need." My voice cracks and I know he hears it. Behind me, I feel Brady approach from the hall. His footsteps are heavier than Laney or Ellie's.

"I just called my grandma. They'll be on the next available flight." I can feel Dr. Parker appraising me as I speak. I flinch as I realized what he's seeing. My shirt is smeared with my mother's blood.

"Whitney, I think it was an excellent first step to have called your grandma. But calling me was the perfect second step. I'll need to assess whether this situation is safe for everyone involved. I don't just mean you... I mean your mother, too."

Realization sinks in as he speaks. It had never, not even once, occurred to me that my mother might hurt herself. I mean, *seriously* hurt herself.

I gesture for him to come in.

"Please, come into the dining room...we can talk there. Mom is upstairs with Delaney and my sister is playing in her room. Can I get you some water or tea?"

"Tea would be wonderful, thank you." He follows me into the dining room and I know that he's examining our house as we walk, looking for any signs of disarray or disorder. He'd be disappointed if that's what he wants to find... our house is spotless.

Other than the blood on my shirt and the bloody bathroom upstairs, no one would be able to tell that anything is out of the ordinary in our household.

"Brady? Why don't you go help Delaney." Dr. Parker's voice is not a request. It's a quiet directive. He clearly wants to speak with me alone. I seat him and put the teapot on the stove. I bring him mom's basket of assorted tea bags and sit down beside him as we wait for the water to boil.

"Dr. Parker, she hasn't been really bad until just a few days ago." That's only a slight underestimate. "I kept thinking that she'd get better... but she hasn't yet. It's hard to describe, but it's like she's not really here anymore. I'm not a doctor, but it seems to me that she's trying to protect herself from her own grief. She and my dad were best friends."

I don't want to confide in him and I grew more afraid with every word that I speak, but I know I have to do it. He has the ability to pick up the phone and call people- of the State affiliated kind- who could make a drastic difference in my life...for the worse.

"I think you're very astute, Whitney." His blue eyes, just like Brady's, examine me. "And I think you are probably correct. Your mother is more than likely attempting to shield herself from the grief that she feels. She has created a safe cocoon for herself- an alternate reality, if you will." He continues to observe me and I realize that he's trying to gauge my own mental health, to see what kind of impact this whole thing is having on me. He's definitely a psychiatrist.

"Everything I've heard from you and Brady lead me to believe that she is aware that your father is gone. Her mind has been cushioning the impact of his passing, though, by not allowing herself to dwell on it. To do that, it seems that she has withdrawn from life in general. Your mom needs counseling, Whitney. I think she's beginning to acknowledge the pain to herself. Sometimes, people manage extreme emotional pain by creating physical pain for themselves... to sort of help distract them from the pain they feel inside. Does that make sense?"

I nod. I've heard enough about 'cutters' in school that it actually does make sense.

He nods too. "I'm wondering if that's why she scratched herself in such a way. I'm sure that she'll be completely fine, with time. But she's probably going to need medication and so forth. Her recovery will definitely require therapy."

I knew he would say that. And I know that he's right. My ears ring as I ponder my new reality.

"Will she need to sleep in a hospital, Dr. Parker? I'm going to have my license this week. I could drive her to therapy every day, instead."

"Whitney, first- call me Joe." He smiles warmly. "With your mom trying to injure herself, I think she needs inpatient therapy. But I do want to assure you—I feel pretty confident that your mom's depression is situational, which means that with the right amount of medication and therapy, she'll overcome it." His voice is encouraging.

"Further, everything is strictly confidential with me. I don't speak about my work at home." He'd astutely guessed that I'd be nervous about that. I don't want Brady to think my family is even crazier than he already does.

It's a relief I feel for exactly three seconds before I suddenly hear someone screaming in my home...for the second time today.

My sister.

Dr. Parker and I both rocket from our seats and run for the source of Ellie's distress.

She's standing in the front doorway, with the door standing wide open. I follow her horrified gaze to find Mom skipping up and down the bricks of our driveway like a child in gym class.

She's still in her bloodstained nightgown.

And my dad's exotic, saltwater fish are scattered around her on the ground, where she's purposefully dropped them.

They flop clumsily while their gills heave open and closed as they desperately try to breathe.

As I stand aghast, I realize that a couple of the happy orange and white clownfish have stopped struggling- they're dead on the hot bricks already.

I dash outside, yanking the fish net from her hand and start scooping up the fish that are still moving, running back inside with them to drop them back in the tank. Mom had pushed the large leather ottoman up to the tank so that she was tall enough to reach into it to dip the fish out. I can't imagine what had made her do such a thing.

I make three trips as fast as I can and am able to rescue eleven fish, including Ellie's favorite yellow and blue Tang. When I come out the fourth time, the remaining fish are all dead; including the Chrysrus Angel that dad had shipped from Africa. I note numbly that it doesn't look nearly as majestic out of water-- It's black and white stripes look dingy in the sunlight.

Brady and Laney appear on the porch. Both of them look shaken.

"Whit, I'm so sorry!" The words tumble out of Laney's mouth. "We were trying to clean the bathroom up for you. We thought she'd fallen asleep."

Of course I'm not mad at them. They were just trying to help.

Brady walks quickly to me, standing comfortingly close. I can't believe that he even wants anything to do with me still. My mom had just murdered a tank of fish for no reason at all.

Dr. Parker leads my mother up to the porch swing where he talks to her softly. I can't hear what he's saying, but he pats her comfortingly on the shoulder.

Why in the world would *she* need comforting?

What about the rest of us?

I quickly get a trash bag from the garden shed and begin scooping up the dead fish, dropping them one by one into the bag. Ellie comes out of the house and sits on the porch steps, watching me silently.

"Whittie, I'm sorry that I didn't see her earlier." She sounds miserable, as she sits hugging her knees with her tiny little arms. I can't imagine how she could possibly feel that any of this is her fault.

I scoop up the last fish and dump the bag in the dumpster on the side of the house, coming back around to sit beside Ellie. I put my arm around her bony little shoulders.

"Ellie. There's no way that you could've known what she was doing. It's not your fault. It's no one's fault."

"It's mom's fault," she whispers.

Deep down, I agree. But I can't say that.

"It's not mom's fault, either," I say instead. "She's sick, and we're going to get her some help now. Okay?"

She nods pitifully and I suddenly feel an urgent repressed anger toward my mother beginning to emerge. How could she let herself get so out of control? Ellie and I had lost our dad the same day that she lost her husband. You don't see us losing it like this. It's not fair. Any of it.

My phone rings and interrupts my shameful thoughts. My grandma.

I fill her in on what had just happened and explain that Dr. Parker is here at the house. She has me put him on and they talk for a good ten minutes. When they hang up, I eye him expectantly.

"Your grandparents will be arriving here tomorrow evening. In the meantime, she wants you and Ellie to stay the night at Delaney's. I'm going to take your mom to my clinic for observation and then I'll decide what steps should be taken. She'll need to stay at least overnight, but it's likely that it will be longer." He eyes me sympathetically.

"It's going to be alright, girls, really. I've seen this type of depression before. I'm confident that your mother will be fine."

Ellie clutches my hand and we walk back into the house to pack our overnight bags.

Delaney and Brady stay outdoors. I assume they want to make sure mom doesn't do anything else.

The first thing I see when I enter my room was Samuel, standing by the windows. He turns to face me with a sympathetic expression on his normally impassive face.

"I'm sorry, Whitney." His aquamarine eyes shimmer.

"Where have you been?" I snap, my eyes red and hot. "Did you know what was going on here?"

"I can't interfere, Whitney." He gazes at me apologetically, which lets me know that he *did* know, and I fight the anger that surges through me.

"They're going to put mom in a hospital," I mutter as I quickly shove some clothes in a bag.

"I know. Your mom needs help, though, Whitney. You've tried very hard, but there are some things that you can't fix."

"I know." I sigh. "I'm learning that more and more every day. Will you be with me tonight at Delaney's?"

"Of course. Nighttime is the most dangerous."

As if that makes me feel better. He seems to forget that even though he's immune, earthly beings feel a healthy amount of fear.

I shake my head and rush to mom's room to pack a bag for her.

So much for my life returning to normal.

Chapter Twelve

"Whitney? Are you all right?"

Brady's husky, comforting voice filters through my phone into my ear. Warmth spreads through me. He cares. And he's not running away.

Honestly, I don't know if I'm all right. I still feel numb.

I'm sitting on Delaney's screened sun-porch watching her and Ellie jump on the trampoline. I just can't bring myself to participate in something fun. All I can do is sit here and mull things over. As I watch my little sister laugh as she kicks her legs out in mid-air, I feel an enormous sense of gratitude to Laney for trying to distract her.

I'm also thankful to Ginny, Delaney's mom, for letting us stay here tonight. She'd gathered us in like a mother hen, which is not her usual demeanor. The attorney attitude she usually wears comes across as a little removed-not very maternal. She typically doesn't get warm and fuzzy.

But I know she cares about Ellie and I- she's known us since we were babies. Laney's dad is out of town on business this week, so Ginny made it sound like we were doing them a favor by keeping them company tonight.

"I think so," I murmur, finally answering Brady's question.

I don't want to admit how upset I am. How unsure, scared, unsettled, horrified... the adjectives for my current state of emotional health could go on all night. But he doesn't need to know about any of them.

"It's going to be all right. I promise." He sounds so sure of himself.

He sounds exactly like I had earlier when I'd lied to Ellie. I can't help but wonder if he's lying to me now in the same way. Honestly, I can't believe that someone who I'm really just getting to know is sticking with me through this craziness. It's sort of mind-boggling. I think a normal person would run in the opposite direction.

"My dad wanted me to tell you that he'll be calling you tonight. He just didn't want you to think he forgot. He hasn't come home from the clinic yet."

Oh. He has been with my mom this whole time? That can't be good.

Maybe she's having a hard time. Or maybe she's freaking out in the strange environment. I feel the urge to go there, to try to help, but I know I can't.

"Thanks. For everything. Really. Thank you for calling your dad. I don't know why I didn't call someone a long time ago."

"It's okay. Really." He copies my phrase and laughed. "Whitney, I want you to know that I understand... about your mom. My mom wasn't in such a good place herself after my brother died. But she got better, and I know yours will too. I don't want you to feel weird about it."

Too late.

I'm just getting ready to reply when I suddenly feel Samuel's presence.

I glanced up to find that he's sitting in the chair across from me.

Oh my gosh. Will I ever get used to his sudden appearances?

"How about breakfast tomorrow? I'll take you and Ellie to grab something to eat and then go with you to my dad's clinic so you can see your mom." Brady's voice brings me back into focus.

"Um- you don't have to do that." I really don't want him to keep witnessing my mom's meltdowns. It's humiliating.

"I know. But I want to. How about I come by Delaney's at eight?"

"Okay." I agree softly. My need for his presence overcomes my need to hide my mom's craziness. It feels good to lean on someone, to focus on something other than all of this….crazy. Besides, his dad is a shrink. Surely he's been exposed to all kinds of crazy, right?

"Sleep well, Whit. I'll see you in the morning." His husky, masculine voice caresses my ear. I find myself wishing that he was here with me instead of just in my phone. I also find myself loving the way he says my name.

"Thanks, you too." I hang up and stare at Samuel.

He's observing me silently; his spine ramrod straight in the chair. Does he ever relax? I glance out the window and find Ellie and Laney still jumping. It appeared that they're trying to do flips. I decide to address Samuel's habit of sudden appearances.

"Can you try not to startle me when you appear?"

"I'll try." His voice has a smile in it.

"My grandparents are coming tomorrow."

"I know." Samuel is quiet. He seems reflective, like he's thinking of other things that I have no knowledge of. I know that's probably exactly the case.

"What do you think is going to happen?" I search his face for any sign of an answer, because I already know he won't give me one.

"I don't know. Your immediate plan is un-folding but I can't speculate on the outcome."

"Why can't you? At least speculate, I mean?"

"Because there's no way I can possibly know. It'll be revealed when it's time."

"You know I'm tired of hearing about 'my plan', right?"

I stare at the beadboard that covers the sun porch's walls. The second hand ticks loudly on the palm tree clock that hangs close to my chair. It cheerfully reads, 'It's 5'o clock somewhere.' A fly buzzes angrily against the window, agitated that it can't get back outside.

"I know." He shrugs his shoulders. "But it doesn't mean that it doesn't exist. You have a plan and it is being executed as we speak. But I'm proud of you, Whitney. You've behaved with grace and your life has been difficult lately."

I stare at him hotly, because the unfairness of it all wells up in the most inopportune times.

"Samuel, why can't you tell me what is going to happen? Do you know? Can you give me a small hint?"

I sound pitiful, and I feel weak and spent. I don't know if I have enough energy to keep going, to keep my strength up for my mom and to keep up the charade that everything is fine.

Because it's not fine. Nothing is fine, and it's frustrating that Samuel knows things that I don't, and that he won't even speculate on what else might be getting ready to happen.

He levels a gaze at me, and his tone is as patient as always.

"No. I can't tell you what I know. But I can tell you this. You're stronger than you think you are. You've never been weak. I want you to remember that. I'm here to protect you, but you're strong enough to act alone, too. Trust your instincts. You have good ones."

His voice is earnest, even as his face is characteristically impassive. I'm reminded once again at how strong he is. Infallible, unflappable. Unafraid. I wish I could be more like him.

Which reminds me.

"What did you do this morning during my driver's test? I know it was something."

He smiles. "I stopped the fencing from hitting your windshield. I thought it might unnerve you. I deflected it over the top of your car instead."

I shake my head. I can't even take the credit for keeping my head, because he's right. I would've freaked out if it had hit my windshield instead.

"Whitney? Who are you talking to?" Delaney's mom comes through the door, holding two icy glasses of fresh lemonade.

"What? No one. Just myself. I guess I'm crazy too." I sigh as I take the glass she offers to me. She sits down in the chair that Samuel had instantly vacated upon her arrival. I glance around to see where he'd gone, but he's nowhere visible.

"Whitney. Your mom isn't crazy. She's extremely depressed. That depression is just manifesting itself in strange ways. She just needs some time and some medication to help her along. I want you to know something—you can trust me. You could've come to me with this."

I look at her as she curls up in the chair. Her red hair is in a neat ponytail, her no-nonsense fingernails grasp her glass and her thin, pale legs are curled beneath her.

"I'm sorry. I was just afraid that you would have to call someone … and that they would have to call someone… and then eventually they'd put mom away in a loony bin and Ellie and I would be separated in foster care."

It's the first time I've actually verbalized the words 'foster care'. I cringe just saying the words out loud.

"Whitney, if you had come to me, I could've assured you that you wouldn't end up in foster care. I'm a lawyer. I've seen situations where kids get taken out of homes. Yours is not like that. Your grandma is coming to stay with you while your mom gets the medical attention that she needs. There's no need to remove you from your home when you have family members that can be with you."

She stares at me sympathetically.

"Your mom's situation is temporary. I can tell you that your mom is one of the strongest women that I've ever met. She'll beat this, and your life will get back to normal. Or a new normal, anyway."

Her last statement acknowledges that my life isn't going to be the same, because my dad is gone. She doesn't have to point that out because clearly I already know that. I've been trying to make myself forget it and it hasn't worked.

My phone buzzes in my pocket again, and then Dr. Parker's voice drifts from the receiver.

"Whitney? I just wanted to call and let you know that your mom is resting comfortably. I've done my evaluation and as I suspected, she's going to need medication and further therapy, but I feel confident that she'll recover.

She's had a horrible shock to her system- just like you- and her body handled it differently. Everything will be okay."

"Thank you." I feel relief that he was able to get her to rest. I don't care if it's medically induced or not. She needs sleep.

"Could you do me a favor, though? Your mom was very bothered that she didn't have your dad's gray sweater. I think she'll rest better if she has it. Can I send Brady over to meet you at your house? If you could find it and send it back with Brady, I think it will make your mom feel more comfortable here."

She'd been wearing that sweater the other morning when I found her sleeping on dad's desk. I don't know off-hand where she'd put it, but it has to be in her room somewhere.

"Sure, I'll run down there right now." I hang up the phone and explain to Ginny.

"I'll just be a little while. I'm not sure exactly where it's at, but I think it's probably in her bedroom. Could I possibly leave Ellie here? She's having fun playing with Laney." And I don't want to take her back to the house tonight. I don't want to remind her of our current reality if I don't have to.

"Of course you can. See you in a little bit."

Ginny carries our drinks back into the house and I slip out the side gate without drawing Ellie's attention.

Surprisingly, I don't feel Samuel with me. I absently wonder where he is, but get distracted when I remember that I'll be seeing Brady again in a couple of minutes. I pick up the pace so I can reach the other end of the street faster. I bound up my steps, unlock our door and walk in.

Our house is eerily dark and quiet.

Even though mom had been mentally absent for the past several weeks, I suddenly realize that her physical presence had still been comforting. Just having her here filled a void and provided a slight sense of normalcy. With her gone, the house is so empty, and it feels really wrong.

It's a glaring reminder that my life is coming apart at the seams.

I walk up the stairs to her room, but I can't see any signs of the sweater.

I look under the bed, in the hamper and on the bathroom floor.

Nowhere.

Great.

The one thing that can provide her with some semblance of comfort- and I can't find it. I check my bathroom, not there. It's not in Ellie's room, either, but I'd known that was a long shot.

As I'm walking back down the hall, the lights suddenly flicker.

The hairs suddenly stand up on the back of my neck, and I feel a chill because I sense something behind me. Something large.

Goosebumps form on my arms and then travel down the rest of my body as I slowly turn around.

But the hallway is empty.

"Samuel?" I whisper.

He doesn't appear and I'm not surprised. His presence doesn't instill fear. Not like this. His presence is warm and safe, and I don't feel that anywhere around me.

The floor creaks in the hallway as I step on it, and it startles me, even though I've heard that creak a thousand times before.

I protect you from bumps in the night- the bumps that you can't see, but that I can.

What can Samuel see that I can't?

I suddenly feel as though those things, terrible things, are near, but I can't prove it. Because I can't seem them. But I do have goose-bumps on my arms and the hair is standing up my neck.

Trust your instincts.

Which instincts? The incorrect ones that told me to slam on the brakes this morning or the ones that are screaming at me right now that something is wrong here? How am I supposed to know what is an instinct and what's just me getting spooked in a dark, empty house?

I take a deep breath. I'm being silly. If there's really something here, something dangerous- I know that I'd feel Samuel here. I've spooked myself at night a million other times.

I instantly argue with myself regarding that logic. The logic itself is valid, but that was before I learned that there are really things out there that I can't see. Maybe I'd been right all along- *all* of those other times. Maybe there actually had been something there- I just couldn't see it.

I shudder slightly and look behind me. It feels like something's following me, something invisible. I feel the need to hurry and leave the house. The silence around me is tomb-like, so quiet that it makes my ears ring. I start flipping on every light switch that I come across.

I want to surround myself with light. Light is good. Light is revealing.

Unless, perhaps, I shouldn't *want* to see everything. Maybe it's too terrifying to see.

I feel chilled again.

Another sound registers with me, rising out of the darkness. A floorboard creaking, and not the one beneath me. It'd come from downstairs ... from the floor in my dad's study. The sound is distinctive. I'd heard it many times before as I walked past dad's massive desk.

The startling realization settles down around me.

I'm not alone.

I creep down the hallway, keeping close to the wall as I descend the stairs. Terror floods me because I have to pass in front of the study to get out of the house.

No matter who's in there, I have to pass them to get to safety.

Cold fingers of dread clamp onto me, pushing my heart up into my throat. I urge my feet woodenly forward, even though my heart is telling me to retreat.

But I can't - I have to get out.

I take the final step, pushing myself into the doorway, prepared to run.

A black figure in the shadows moves slightly- startled by my appearance. It seems to hover for a minute, and my breath lingers on my lip as it steps into the light of the hall.

Brady's face is illuminated, visibly showing his relief when he sees me. I feel that same relief. I'm not going to be attacked. There's no intruder. I'm an idiot. My knees feel weak again- with overwhelming relief.

Brady smiles and quickly crosses the room to get to me.

"Whit- thank goodness! Your house was freaking me out for some reason."

Him and me both.

"I let myself in so that I wouldn't startle you with the doorbell-I didn't think you would mind- but then I got turned around. Your house is enormous."

Relief allows me to find that funny. Our house *is* enormous. An architectural monstrosity. I laugh softly, my relief clearly evident in my voice.

"Thank you for being here. I was freaking myself out, too. It's so nice to see your face."

I feel self-conscious for a brief second after the words leave my lips, but only for a second.

Because suddenly he's reaching for me, pulling me to him with his strong arms and suddenly all I can think about is him. His broad chest is the most comfortable place in the world.

He stares into my eyes for a second, and then lowers his head and kisses me. Yet again, his lips render me senseless, tipping me up on an axis and spinning until I'm dizzy. He finally pulls away, and I feel like I need to cling to him, so that I can remain upright.

"Did you find the sweater? Apparently, your mom really wants it."

I shake the dizziness from my head. "I haven't yet. I looked practically everyplace upstairs."

"Well... could it be in the basement? Does she ever go down there? Maybe it's down here somewhere." He starts to move towards my dad's desk. "Hey, wasn't it gray?"

He circles around the desk and picks up the large, gray sweater from dad's chair, holding it up for me to see.

"Is this it?"

I nod silently. I should've thought to look here in the first place. She sleeps down here half of the time, for Pete's sake. Plus, it's the last place I had seen her wearing it. Once again, I like an idiot.

"Okay, well, I'll get this to her, then. I think it'll make her sleep better tonight." He walks with me toward the door, pausing to look at me.

"Are we still on for breakfast?"

I inhale his masculine scent and nod again. I'm not very good with words tonight, apparently. He smiles and my knees feel weak again, this time from his close proximity.

"Good. I can't wait to see you again."

He lightly puts his hand on my elbow, just like he had the other day and guides me to the front door. It feels even more protective tonight in the dark than it had in the daylight.

He pulls me gently to him on the porch, kissing me lightly on the forehead.

"Good night, Whit."

I'll never get tired of hearing his voice.

"Good night." I reply softly.

Out of the corner of my eye, I notice Samuel sitting on the porch swing motionlessly observing our exchange. Had he been out here the entire time?

Brady bounds down the steps, heading in the opposite direction of Laney's house. When I turn back to face Samuel, he's gone.

Chapter Thirteen

Eight a.m. can't come quickly enough.

I'd tossed and turned all night in Delaney's guest room with Ellie, until she'd woken me up at five a.m. with a nightmare. She was screaming. I woke her up to calm her and she couldn't remember her dream. But she was still unnerved. She finally drifted back to sleep and I woke her up again at seven, letting her splash around in Ginny's big bathtub for half an hour. Her nightmare was apparently all but forgotten.

The doorbell rings promptly at eight a.m. After assuring Laney that I don't need her to go with us, I open the door and greet Brady. He's dressed in khaki shorts and a button-up white shirt with the sleeves rolled up to his elbows. His blonde hair glints in the sun and his blue eyes appraise my face as he smiles his brilliant Hollywood smile at me.

How had I gotten so lucky?

He walks toward a black Jeep Grand Cherokee, and moves ahead of me to open the passenger door for me.

"Yours?" I ask. I haven't seen it around town.

"Yep. It was a present from my parents. A sort of 'thank you for passing Driver's Ed gift'." He smiles. I slide into the seat and then he opens the back passenger door for Ellie. She smiles up at him at he helps her into the backseat. He'd definitely won her over, too.

"I don't have a car seat. Do you think she is okay just buckled in? We're not going far, just down to your house to get yours."

How did he even think of that? Because I'd honestly forgotten. I smile at him gratefully as he carefully buckles Ellie in, making sure that the clasp clicks.

"Okay, young lady, I want you to keep your hands and legs inside the moving vehicle at all times, you hear? Don't be pulling any shenanigans." He grins and she grins back-her sincere impish little smile that I haven't seen for awhile.

"I'll try." She promises.

We stop by the house for just a minute to get Ellie's car seat out of mom's car. The house looks just as empty now as it did last night. Even in daylight, the dark windows look creepy. I put the thought out of my mind as I get Ellie situated in the backseat and then climb back in the front.

"This is really nice," I comment as I look around the cab. Leather seats, wooden inlay on the dashboard. Brand new- definitely top of the line. His parents had spared no expense. This is quite a gift.

"Well… ever since Bryant died, my parents have spoiled me a little bit. I'm not ashamed to admit it." He glances at me. "I don't take advantage of it or anything- it just seems like it makes them happy to do it."

It never crossed my mind that he took advantage of it. It just didn't seem like something he'd do.

The ride to the clinic is extremely short- only ten minutes. I try to memorize the way there so that I can drive it myself. Ginny's taking Laney and me to get our licenses this afternoon, so I'd be able to drive my grandparents to the clinic tomorrow.

As we walk through the front doors of the clinic, soothing nautical blue walls envelope me. A soft perfumey scent wafts in front of my nose- definitely not the normal clinical smell. Soft music is piped in and a professional looking secretary is sitting at the reception desk.

"Brady!" she exclaims as soon as she sees us. "It's been months since you've been in here!" She stands up to give him a hug. "Are these new friends?"

"Eleanor, these are Maricel Lane's daughters, Whitney and Ellie." She briskly walks closer and holds her hand out. I shake it.

"It's nice to meet you, girls. Your mom is resting comfortably. I think she might like it here."

Looking around, I can see why. Every piece of furniture is upscale. The floors are marble. The atmosphere is a far cry from the usual sterility that you generally encounter in clinics. Instead, it feels refreshing and soothing. Like a spa. My mother loves spas.

"Can we see her?" I ask Eleanor.

"Of course. Brady, do you want to take them back? Or would you rather I do it?" She asks me.

"No, Brady can. If you want?" I turn to him hopefully. I definitely prefer that he stays with us.

"Sure, right this way, ladies." He holds out his elbows like he's escorting us into a formal dinner. We each take one and walk with him down the hall.

We don't have to go far.

Down a short carpeted hallway, we stop at a door on the right. I peer in to find mom sleeping soundly, curled up in a ball. The morning light floods in through one window, making the room seem cozy and warm. My dad's sweater covers mom like a quilt- she has it grasped tightly in her hands under her chin.

I'm a little surprised to see an IV bag was dripping into a tube, connected to a needle in her arm.

Dr. Parker's voice startles me from behind. I turn around to look at him as he spoke.

"I started an IV to give her some fluids. She was pretty dehydrated last night. I'm also giving her a mild sedative to keep her calm and help her sleep."

I know that she's probably more than a little dehydrated. She hasn't wanted to eat or drink for weeks. I wonder how much difference some fluids would make. Maybe even the fact that she's been dehydrated had contributed to her present state of deterioration. I ask him about it.

"Yes, I would imagine that it contributed- at least somewhat. Once our electrolytes get out of whack, it can cause us to do all sorts of strange things. She might have even ended up in the hospital eventually."

I gulp. I feel even guiltier about not calling someone sooner. But I'm also encouraged. This is another puzzle piece to her strange behavior. And we have a remedy for this piece. Maybe she really will start to recover soon.

Ellie walks past me into the room and stands at mom's side, looking down. She puts her little hand on mom's arm.

"You're going to be alright, mom," she whispers. And then she leans down and kisses her nose. I feel a lump form in my throat. I push myself forward and wrap my arms around Ellie.

"She is, you know," I murmur to her. "She's going to get better and she'll come home."

I stare down at mom's motionless form.

She hasn't moved a muscle. The sedatives are doing their job. Her face is pale against her light blue designer pillowcase. Ellie twists around and hugs me, burying her face in my waist. Brady looks from her to me.

"Do you want to go get that breakfast, now?" he asks. We'd thought it best to come straight here instead of stopping for breakfast. My stomach's rumbling though, and I'm sure he heard it.

"Are you hungry, El?" She nods, so I turn to Brady.

"Sure. I have to be back at Laney's by noon though. We're going to get our licenses."

We turn to walk out. I turn back around once, and mom's still the same- she hasn't moved. We quietly walk out of the room and down the hallway.

***

Brady drops us back off at Delaney's with plenty of time to spare.

We find Ginny and Laney lounging on the sun-porch, drinking hot tea. Laney stands up and hugs me- she can probably see on my face that I'm spent already. It's one of the benefits of having a life-long best friend – she knows me.

"Hey, Whit... Laney was telling me that Ellie is supposed to have swimming lessons today," Ginny mentions, reminding me with a jolt. It'd completely slipped my mind. "Why don't we drop her off on the way to the BMV, and then we'll swing back by and pick her up when we're finished?"

"Thank you, Ginny. I totally forgot, with everything going on. That'd be great. I don't want her to miss those lessons." I squeeze Ellie's skinny shoulder.

"I already ran down to your house and got a swimsuit for her," Laney informs me with a mischievous smile. "See? I always knew it would come in handy for me to know where you keep your extra key!"

"You just wanted to be able to run in and get my clothes whenever you need to!" I tease. I love her. I really do. I'd lucked out in the friend department, too. I guess Samuel was right. My instincts are good. I'd gravitated toward Delaney when we were just little kids- I had known, even back then, that she'd be good for me.

We pile into Ginny's silver BMW and it doesn't take us long to reach the Aquatic Center in Traverse City. Delaney and her mom wait in the car, bickering between themselves about Delaney's future car while I take Ellie in.

I can see on her face that she's nervous.

"Don't be nervous, Bellie. You're gonna love it!" I don't emphasize how important it is that she learns to swim. All things considered, I'm sure she knows.

We enter the steamy pool area, looking around for Miranda. The air changes the instant we step into the room- the humidity from the pool drifts upward and forms condensation on the observation windows. The thick smell of chlorine floods my nose.

A group of kids are already in the pool, but I still don't see Miranda. We find an empty bench by the wall and put down Ellie's bag. I'm helping her pull off her shirt when a voice approaches me from behind.

"Excuse me, Miss?"

I turn around. The voice belongs to Carter Kelly.

I can tell from the expression on his face that he hadn't recognized my backside.

"Oh. It's you."

He obviously recognizes me now. His resigned tone of voice is almost humorous.

"You can't wear your street shoes in here on deck. You have to either take them off or bring unworn shoes to wear in here."

His dark eyebrows are knitted together and he looks as though he can barely bring himself to address me. What the heck is wrong with him?

"Um, this is my sister Ellie. She's here for swim lessons. Do you know where Miranda is?"

I force myself to remain pleasant, but it's difficult. It's hard to be nice to someone when you can tell they're struggling to just be civil.

"Yeah, she's not here. But I am. I teach the beginner's swimming classes on Tuesdays and Thursdays." He kneels down to look at Ellie.

"Ellie, I'm Carter. I'm going to be your swim instructor. Can you swim at all? Doggie paddle?" She nods at doggie paddle.

"Perfect!" He smiles. I hadn't even realized he was capable. But he actually has a nice smile. Very nice, in fact. And it disappears abruptly when he glances back at me.

"Do you see that group of swimmers way down there?" he asks Ellie. "You can go down there and join them, okay?" She nods and looks quickly at me.

"Its okay, El. I'll be back before your class is over, okay?"

She nods again and leaves to join her designated group. I watch as she slips into the pool and wades over to stand with the group.

"An hour, right?" I turn to ask Carter, but I find that I'm talking to the heavily chlorinated air. He's already gone- walking around the pool to the other side.

He hadn't said a word to me. Nice.

I'm still fuming as I drop back into Ginny's BMW and slam the door.

"What?" Delaney turns around to demand.

"Nothing. Except that Ellie's swim instructor is this new guy, Carter Kelley, and I'm pretty sure he hates me but I can't figure out why. I haven't done anything to him." I totally lost her though, with the words 'new guy'. Because new guy equals new challenge.

"What new guy? When did you meet him? You didn't mention anything." Her face is comical- like she suddenly discovered that I have withheld the ability to create fire with my fingertips from her.

"It didn't seem important, and then I forgot about it. I bumped into him and Miranda Eli at the store awhile back. I barely talked to him," I reassure her. He's definitely still uncharted territory for her to explore.

"You know," Ginny ponders, "That name is familiar to me for same reason. But I can't remember why. It's nothing bad," she assures me," He's not a client or anything. I can't think of where I know him from. Or maybe I know his parents? I don't know. When I remember, I'll let you know," she promises.

"It doesn't matter because I don't care about him," I say petulantly. "I don't want anything to do with him. I find his whole attitude annoying."

We pull into the License Bureau at just that moment, though, and my attention is diverted by the process of getting photographed and having my license handed to me.

Thirty minutes later, we're on our way back to pick up Ellie with our freshly printed licenses in our pockets. We are now licensed drivers.

"Whitney, can you drive to the airport to pick up your grandparents this evening? I think their flight arrives at 7:30. Do you feel comfortable driving there, or should I do it? I have a teleconference, but I can cancel it if you need me." Ginny looks at me. I actually feel confident. The route to the airport isn't confusing.

"No, it's okay. I've got it," I assure her.

"Do you want me to come?" Delaney asks.

"No, it's all right. I'll be fine."

"Okay. But I'm going in with you to pick up Ellie... I want to see this new guy!" I roll my eyes, but wait as she climbs out of the car.

When we enter the pool room, with our shoes in our hands, Ellie's still in the pool.

Carter now stands on the side of the pool in only his swim trunks and a whistle around his neck, calling instructions to the kids. He's shirtless.

Delaney lets out a low whistle, not unlike what a guy would do for a curvy hot girl.

"Holy cow, Whit! You didn't mention that he's gorgeous." Her eyes haven't left his body.

"That's because I didn't notice."

Until now. But she's right. He's gorgeous.

In a sulking, completely opposite of Brady kind of way.

He's lean and muscular, as opposed to Brady's bulkier football player's frame. His legs are long and tan and you can tell he spends a lot of time in the sun. And then I notice that his dark eyes are staring a hole through me. Again.

"Yikes, you were right. He does look ticked at you! What in the world did you do to him?" Laney's face is puzzled.

"I told you! I'm not imagining things. He hates me. And I didn't do anything!"

I feel his dark stare piercing me as I make my way toward Ellie's little pile of clothing. I feel him approach before I even see it-from the palpable heat of his stare.

"Whitney, I don't know if Miranda told you or not, but it would be very helpful for Ellie if she had some goggles and a swim cap." His tone is accusing, as though he thought Miranda had told me and I had irresponsibly chosen to ignore it. Wrong.

"Um, no, I didn't know that. But it's not a problem. I'll make sure she has them next time."

I don't like the tension in the air between us.

I've never been a person that likes conflict or discord. And when I don't even know what I had done, there's no way I can diffuse the situation. Before I can even think it through, careless words had tumble out.

"Have I offended you somehow, Carter?" My voice is slightly defensive, but still inquisitive.

He spins back around to look at me. The look of surprise is clearly evident on his face for a moment before he masks it again with an impassive expression.

How can he be surprised by the question? He'd done everything but burn something in effigy in my honor.

"Offended me? Of course not. I don't even know you."

His tone is matter of fact, but he stares at me like I'm an idiot.

"You just seem... angry with me. I was wondering why." Now I just sound pathetic. Why had I even opened my mouth? I swear, I never think before I speak.

"Maybe you're just a little sensitive." Carter suggests, before he turns to walk away. "See you Tuesday." He doesn't look back.

I'm speechless and for once, so is Delaney. We look at each other, before she starts giggling.

"You're an idiot!" She laughs.

"Whatever," I scowl.

"Seriously, have you ever considered the benefits of just being mysterious? You could've just gone on about your business and left him to wonder why you don't care that he clearly hates you. Men always want what they can't have."

She nods knowingly. My best friend, the sage.

"I don't want him to want me." I'm positive about that fact.

"Well, I'd take him," Delaney states firmly.

We both watch as he kneels down to help a little swimmer out of the pool. The muscles on his back ripple like a wave. "And I have the added advantage that... well, he doesn't seem to hate me."

I shrug in response, but for some strange reason, I can't pull my stare away from him. Until he abruptly turns to face me, and his dark eyes burn into mine.

Heat floods my cheeks and I quickly hurry over to get Ellie, rushing out of the room in retreat.

Chapter Fourteen

I hadn't realized how much I'd missed the familiar comfort of my grandparents until they step off the plane and I see their smiling faces.

They exit the terminal and rush to us, gathering both Ellie and I up in their arms in bear hugs. One thing about Venezuelans... they don't shirk away from affection.

My grandpa holds me away from him so he can get a better look. His white panama hat shades his face from the fluorescent lights above us.

"Whitney Diane, I think you have grown four inches since I saw you last!" Grandpa finally announces.

"And just look at her, Vin... she's so beautiful!" My grandma cries. "And you, mija," she hugs Ellie again. "You look enough like Whitney to be her little twin!" Ellie laughs happily. She loves it when people point that out.

"How's your mom, Whitney?" Grandma's face is suddenly no-nonsense and all business, searching mine for tell-tale signs that something had changed for the worse.

"She's the same, Grandma. She has been sleeping a lot at the clinic, but I think that's because she's so sleep-deprived. They've been giving her sedatives, too. She needs the rest."

"Has she spoken to you since she was admitted?"

"No. She's mostly just slept. She hasn't been awake when we've been there. Maybe when we go there tomorrow." I hope so. I'm desperate to see some glimmer of my mom's normal self. Just a glimpse would tide me over until she recovers.

Grandma clucks about that and we head over to pick up their luggage. Everything at home is ready for them. I'd spent the afternoon putting fresh linens on their bed, cleaning the guest bedroom and cutting fresh flowers to put on their nightstand. It's what my mom always does when they come.

I'd driven dad's silver Land Rover to pick them up. As we approach it, I hear grandma's sharp intake of breath as she recognizes it. She doesn't say anything though. Honestly, it's just as strange for me to drive my dad's car as it is for her to ride in it. Because it was his.

But at the same time, it seems wasteful to let it sit in the garage. It's only a year old and it feels like my dad. It actually makes me smile to drive it, not cry like I would've several weeks ago.

I must be making progress.

They haven't eaten yet, so I make them sandwiches when we get home as they get settled into their room. Ellie helps layering the tomatoes and lettuce after I slice them. I'm just setting their plates down at the table when my cell phone rings. I glance at it, see Brady's number and walk quickly into the privacy of the empty family room.

"How are you doing? Are your grandparents there yet?" Just the sound of his voice is soothing. I almost sigh out loud.

"I'm fine. And they're here. They're just getting ready to eat something." I stare at the aquarium. It looked empty with so many fish absent. The rest of the fish them seem back to normal though, as though they've forgotten about their near-death incident. A three-second memory must come in handy sometimes.

"I was thinking… maybe I could come over? Would you like some company?" Even though I want him to, I hesitate.

"Or do you need to focus on your grandparents tonight?" he quickly adds. "I hope I'm not being rude. I just can't stop thinking about you."

"I want to see you, too." I murmur. "I really do…you have no idea. But I'm probably going to be tied up with my grandparents tonight. How about tomorrow afternoon?"

"Perfect!" He quickly agrees. I love that he never tries to make me feel badly for having to put other things or people first. I have yet to find a fault in him. I'll have to keep looking—no one is perfect.

Grandma walks in just as I'm putting my phone back into my pocket. She eyes me curiously.

"Hi Grandma. Are your sandwiches okay?"

"Of course. You learned to cook from your mother, who learned to cook from me. They're perfect," she assures me.

Her words are as confident as her appearance.

Grandma always looks perfect- which is where my mom got it from. I can only hope that Ill eventually inherit that trait.

This morning she's dressed in a tan pantsuit and tan leather sling-backs. Not a strand of her silver-white hair is out of place. It's smoothed into a sophisticated bob.

"Were you talking to someone, sweetie?"

"Just a boy. Brady." Only the most beautiful boy on the face of the planet. "His dad is mom's psychiatrist." Grandma looks at me with raised eyebrows.

"Don't worry, you'll like him. He's nice. You'll meet him tomorrow- he's coming over."

Her face is unreadable as she says that she can't wait to meet him. I follow her back to the kitchen to wash up their handful of dishes and then climb the stairs wearily to my bedroom. It's been a long day.

I'm just wearily dropping into bed when my phone buzzes with a text.

I think I am falling for you.

I smile and clutch my phone to my chest, my heart thumping wildly. I'm pretty sure I'm falling for him, too.

***

Sunlight washes over my face the next morning, waking me from a sound, satisfying sleep.

I squint and look at the clock. Holy cow, it's nine a.m. I haven't slept this long in quite a while. The other side of my bed is empty which means that Ellie is already up.

I take a shower in record time, taking pains to keep my hair dry. I don't want to take the time to wash and dry it. When I walk back into my bedroom, Samuel is sitting beside my bed.

I don't feel startled this time. Maybe I'm getting used to it.

"Good morning, Samuel." I smile at him. His aquamarine eyes shimmer in the morning sun.

"Good morning, Whitney. You slept well last night," he observes.

The average person would have formed that phrase as a question, asking, "How did you sleep last night?" Samuel didn't have to. He already knows. I wondered if it's weird that I'm not creeped out by that. I've gotten accustomed to him quicker than I would've thought.

I smile at him again. "I know. I feel... better this morning than a long time. I don't know why. Probably because my grandparents are here."

He cocks his head and looks at me. "Do you think it's that, or do you think it has something to do with Brady Parker?"

My face immediately flushes and I don't know why. I'm human, and it's human nature to develop crushes from time to time.

"Does it matter?" I ask lightly. "It's probably a little bit of both. I'm just so happy to be... happy for once. It's been a while." He nods expressionlessly.

"I can understand that."

"It feels good to have my grandma here to worry about things instead of me. And it feels good to think about Brady, like a normal girl." He regards me silently, but his eyes shimmer again.

"Why do your eyes do that? It's like they ripple or something." I watch his face. I keep waiting for one of my questions to offend him, to get too personal, but he never seems to mind.

"My eyes shimmer sometimes because they aren't really mine. It's just how my real eyes react when I take human form."

Well, that makes sense.

"Is it easy for you... to be human?"

"Well, you have to understand that I'm not really human. I'm just in human form- I only look like a human. I don't have to worry about the... shortcomings of being human, like being ruled by your hormones or emotions, because I still keep my own traits. It's different for fallen angels, though. They have their own rules—it makes it easier for them to manipulate humans."

I can hear the acidic derision in his voice.

"I can't imagine why any angel would choose to fall. Not since they know for a fact that Heaven and God are real." I'm extremely bewildered about that, actually. Why would they choose such a dark path when they know it's going to end really badly for them?

"It is hard to imagine," he agrees. "But it happens- for different reasons. Remember me telling you that angels are obedient- always? No matter what the order is, we follow it. We have to. Well, some of my kind chafe at that kind of restriction. They grow tired of it and want to make their own decisions. And then there are the ones who want to procreate."

That catches my attention.

"You've got to be kidding me. I thought you don't have those urges!"

"I don't. We aren't like humans." He scoffs at the notion, like I should've known it was ridiculous. "When they fell, though, they gained a few human traits, although they don't procreate for pleasure's sake." I stare at him waiting, still slightly confused.

"They do it to increase their number. Most of the evil on earth is created by Helel's legion, it's comprised mainly of fallen angels and demons. Some humans don't understand, but there *is* a difference between the two. Angels were created by God. There are a specific number of us in existence and that number won't change. The only way for Helel to increase the size of his army is to create something different."

"Demons?"

Samuel nods.

"Why do you call him Helel? I've never heard that name."

"That's what we've always called him. Lucifer is how humans translated his name into Latin... from Helel." I can't stop wondering how much of the supernatural world I didn't know about- and it's been under my nose the whole time. I just didn't know it.

"It is important to Helel to increase his legion. The more he has in numbers, the more souls that he can reach here on earth."

"And how…" My voice trails off. I'm not sure that I want to know, but at the same time, I'm pretty sure I need to know.

I also have the strange feeling that Samuel is leading me down a path. Even though I initiated this conversation, this is something he wants to talk about. He's extremely willing, almost eager, to share this information.

"I'm getting to that. A demon is the product of a coupling of a human and a fallen angel. While they live, they're part of the Rephaim. They're half angel and half human. But their physical bodies are mortal—they die. Their spirits continue though, so they need to find a body to inhabit when they walk on the earth. After a Rephaim's body dies, it becomes a demon, a minion of Helel and fallen angels. This is how he increases his number."

You've got to be kidding me. This is the stuff of a horror movie.

I stare at him aghast, with my mouth literally open. I snap it closed.

I never in my wildest dreams would've thought that an angel could procreate with a human. Samuel had been right. There's so much around me that I can't comprehend and I'm starting to think I never really will.

"Fallen angels are incredibly dangerous," Samuel continues. "Because they have no code to live by. They aren't bound by decency or goodness. One of Helel's Generals, Azazel, leads them. To give you an idea of his moral fiber... he was the one who introduced the art of warfare and adultery to humans."

"So he was a nice guy, then?" I raise an eyebrow. We could attribute WWII and the current divorce rate to him.

"You mean *is*. He's still alive and wreaking havoc on the human race, unfortunately. One of the gifts that they acquired when they fell was a heightened ability to seduce human women." Samuel shakes his head regretfully.

"Okay. So, just to recap... fallen angels and Helel try to make their army bigger by having babies with humans. Their babies grow up to be half-immortal, but when they die, they become demons?"

Samuel nods. "And the demons need bodies if they want to be on the earth... so demon possession is real?"

I'm hesitant about that last part. I *so* don't want to believe it. Scenes from the Exorcist are going to haunt me from now on, I can tell.

"How do they do it? I mean, how do they take over a person's body?" I sense that this might be good information to have.

"Demons wait in the darkness and shadows until a human is vulnerable, weak or overwhelmed. They always act when the human's defenses are down."

Like my mother.

My heart seems to stop beating.

I feel Samuel's gaze upon me- I look up and meet it, his aquamarine eyes holding mine with all the strength of steel.

I suddenly know that *this* is what he'd been leading me toward.

"Samuel... how do you know when someone has been possessed?" I can't breath and my ribs are constricted.

"I can tell right away from the scent. Humans though- it's much harder for you to make that determination, even after your mind has opened to the possibility. You'd have to watch for strange behavior. Becoming violent, hurting animals, mood changes, changes in hygiene.... There are a lot of different indicators. But mainly, you'd watch for a drastic change in behavior. Sometimes it is mistaken for seizures and multiple personality disorders and so forth."

Or extreme depression?

My breath exhales in a rush. How common was this- that we simply assume a possessed person is crazy?

Chills run down my spine and I can't move.

"Samuel. Is my mother possessed?" The words come out haltingly, stilted.

I almost can't form them with my tongue, which has suddenly become dead and wooden in my mouth. I can't feel anything. I wait for what seems like an eternity, watching Samuel's blank face.

Finally, he nods once.

Pictures flash through my head like a movie reel. My mother listlessly wandering through the house never sleeping, never bathing... my mother killing all of dad's fish.... My mother staring maliciously at me while I slept....my mom scratching herself. My heart feels like a lump of ice in my chest.

"Is she still in there?" I whisper. What happened to a person's own soul when their body is possessed?

Samuel nods. "Yes, she's still there. But the demonic force suppresses her human one. It's too difficult for her to overcome it. If the demon is displaced, your mom will re-emerge. She won't remember anything."

"You knew this? The whole time!" My tone is shakily accusing. My glare flashes upon his face like thunder. He actually winces away from it.

"I'm sorry, Whitney. I don't like it. I don't enjoy anything about it. But I can't interfere. Your mom's guardian couldn't stop her from allowing herself to become vulnerable. She became despondent. We can't control the emotions of the ones we protect." He shakes his head slightly and I know he's thinking of the shortcomings of humans. It doesn't ease my fury.

"You have allowed me to believe that she was just extremely depressed... that an inpatient clinic would help her!..."

My voice trails off. I can't even think of anything else to say. I know he's not at fault- but he'd allowed me to remain misinformed. He's guilty by omission.

"Whitney, I couldn't say anything. You know that I have to let these things unfold the way they will. *I am not allowed to interfere!"*

His voice thunders with his own agitation, loud enough that my bedroom windows vibrate, as though he's offended that I might think so little of him. Finally a reaction from him that I can accept. I had found what would offend him, but I don't care anymore.

"How do I get it out?" My voice is shrill and shaky. I know he knows the answer. But he's gone.

Ellie bursts through my door, her face panicked.

"Whittie, what's wrong? Why are you yelling?" She's shaking as she stands next to me, waiting for an answer, her eyes searching my room for someone else or an explanation. She doesn't find one, of course. He's already gone.

I find that I'm shaking, too. I sink onto my bed, pulling Ellie down with me.

I hug her tiny body close to me and whisper that everything is fine. But it's not.

I know that now.

Chapter Fifteen

As Ellie leads me out of my room for breakfast, I look back over my shoulder and Samuel is standing by my windows. His expression isn't angry anymore. Apparently, angels can quickly get themselves under control. He actually looks more apologetic than anything. I don't know why- I wasn't offended. I'm actually glad to see a flash of temper. It's nice to know that he really is capable of emotion.

After we eat, my grandma insists on cleaning the kitchen up herself, so I take advantage of the few minutes of free time that I have until we leave for the clinic. It's nice to be off of cooking and cleaning detail for once. I duck into dad's study and boot up his computer. I keep expecting Samuel to appear next to me, but he doesn't.

I type in 'demon possession' into a search engine. More links that I can even count pop up. I sift through them, skipping the sections that detail how to determine if someone is possessed- and just search for how to get one out. All of the websites are speculative, and all of them continually state that exorcising a demon is dangerous business.

As if I need to be told that.

I really need Samuel's input right now, but he's nowhere near. He's probably avoiding me, knowing that I'd have another hundred questions for him. I return my attention to the search engine and type in "Rephaim."

It turns out that there are lots of different theories concerning Rephaim, but a few of the websites had the gist of the truth. I know I have the truth- I'd gotten it straight from the mouth of an angel.

As I sift through the mountains of information regarding this strange species of half-angel and half-human, I wonder how it is that I've never even heard of such a being before. How can so much information exist about something and I've been entirely oblivious to its existence?

I guess humans truly are oblivious to our surroundings.

As I gaze absently at the icons on the bottom of the screen, the email icon comes into focus... which reminds me of my email to Josef Amir.

With all of these other distractions, I'd completely forgotten about it.

I pull up my dad's email and search for one from Mr. Amir. There isn't one, but there *is* one from a Shirav Lotan, with Josef Amir's name as the Subject. My breath speeds up and I open the message.

Dear Ms. Lane,

I hope that all is well with you today and that your family is in the best of health. First, I would like to pass on my deepest regret about the death of your father. He was a kind, wonderful man who will be missed by everyone who knew him.

Second, I need to pass on the regretful news that my employer, your father's colleague and friend, Josef Amir has passed away also. He had an accident in the Magdala dig site that your father and he had been working in. The accident was tragic and I am sorry to bear the bad news to you.

Last, I am unsure what to do with the box of relics that you referenced in your email. Someone will be replacing Mr. Amir, but we are unsure at the present who that will be. If you could kindly keep the box with you until I get that information, I will let you know as soon as possible.

Thank you so much for your email and your concern about these important artifacts.

Best regards,

Shirav Lotan, Executive Assistant to the late Josef Amir

I'm stunned as I finish reading. Josef Amir was dead, too

What are the odds of that?

My phone suddenly vibrates on the desk, rattling loudly against the wood. I stare at it motionlessly for a moment before I pick it up.

"Good morning, beautiful." I smile. Somehow, even with all this new craziness, Brady's voice washes over me like warm milk, soothing me. His voice is deep and calm, like a balm for my stress.

"Good morning."

I want to tell him to come to me. Right now. I want to tell him everything and have him say that everything is going to be all right. But I can't. He'd think I was insane.

I can't even tell Delaney- the person who knows me best in the world...because she would, too. I mean, how could they not? The average human doesn't believe in demonic possession and angels. I hadn't either- until I'd come face to face with all of this stuff. I don't know what my next steps should be.

"Hey, are you going to the clinic this today?" Brady's voice brings me back to earth.

"Yeah, we're leaving here shortly. My grandparents haven't seen my mom yet."

I didn't even want to go now that I know the truth. But on the other hand, Samuel said that she's still in there, deep down. Maybe she could still hear my voice. I need her to know that she's not alone- that I'm going to try and help her.

"Do you want me to meet you there?" Brady sounds hopeful. I decide that the clinic is as good a place as any for him to meet my grandparents.

"Sure. I think we're leaving in just a few minutes." I can hear my grandpa telling Ellie to get her shoes on which means we have approximately five minutes until she actually finds them.

"Great, I'll make sure I'm there." I can hear the smile in his voice. It makes me wish I felt like smiling.

As I set my phone down, I notice two missed calls from Laney this morning. What the heck? My phone didn't ring. There has to be something wrong with it. I decide to call her on the way to the clinic and then put it out of my mind as I search for my sandals.

On the way out the door, grandpa announces that he'll drive. A few months ago, I might've been offended. Now, I don't care, I just stare absently out the window.

Children play on the sidewalk while the sun shines down on them happily. Old people sit on porch swings, and all the while, no one is aware of all the darkness that surrounds us. I fervently wish I was one of them again.

My phone buzzes in my lap. Delaney. Crap, I'd forgotten to call her.

For the remainder of the drive to the clinic, I listen to her chatter pointlessly about things I normally would've taken an interest in.

She bumped into Courtney at Target and had 'accidentally' rammed her with the cart. Her mom had bought a box of apricot squares from the bakery for Laney to give to my grandparents. Oh, and her dad was going to take the *No Problem* out to the docks for me tonight from storage.

I find it all slightly interesting, but my mind is still numb with the information that I'd been presented with earlier today.

Somehow, the knowledge that your mom is possessed by a demon trumps everything else. I desperately wish I could share all of this with Laney... all about Samuel, my mom.... But I can't.

For the first time in my life, I can't discuss something vitally important with her. She'd just think that I'd gotten overwhelmed with all of the stress surrounding me. She'd call Dr. Parker herself and I'd end up in a clinic bed, too.

Gah. I feel sick to my stomach.

We pull up to the clinic and Brady's Cherokee is already there, shining in the sunlight. It looks like it had just been washed, the chrome wheels glittering brightly.

I hang up with Delaney, promising to call her later and jump out of the car. I grab Ellie's hand and lead the way down the hallway to my mom's room. I don't see Brady anywhere, but I know he's here somewhere. He'll find me.

I pause at mom's door and peek in. She's sound asleep. The sedatives are doing their job.

It actually makes me more comfortable this way. If her body is sleeping, then maybe mom isn't aware of what's going on. I hate the thought of her distress. She's been through enough already.

All of us have.

My grandparents nudge past me and into the room. Grandma stands speechless at the foot of the bed with her hand over her mouth- staring down at her listless daughter. My grandpa wraps his arm around her.

"It's okay, Ava. She'll be fine. She's strong- like you," he murmurs into her silvery hair.

Yeah, right. I thought that myself the other day. I look away.

Grandma Ava and Ellie pull up chairs next to her, holding her hands and talking softly to her. I sit in the chair by the window, watching the hummingbirds eat from their birdfeeder. I can't bring myself to touch her. I don't want to get that close to a demon. It makes me feel horrible, because regardless of anything else, she's still my mother.

Brady taps on the door softly before he quietly walks in. I feel my face light up as he enters. Pathetic. Maybe Laney's right. A little mystery would be good. But I have enough mystery around me. I don't need to play dating games, too.

I feel myself melt into his hug, closer to him than is appropriate with my grandparents in the room. He looks at me quizzically, surprised, but rubs my back for a minute before he backs up. He looked concerns as he introduces himself to my grandparents.

He shakes grandpa's hand and then chats with grandma. I feel her examine him- taking his measure, she would say. She smiles at him, so I guess he measures up.

"Have you spoken with my father yet?" he asks her. She shakes her head.

"No, we just got here a few minutes ago." Her gaze returns to my mother's motionless face.

"Well, he's in his office. He's been waiting to see you. Would you like for me to take you to him?" She nods and Brady leaves to show them the way.

I think he must have sensed that they wanted to speak with his dad away from Ellie's nervous ears, and maybe even away from my own. I almost laugh humorlessly. They have no idea that Dr. Parker can't help us now. It then suddenly occurs to me that I have a rare opportunity to speak to my mother alone.

"Ellie, can you do me a favor? Can you go ask Eleanor for some ice chips? I think mom would like them- if she wakes up while we're here." The lie rolls off my tongue so much easier than I would've liked. Ellie doesn't detect the deception at all... she's just happy to help and eagerly leaves to find Eleanor.

I hesitantly approach the bed and stand by my mom's elbow. Staring down at her, she looks so peaceful while she sleeps. Maybe Samuel was wrong. Yeah, that's unlikely.

"Mom... I know you're in there somewhere." I say gently. "If you can hear me...I'm sorry. I don't know why this is happening to you, but I'm trying to figure it out. I'm going to help you, I promise." I glance at the clock on her wall. My grandparents had been gone for a couple of minutes already. They'd be coming back any minute.

I return my attention to mom and am startled to find her eyes wide open and staring at me. Her blue eyes aren't warm and sparkling as they usually are. They're the same wide open, unblinking eyes of a dead fish. The temperature of the room dramatically drops, and my breath releases in a white puff.

"Mom?" I whisper, my heart icy with dread.

"Mom?" She mimics in a raspy, imitating voice. The cold amplifies, and the windows frost over, icy tendrils of designs winding across the glass. With a start, I realize that the cold comes with an evil presence. That night in my room… I bet I hadn't been dreaming.

My mother stares at me, only it's not my mother.

The expression on her face has turned to malevolence… the same expression that had been on her face when I'd woken up and found her watching me sleep. She sits up somewhat in her bed, but her arms remain motionless at her sides. I instinctively back up.

"Whitney," she rasps in a guttural whisper. "Do you really think you can help your mother?"

"Who are you? What do you want?" I can't help but watch her face in horrified fascination. My mom's mouth is moving and speaking, but it's not her. I've never witnessed such a terrifying thing in my entire life. My stomach rolls with revulsion.

"Who am I… Who am I…." The voice taunts me again, sing-songing. It doesn't even sound like my mother now. It's pure evil.

Samuel suddenly appears on the other side of the bed, staring down at my mother with the all the contained fury of an angel.

He's in his terrifying true form, his enormous muscles taut as he grips the bedrails and his massive wings open so that they fill the entire other side of the room. His black eyes stare hard at my mother's face. I close my own.

"What is it you want, Malphas?" He demands.

Malphas. *M*.

The picture of my mother, kneeling down on an anthill with her nightgown dragging in the dirt explodes into my mind. Her finger had drawn a shaky 'M' in the sand. Bloody M's all over the bathroom…M for Malphas. Not Maricel as I had thought.

Had she been trying to tell me? My mind whirls and I open my eyes.

"What do you *think* I want, Angel?" My mother's mouth asks Samuel, twisting into something ugly.

The evil exudes from my mother's body with such unmistakable force that I take another step backward. I need to get away from her. She terrifies me now.

"I want *her*."

My mother's eyes are staring at me again. But my mother isn't behind the stare. The demon, Malphas, is using my mom's eyes in a way that she had never. He's glaring at me with unrestrained malice and hatred.

"You know you're not going to get her, Malphas." Samuel confidently states.

"Won't I?" My mother rasps. She had leaned slightly upward to speak. "I think I will. It will be out of your hands. Whitney loves her mother." The voice snakes out of her mouth like a viper swaying upwards out of a basket.

"What does that mean?" I blurt, frightened. Samuel shakes his head at me. Clearly he doesn't want me to engage with the demon.

But what does my love for my mother have to do anything? For that matter, what do *I* have to do with anything? Why does he want *me*?

"You love your mother, Whitney. That's all I mean. You wouldn't want me to stay here forever, would you? You can help her." His raspy voice sends chills down my back.

It's absolute evil. There is no mistake.

I've never heard such a terrifying sound in my life. *This* is the evil I imagined in my head when I jumped into bed without my feet hitting the floor. *This* is the evil that I couldn't picture but felt like it was outside my bedroom door.

I wonder now if it had been…all along.

"You also love your sister. More than anything. Foolish human." I can hear the contempt in his rasping voice. "If you give me what I want, I'll leave your mother. If you give me what I want, I won't be forced to take it from your sister."

The threat hangs in the air, so real I can practically reach out and touch it with a shaking finger.

"What do you mean, my sister? *What do you want*?!" I cry.

But my mother's body slumps back against the bed limply, her eyes closing abruptly, her head rolling to the side. Samuel disappears, along with the frost on the glass.

Brady walks back into the room, carrying two cokes. He hands one to me and I take it with shaking hands, trying to get myself under control so I don't collapse into a heap on the floor.

"What's wrong?" His eyes flash from my shaking hands, to my face and down to my mother in alarm, logically thinking that mom had woken up and distressed me somehow.

Her eyes had opened all right, but she wasn't the one who'd distressed me.

His free hand rubs a circle on my back and I lean my head on his shoulder. I don't know how much longer I can bear it alone. I have to remind myself that I'm not. I have Samuel and I can feel him near me right now.

I glance up, but of course I can't see him.

"Nothing. It just upset me more than I thought it would to see my mom like this." I'm disturbed by how easily the lies roll off my tongue these days. I've never been a great liar and now, it seems like I've perfected the art. I don't like it.

Brady looks at me sympathetically. "It's going to be alright," he murmurs, just as Ellie comes bounding back.

"Sorry it took so long, Whit! I couldn't find Eleanor and then she wanted to give me some Jolly Ranchers..." she looks to see if I'm upset. I smiled weakly to show that I'm not.

"It's alright, Monster. Did she give you any lemon ones?"

Lemon is my favorite kind. I don't really want candy, but I want to distract her from the heaviness in the room. She remembered and proudly handed me two pieces of lemon. Malphas' threats toward my sister echoed in my mind. I can't shake them. I don't know how to protect her from him. She's so small.

And we're so very human.

Grandma and Grandpa return with Dr. Parker, and I look at him sympathetically now.

He really still believes he can fix my mother with happy pills and therapy.

He talks with me in medical jargon about decreasing her sedatives to bring her out of her sedation and I nod like I'm encouraged. But I'm not. She's not coming back to us anytime soon. Not until I figure out what Malphas wants. And even then, who knows?

Grandma settles into a chair and reads to my mom. She wants mom to hear her voice. I have the sudden compulsion to hand my grandma a bible and tell her that mom would love to hear some scripture, but I think the better of it. It's probably best not to antagonize a demon.

Ellie is getting restless cooped up in the small room, so Brady suggests that we take her outside to the duck pond to feed the ducks. We make a quick stop at Eleanor's desk to get some crackers and head out back to feed them.

The back of the clinic is tranquil, an entirely different world. It's surrounded by a perimeter of trees and contains a huge pond with a gazebo. Brady helps Ellie feed the ducks, while I sit in the shade of the gazebo.

Even the tranquility of this nature reserve can't calm my nerves. My legs are still weak from my encounter with Malphas. As Brady and Ellie work their way around the other side of the serene pond to the reach a larger group of ducks, I feel Samuel's presence.

"I know you're here," I whisper.

He appears next to me, hidden from the view of Brady and Ellie by one of the side-beams of the gazebo. I'm not hidden though, so I try to speak discreetly. I do *not* want Brady to witness me talking to myself. We're already at the clinic, so it wouldn't take much for him to lead me inside and have his dad hook me up to an IV.

"Can you explain?" I try to sound as assertive and demanding as I can with my quiet whisper. He gets the point.

" I've been trying to discover what Malphas is doing here. It's significant that Malphas himself has emerged on earth," he explains. But then he seems to remember that I'm not of his realm. I still belong to the earth and so I have no clue what he's talking about.

"Malphas is... a leader of sorts among demons. I guess you could call him the equivalent of an earthly prince. He's important to them. He doesn't usually get involved with earthly issues. Most of the time, he's the liaison between the lower demons and Helel or other fallen angels. That's what makes this so puzzling." The truth I s reflected on Samuel's face. He honestly doesn't know what the demon wants.

"I've never seen him possess a human before. He usually thinks that's beneath him." The troubled tone of Samuel's voice doesn't reassure me. I gaze across the pond, watching Brady and Ellie laughing together, as Ellie chases a couple of the ducks.

"Samuel, he threatened Ellie. I have to find out what he wants. How do I do that?" I can't handle any BS about not being able to counsel me or him not knowing. He stares at me seriously, contemplating his answer.

"Whitney, the only thing you can do is wait. We have surveillance in place to better observe everything that is going on around here. When one of them moves, we'll know it."

"When one of who moves?" He might not know what Malphas wants, but he knows something else. I can tell.

"I can't say any more than I already have. I just want you to promise that you won't try to speak with Malphas again alone. You have no idea how dangerous that can be."

His words are chilling, but I actually do have a good idea. All of the websites about demons had strongly warned against trying to interact with one. I don't want to imagine the consequences.

"You're not alone, Whitney. I'm here. There are so many of us involved, trying to figure this out, that you don't need to worry about it right now. You just concentrate on keeping calm and taking care of Ellie. Ok?" He wants me to agree. And to mean it.

But I can't.

I've found myself lying a lot lately, but I don't want to lie to Samuel. There isn't really a point anyway, because he would see right through me. He knows my face.

So, instead, I just shake my head and go to meet Brady and Ellie as they return from feeding the ducks.

I can hear Samuel sigh as I walk away from him.

Chapter Sixteen

I can't see.

The water is icy cold and I lift a shaking hand to push my wet hair out of my face.

Water pours in on me. My eyes adjust to the darkness and I see that I'm in a half-submerged room with no ceiling. The night sky envelopes me. I'm tilted at an angle and it's hard to stand without slipping.

My head is throbbing. I lift a hand to my temple and it comes back covered in blood. I move to push my way to the door and kick something with my foot.

I tentatively poke my foot at it.

A small hand floats to the surface of the water in front of me.

My own screams wake me up.

I'm twisted in my sheets again, my comforter kicked to the bottom of the bed.

Ellie sleeps peacefully next to me. Maybe I'd only thought I screamed or maybe I had been screaming in my dream. My hair is wet with sweat. This dream was just like my others… devastatingly real.

I stare at Ellie. The size of the small hand was exactly the size of hers.

I jump up and run to the bathroom, throw the toilet lid back and start heaving. I vomit over and over until there's nothing left in my stomach and then I slump to the cool tile floor.

The tiles feel good against my flushed cheek. Out of nowhere, a large hand hands me a towel. I take it and sit up, wiping my mouth. Samuel leans on the counter, watching me.

There's no concern on his face because he already knows I'm fine. But there *is* sympathy. I stare at him pensively.

"Why did I have that dream? Does it mean something?"

"I don't know. I wish I did. One of our shortfalls lies in not being omniscient. I can only see the future if He deigns it to be pertinent. He hasn't shown me anything yet." I decide *He* must be God.

Then I decide that I'm probably going to lose my mind soon. Normal people don't have these conversations. And more importantly, normal people don't sit on their bathroom floors in the middle of the night having any kind of coherent conversation with a heavenly creature.

"Samuel... I'm afraid." My voice is child-like. "I dreamed that Ellie was dead and it was so real."

It doesn't matter to me that I'd obviously been in danger too. My head had been dripping with blood, but all I can see in my head is an image of Ellie's small white hand floating on the water.

I shudder so hard that my teeth snap together.

"I'm sorry, Whitney. I really am. Don't be afraid. Everything will work out exactly the way it's meant to. You can have faith in that."

He sounds so completely sure of it, so unaffected that I shake my head. Maybe that's what I'm afraid of, too. Maybe I won't like the way it's meant to work out.

My dad's drowning hadn't turned out so well for me, after all.

I brush my teeth and try to force all unpleasant thoughts from my mind. My mind needs a rest. I'm so freaking weary.

I return to bed and curl up next to Ellie, willing my whirling thoughts to still.

Suddenly, Samuel's presence surrounds me again. And then he's right behind me, with one giant wing wrapped under me and the other tucked over the top, covering me and Ellie both.

Peace descends upon me like a favorite blanket.

I've felt this feeling before- I just hadn't known back then that it was him.

I'd been mistaken… his wings are soft, after all. I feel like I'm enveloped in goose-down pillows. He doesn't say a word; he simply offers a safe haven from my troubles. I'm hidden inside the shelter of his wings.

And I've never felt so protected in my life.

My eyes flutter closed and sleep comes quickly.

***

The next morning, everyone is gone when I wake up, including Samuel. There's a note on the table from my Grandma.

Whitney,
You were sound asleep and I couldn't stand to wake you up. We're going to the clinic, but we'll be back by

dinnertime. You should stay home and rest. You deserve
it.

Love you,
Grandma

I'm still standing at the table with the note in my hand
when the doorbell rings. I look at the clock in surprise and
am even more surprised to find that it's 10:00 am. I'd slept
in.

I open the door, with my disheveled hair and pajamas,
to find Laney waiting impatiently on the porch. She stares
at my appearance for a second before she giggles. I rub at
my sleep-blurred eyes and glare at her. As much as I love
her, finding her on my doorstep before I'd had any caffeine
doesn't make me ecstatic.

"What are you doing here so early? And what's with
the doorbell?" Usually, she just walks right in.

"Well, with your grandparents here, I didn't want to
startle anyone by walking in like I owned the place." She
pushes past me into the house and heads for the kitchen.

"Please, come in," I mutter grumpily, which she
happily ignores.

"I've come to give you a distraction. You're
welcome." I hadn't said thank you, but I let that slide.
"You need some sun. Plus your grandma called me. She's
worried about you and wants you to do something today
besides sit at the clinic."

I should've known that was coming.

Delaney stops in front of the fridge and takes out a
cold soda.

"Let's go sailing. Your boat is already at the lake and
I know you're dying to get out there."

She takes another appraising look at me, then cracks
open the coke, handing it to me instead of drinking it.

Apparently, she thinks I need it more than she does. I set it on the counter.

"I don't think so, Laney. I'm not in the mood today." For anything. Except maybe moping around the house feeling sorry for myself.

"You're not in the mood for your boat, the lake and sun? Who are you and what have you done with my best friend?" She stares at me incredulously. Somehow, a comment about someone not being who they should be makes me scowl.

"I just don't want to go, okay? In case you haven't noticed, my life is not a party right now!" I snap, slamming the fridge door closed as she's getting ready to reach inside of it again. Her face freezes and she stares at me in surprise. I very seldom snap at her. In fact, I can't even remember the last time. I instantly wish I could take it back.

"I'm sorry, Whit. I wasn't thinking. I didn't mean to imply...never mind. I'm sorry."

I register the hurt on her lovely face and am ashamed. Nothing about my shambles of a life is her fault. She'd gotten up early to make me feel better. I feel like I just stepped on a butterfly.

"No, I'm sorry, Lane. I am. I'm stressed. And you know what? Maybe you're right. Maybe a couple of hours on the lake would be good for me." Her answering smile makes me feel better, as I hand her the untouched coke I abandoned. I jog up to my room to throw some clothes on and run a brush through my hair. Ten minutes later, we're walking toward the harbor.

True to Laney's word, my little boat bobs gently in her slip. The tiny mother-of-pearl chips in her white hull glitter in the sun. She's spotless. It looks like Delaney's dad, Mark, must have washed her, before he lugged her down here to the marina. I would have to remember to thank him. I already know exactly what he'll going to say. He's going to grin and say that it was 'No Problem.' He's super-corny, but a really nice guy.

Maybe Delaney had been right after all, because I feel better just walking down the wooden planks of the pier. The smell of the lake hangs around me in the air and I feel at home. My boat brings back happy memories.

Delaney swings her leg into the boat and wedges a small thermal lunchbox beside her. The one downfall of sunfish boats is that they're extremely cramped. I'm just lucky that my boat is a two person boat- many only hold one.

"I brought us some sandwiches. I know how grumpy you get when you're hungry." Or when my best friend tries to cheer me up, I think guiltily, but I don't apologize again. She already knows. That's the kind of friend she is.

I situate myself on the other side and loosen the sails, then tighten them on the boom. Then I release the lines that keep us anchored to the pier. I steer the rudder to guide us out of the harbor and inhale a big, appreciative breath when we're in open water.

The wind picks up and we gain some speed, taking us further from shore... further from the clinic and further from the craziness that surrounds my life.

I push my sunglasses up on my nose and sit back, looking around me in pleased satisfaction.

The water is sapphire blue today, perfectly motionless. The sky is blue, the clouds are white and my best friend is unusually silent, giving me time to just relax on the water. To top it all off, the sun shines gently down and warms my shoulders. I watch as a jet-skier throws plumes of water behind him, making a wide arc around our boat. The colorful sail snaps in the wind and I inhale contentedly, trailing my fingers lightly in the cold water.

"Thank you for making me come," I sigh to Laney. "This feels good."

"I know. I knew you needed it." Her voice is quiet as she watches me pensively.

"What?"

"I've just been worried about you. That's all. You're not yourself." She quickly adds, "But you have good reason."

She doesn't know the half of it. God, I wish I could tell her. Maybe she could help keep me sane. I contemplate that for a moment, trying to choose my words carefully.

"Lane... I'm sorry that I've been so grumpy lately. Nothing that's going on in my life is your fault."

"I know, Whit. And you don't need to apologize. God knows, you've put up with me a million times over the last 16 years."

"You've got that right!" I smile, then sigh. "But seriously. You deserve better. You're the best friend anyone could ask for."

I can't help myself. Now that I've ingested my morning dose of caffeine and have fully woken up, I feel overwhelmed with appreciation for her. Out of all of the crazy, scary things in my life, Delaney is one of the only sane, comfortable constants.

"What's with all of this... sentimental stuff?" She regards me suspiciously. "Are your grandparents making you move back with them?"

"No, of course not! Why would you even say that?" I'm startled by the idea. Surely that hadn't crossed my grandparents' minds, had it? Had they spoken to Ginny without my knowledge?

"I don't know. It's just... you've been so distracted and with the situation with your mom and everything... I thought maybe your grandparents had decided that it would be best to pack all three of you up and take you back with them. No?"

"No! Absolutely not. Our life is here. And besides, my mom isn't licensed to practice medicine in Venezuela. We have to stay here." And hopefully someday mom will be herself again and can practice medicine in the practice she had worked so hard to build.

"Well, that's a relief. I've been worried about that." I can literally see the relief on Laney's sun-flushed face. Apparently she's been stressing pretty hard, herself.

"Why didn't you say anything to me?" I query. It isn't like her at all to hold something inside without just blurting it out.

"I didn't want to give you anything else to stress about. Forget I mentioned it. If your grandparents were thinking along those lines, I'm sure they would have said something by now."

Well, you'd think. But I still feel the need to clarify that with my grandma when I get back home. But right now, I just shrug.

"You know what? I'm not going to worry about it. I think everyone has a plan, and everything will work out the way it's meant to."

I'm sure that Samuel is probably ready to explode with ironic laughter right now as he listens. Laney stares at me thoughtfully, getting ready to say something, but then her eyes shift and she says something else.

"Not to change the subject, but isn't that the new guy, Carter?" I follow her gesturing finger.

Sure enough, there he is, windsurfing a short ways away from us. His strong arms hold tightly to the bar on the rig, as he leans away from it to maintain his balance. I watch as he lightly steps across the board in his foot-straps, maintaining his stability in the rolling waves.

He's good. I'll definitely give him that.

He rises and falls with the waves effortlessly. His lean biceps bulge and I can tell that it takes effort. I've never windsurfed, myself. But it looks like it takes some strength to remain upright for any significant amount of time.

He wears a pair of dark sunglasses and blue swim trunks. His chest is bare except for his harness. I find that I can't tear my eyes away.

"Wow." Delaney murmurs.

Indeed. He's so graceful as he skims on top of the water that he makes it seem like art.

"Hey, Carter!!" she yells suddenly, waving at him and smiling. I want to duck, but there's no place to duck down to. Sunfish boats are cramped. Dang it. I had no idea she was going to yell at him. I was perfectly happy just watching him. I don't want to deal with his heat filled glare today.

"Laney!" I hiss.

But she doesn't pay any attention, and in fact, yells his name again.

This time, he hears her and turns his head to locate her voice, pushing his sunglasses onto his head to get a better view. When his eyes register our boat, the look of surprise is blaringly evident on his face. He curiously waves back and continues to stare in our direction.

For once, his gaze doesn't burn me.

Unfortunately, a wave chooses that exact moment to crash into his translucent sail.

With his attention diverted, he loses his balance and tumbles into the lake.

We can't help but laugh as he plunges sideways into the water. The wave hadn't been overwhelmingly large, so we know he's fine. A little dunking will be good for him- he's a teench arrogant, a little too sure of himself. I know it'll annoy him that he'd fallen because he let us distract him. I smile to myself.

His head bobs to the surface a second later, and he spits out lake water.

Now he's glaring. My smile stretches even wider as I watch him float beside to his windsurf board. He leans his head back to re-wet his hair and then shakes it like a dog. Then he floats aimlessly on his back with his face tilted up toward the sun, pointedly ignoring us and apparently enjoying his cool dip in the lake.

As I watch his dark head bobbing up and down in the water, a heavy feeling of apprehension rises from my stomach, making its way to lodge directly in my throat as recognition slams into me.

It can't be.

But it is. I remember with absolute clarity another day when a dark head had bobbed up and down with the waves. A dark head that looked just like this one. My hand grips the side of my boat hard enough to turn my knuckles white.

He's the same boy.

The heavy, sick feeling in my chest shouts the truth loud enough for me to listen.

Carter Kelly is the boy who killed my dad.

My ears roar, and the light pixelates, and then all I can see is crimson closing in from the corner of my eyes like spilled ink, spreading inward.

Then nothing at all.

"Are you alright? Whitney! Are you okay? Wake up!"

An assertive male voice persistently asks me questions and demands to be heard.

Am I asleep? I do a quick assessment. I don't think so- I'm wet and cold. And I'm not sure if I'm ok. I don't know what had happened.

It occurs to me that I'm weightless, my shirt clinging to my ribcage like a wet towel.

I open my eyes. I'm in the water next to my boat. Carter is floating with me, supporting my weight with his arms, his strong hands gripping my sides tightly.

I must've passed out and fallen into the water. I take a moment to get my bearings, looking up onto the boat into Delaney's pale, scared face and then back at Carter.

And I remember.

All of it.

Rage rushes into me with all the velocity of a charging bull.

"You!" I spit with as much hatred as I can muster, twisting out of his arms so I can hold onto the boat myself. "Get away from me!"

I don't want a single finger of either of his hands touching me. I can still feel the imprint of his hands on my body and it makes me sick. My stomach rolls.

Carter looks confused, and Delaney is shocked as she watches my face turn into something venomous and hateful, something she's never witnessed before. I can't help it.

More contempt than I've ever felt in my life- more malice, more venom, more hate-bubbles up in my chest until I feel like I might burst from all of the negativity congealed there.

"You. Killed. My. Dad."

Short, stilted words shoot from my mouth like daggers aimed at Carter's head.

He has the grace to look ashamed. He drops his gaze guiltily, hiding it behind his wet dark lashes. Delaney's mouth forms a perfect O. She clasps her hand over her mouth and looks quickly back at Carter.

"Whitney... I'm sorry. Very, very sorry." His words are quiet, very nearly drowned out by the lapping of the water against the boat. He still isn't looking at me. All of the arrogance is gone from him now. I take no satisfaction in that.

"I didn't mean to hurt anyone." His voice is tired.

As if I care.

He'd ruined my life. And then he had entered it, without even acknowledging who he *was.*

He had the nerve to act angry- as though I had offended *him* somehow. I'd actually wasted my time wondering what I had done to offend him*!* Well, he offends me now just by breathing.

It should have been *him.* That's all I can think right now. I can't see past my ugly anger.

"Do you think that matters?" My voice is incredulous and hateful at the same time. "My dad saved you. You're only alive because of him." My words are a simple statement of truth. He knows it and I know it. "And you killed him. Your *stupidity* killed him."

We both know that, too.

Chapter Seventeen

"Whitney, I'm so sorry. That's exactly who he is. I couldn't recall it other day, but I wracked my brain, trying to remember where I'd heard his name. It was from the newspaper. There was a story right after your dad died, about how he saved a 16-yeard old boy... named Carter Kelly."

Ginny's voice is sympathetic and apologetic at the same time.

She hands me a glass of her special lemonade and sits down on the sun porch beside me. I find myself wishing that she'd spiked it. I've never even tasted an alcoholic beverage before, but if ever there was a time for a drink, this is it.

Knowing that my grandparents would still be at the clinic, Delaney had rushed me to her house as soon as we had docked the boat and had settled me onto a chaise lounge on her sun-porch.

I had scared her with my shaking. I had shaken so hard, like I was frozen to the bone. That's because it feels like my heart has frost-bite. It's just one thing after another after another.

I'm pretty proud of myself though, for the way I'd handled it.

I had simply twisted away from Carter and climbed back onto my boat without another word...turning it towards shore and completely ignoring Carter's pleadings for me to listen.

There's nothing he can say that would quell the rage in my chest. I can't even listen to the sound of his voice. I can't look at his penetrating dark eyes as he implores me to hear him.

In my head, I see him bobbing in the water watching us sail away from him. His gaze had scorched my back as I fled. I shudder. There's something intense about that guy, completely separate from the fact that he had killed my dad.

Delaney sits next to me, as close as Velcro. She wrapped a blanket around me even after I insisted that I wasn't cold. She sits with her arm around me now, rubbing my arm as if to warm me up.

"When did you recognize him, Whit?" Her voice is curious even as her face is lined with worry.

"I'm not sure exactly. I was watching him float in the water and all of a sudden, I just knew."

She shakes her head in sympathy. "I'm sorry, Whitney."

"Laney, It's not your fault. It's his."

Ginny's concerned face hovers next to mine.

"Whitney, I know you're upset, and of course you have every right to be. But your dad's drowning was an accident. I'm sure that Carter didn't want it to happen. He almost drowned himself that day." Her voice is gentle.

She isn't reprimanding me or even lecturing me. She's just trying to offer an objective view- a sensible opinion of someone who isn't immersed in emotion. My head knows that she's saying is true. But it doesn't help my heart.

"Ginny... I know." My voiced is resigned. "I'm not upset because he was in that situation. Well, maybe a little—there was a red flag up and he went out anyway! But really- what I'm most upset is that he fought against my dad so hard. My dad was out there for so long, exhausting himself, because Carter wouldn't stop fighting him. He wouldn't let my dad help—and that's why my dad died. *That's* how Carter killed him."

Delaney and her mother are both silent, thinking about what I said.

After a minute, Ginny stands up, squeezes my shoulder gently and goes inside, leaving Delaney and I alone. Well, almost alone. I can feel Samuel nearby.

"You think I'm wrong, don't you?" I ask Laney softly.

"No. Feelings are never wrong. People can't help how they feel. They can only help how they react." Her voice is gentle. And wise beyond her sixteen years. Maybe she really is a sage.

"Seriously, Whit. I have to say this. I saw Carter's face. I can tell it's killing him. I barely even know him and I can see that."

I nod wordlessly, watching the beads of condensation run silently down my glass and pool on the table. I know she was right. But I know with just as much certainty that it doesn't matter to me right now.

My phone buzzes and I pull it from my pocket to find a text from Brady.

R U home?

Laney watches me with one eyebrow practically raised into her hairline. It looks as though she'd been at it again with the tweezers. I ignore her stare and answer his text.

No. Why?

He answers within a couple seconds.

I miss U. I thought I might come over? Yes. Please. I almost exhale with a relief that I hadn't realized I felt. I'd missed him without even realizing it. It's strange how quickly I've grown to feel close to him, to rely on him to lift me up. I text him back.

Please do. I'm at Laney's- will be home in a bit.

I stand up. Laney watches me silently, wanting to ask questions, but for once in her life refrains from vocalizing them. I hand her my empty glass and then bend down to hug her quickly.

"Thanks, Lane. I love you- you're the best. Call you later?"

She nods and I duck out the door, walking in a clipped pace toward home.

I catch a glimpse of a black t-shirt sitting on my porch steps as I approach. I smile. He'd beaten me here. I practically bound the rest of the way, anticipation building within me, and then pull up short when I realize that it's not him.

Carter is waiting for me.

He'd changed from his swim trunks into khaki shorts, a t-shirt and black flip-flops. His dark hair is dry now, but the expression on his darkly handsome face is still the same. Apologetic. I shake my head. I need more than that.

"What are you doing here?" My words stab through the air like icicles.

"Waiting for you." His words are as soft as mine were sharp.

"I can see that. Why?"

"Because I need to say something to you. Will you please listen, just for a minute?"

I want to say no. I want to turn around and walk away, but there's a pleading in his voice that I can't ignore. My attitude toward him is iniquitous- completely unfair. I know that. Laney's voice rings in my memory... *People can't help how they feel- they can only help how they react.*

I truly don't want to be an ugly person. Carter's voice is sincere. His expression is remorseful. I stop moving.

"I'm listening." I can't quite get the ice out of my voice, but at least I'm standing here. He can't expect much more than that.

"Okay." He suddenly seems flustered as though he doesn't know where to start, as though he hadn't been expecting me to listen.

This doesn't fit with the image of him that I keep in my head- of cocky, arrogant Carter. The Carter with the dark hair slanted down over his eye and the heat-filled glare. This isn't him. This is contradictory.

" I want you to know that if I could change everything, I would." His voice is low and husky. "I hate what happened. I don't know how it happened- and this will probably make you mad, but I don't even remember much. The details are gone- it's all a blur to me. I'm an excellent swimmer. It shouldn't have happened."

He rubs his forehead with long fingers, as though he has a tension headache. "I couldn't even bring myself to go into the lake again for weeks- not until today, in fact. I can't tell you how sorry I am. There aren't words."

He studies me with his intense dark eyes and I find that I can't find it within me to continue hating him. This Carter is completely different than the one I thought I knew.

This Carter is vulnerable, sorry and so... human.

It's obvious that he lives with what had happened on a daily basis. He hadn't just put it out of his mind like I had assumed. It had been so traumatic for him that he'd blocked it from his memory, just like I'd blocked his face from mine. That has to mean something, right?

I took a step closer, just a small one.

"Okay." I murmur. "I know it was an accident."

He nods slowly, his eyes never leaving my face.

"I can't forgive myself. It shouldn't have happened. Period. I'm a swimmer- a good one. I shouldn't have been in distress and I shouldn't have fought against your dad when he tried to help. I know better than that. I wish I could remember what was going through my mind, but I just can't."

Pity floods through me in a warm wave. He's hurting, too. I can't imagine living with the guilt of knowing that someone was dead because of something that I'd done.

"My dad died to save you. That means something, something big. You have to forgive yourself and move on, and then make your life something great so that it was all worth something."

My dad can't have died for nothing. Carter needs to make sure of that. He watches me carefully speak every word as he stares at me.

He flashes a brief smile, which disappears as quickly as it emerged.

"Do you think you can forgive me?" His dark eyes assess my face, searching for any sign of acquiesce.

I try to nod, but find that I still can't.

"I'll try. I will. I don't want to carry this anymore."

I sit weakly down on the step next to my dad's killer. I'd have to stop thinking of him like that because it certainly wouldn't help with the healing process.

"If you can, I'll be impressed." He studies me carefully. "When my mom died, I was furious at the entire world for at least a year. I was a punk. I made it even harder for my dad than it already was. But I was just so mad at everything…and everyone."

Surprise filters through me. "Your mom died? I didn't know that. Miranda said that you and your family had moved here from Chicago, so I just assumed that she meant your *whole* family."

He nods slowly. "What's left of my family moved here. My dad, my sister and I. I think my sister, Mia, will be in your class next year. My mom died a year ago from cervical cancer. She was sick for quite a while- she fought really hard. Dad wanted to move away and get a clean start- away from everything that reminded him of sad things. He took it as some sort of weird sign that I had almost drowned here, but didn't. So he started thinking that this was the place where we should get a new start. I was against it, though. I didn't want to run into *you*."

"How did you even know about me? You were out of it that day."

"I saw you waiting on the beach while the paramedics were with me. I saw your face- and your little sister's. And I never wanted to have to face you and let you look at me like you looked at me earlier." His voice cracks, but he stares at me steadily.

"I read the article in the paper about your dad and how he had saved me. I remembered your name- but I didn't need it. I have never been able to get your face out of my memory. I've even dreamed about it. Then when we actually moved here… I guess I just wanted you to hate me. I felt like I deserved it."

"Carter, I …"

Brady's cheerful voice interrupts my statement and my train of thought. He confidently strides up to the porch and stands still at the bottom of the steps, his gaze fixed upon Carter.

"Hey, Whitney," he greets me, his eyes still on Carter.

"Hi," I answer softly, not sure how to handle the situation. Brady looks curious, but not worried. Carter seems hesitant as though he's not sure if he should stay or go. I have a feeling that he wasn't finished talking yet- that he has more to say.

"What's going on?" Brady asks.

I guess he can feel the uncertainty in the air, too. His electric blue eyes search my face for an answer. I'm not sure what explanation to give him.

"Um, Carter wanted to talk to me about something. He knew my dad."

It's the truth- sort of. He'd been with my dad for a few minutes, even though I can't say that they'd actually formerly met.

"Really?" Brady turns to Carter with interest. "You were lucky. I wish I could have met him. The world needs more people like Peter Lane. It's incredible how he risked his own life to save a kid that he didn't even know."

For a reason that I can't explain, I get the impression that this was said for my benefit, maybe even to make me feel good. But I don't care. It's the truth. The world definitely needs more people like my dad- then it would be a better place.

"Oh, I know," Carter answers, bringing me back to the present. His voice isn't cocky or arrogant. It's just softly matter of fact. "I was that kid."

"What the--?" Brady moves quickly, shoving Carter angrily up against the side of my porch. "And you have the nerve to be here- to stand in front of Whitney, to breathe the same air? Do you have any idea what you've done to her?"

His voice is instantly furious, his hands wrapped in Carter's t-shirt. Carter stands several inches taller, but

Brady definitely outweighs him. They scowl into each other's faces like angry pit bulls and I freeze in alarm.

"Stop, please. It's okay." I move closer to try and tear them apart, to push myself in between them, but I can't wedge myself in.

"It's *okay*?" Brady turns backward to look at me incredulously, his hands still grasping Carter. "Your dad would still be alive if it wasn't for this punk!"

It registers with me that he used the same name to describe Carter as Carter himself had used. I wonder how he'd feel about that- if he knew that Carter was sick about everything, that he was angrier at himself than I could ever be... but I didn't think it would matter.

"Get your hands off me!" Carter's voice is steely as he shoves Brady's hands away and wrenches clear from his grasp.

Brady doesn't appear to have noticed- his attention is still on me. His anger has shifted to me, as though he can't believe that I'd side with Carter when he was just trying to act in my best interest in the first place. He looks betrayed.

"It's not okay that my dad is dead, but Carter didn't purposely do it. It's not like he held him under water until he drowned." I flinch at my own words. "My dad meant to save him and he did. He did an honorable thing. The fact that he didn't come back isn't Carter's fault." I'm just as incredulous at what I'm saying as Brady is. He stares at me in amazement.

"Are you being serious right now?"

He continues to stare at me in shock and I realize that I've finally found his imperfection.

He had a temper. I should feel good that it had flared up in my defense, but for some reason I don't. All I felt is sudden weariness.

"Please. Just stop. He came here to apologize. I don't want to talk about this anymore."

I tug on his arm and he takes a step away from Carter, as Carter backs further down the stairs. His intense eyes burn a hole in Brady. Brady obviously doesn't care. He steps closer to me and wraps his arm protectively around my shoulders.

"You should leave. You don't belong here." His words immediately irk me.

Why does he think he has the right to dismiss someone on my behalf? I feel guilty because I know he's just trying to help me- like Delaney. Everyone is trying to help me.

But something about Brady's attitude has my back up. I'm entirely capable of deciding who I speak with and when. But I don't want to make an issue out of it at the moment. His show of temper annoyed me and I just want to get away from it.

All of it. Including Brady, for a while.

"Actually, I'm tired. Can we take a rain-check, too?" He looks at me in surprise. I shrug out of his arm and instantly feel the absence of warmth. What the heck am I doing? But I don't take it back. I need some time alone.

"Sure, if that's what you want." He seems a little hurt, but I can't think about that. Carter looked interests... and then satisfied.

"Get some rest, Whitney. I'm sorry about earlier, too." I decide he must be referencing when I fell out of the boat after I recognized him.

"Thanks for helping me. I'm sorry I wasn't more gracious about it."

"You're welcome. Anytime." He smiles quickly and walks away. He doesn't look back.

"Are you sure, Whit? I can stay if you like- until your grandparents get back. Or I can go with you to the clinic?" Brady was gently persistent. He apparently thought it was a bad idea to leave me alone. I was just as persistent, though. I wanted to be alone. Or as alone as I could be with Samuel around.

"No, I'm fine, really. I think I'll take a quick nap before everyone gets back."

Well, when everyone gets back except for my mom- because she's stuck in a hospital bed with a demon in her body.

My words seem to soothe him. He nods understandingly, the anger he had shown earlier completely dissipated, as though it had never even happened.

Well, even though he had a temper, at least it's just a quick flash. It's like a brief summer storm- quick and fierce, but over with in a blink.

He gives me a quick hug. "Call me if you need me, okay?"

I nod and watch his broad back as he walks down my driveway.

I feel a strange feeling of relief that he's gone.

What in the world is wrong with me?

I felt like I'd just pushed away from the Mad Hatter's tea table.

Nothing makes any sense.

Chapter Eighteen

"Mija?" My grandma's soft voice interrupts my concentration.

I look up from where I'm curled up staring off into space to find her standing in the door of the family room. I smile at her endearment—*my girl* in Spanish. It's comfortingly familiar. My mom uses it, too. Grandma smiles back, but the expression on her face is marred with concern.

"We're back from the clinic. Ellie and grandpa are eating ice cream on the porch. Your grandpa's worried about you."

I smile again because grandma always did this. She never, ever expresses her own concern. It's always 'grandpa' who's worried. She likes to appear that she's unflappable and collected all of the time. She has no idea that we all see right through her.

"I'm sorry, Grandma. What is he worried about?" I try to conceal my smile as I play along.

She crosses the room and sits lightly on the end of the chaise lounge, patting my leg.

"Well, sweetheart, he's concerned because you're not yourself. You haven't relaxed since we got here, and he wants you to know that we're here now. We're going to take care of everything. You don't need to worry."

I lose all trace of the humor that I'd been feeling. They have no idea what we're dealing with. They can't take care of it. It's not possible. I take deep breath.

"I'm sorry, grandma. I just... can't help worrying about her. It's been hard lately and..." My voice breaks without my permission.

I sit in silence as I try to collect myself. *Do not cry*. I repeat that to myself silently, like a mantra. Grandma leans over and takes me in her arms, stroking my hair lightly.

"Sweet girl, you've been amazing- so strong! The way you've taken care of everything... your dad would be so proud of you! I'm proud of you, too. But you can rest now. We're here and you don't need to worry about anything else."

Right. Except for one powerful, malicious demon that has taken residence in my mother's body. Yeah, I guess I don't have anything to worry about except for that.

Grandma's hands are still stroking my hair, comforting me in the way that only a grandmother can. I breathe in the scent of White Diamonds and lie perfectly still in her lap.

"Grandma, do you believe in things we can't see?"

There's a pause, and her hands still.

"What do you mean, sweetheart? Like ghosts?"

I shrug. "Maybe. I guess anything we can't see. Like angels."

Her hands resume. "I definitely believe in angels. There's no other explanation for how we stay safe sometimes, my love. Look at your dad. He traveled to some very dangerous places, and he was safe for years."

"Until he came home, and wasn't safe anymore." My voice is quiet because of the ridiculous irony. He came home from the dangerous places to die on home soil.

My grandma strokes my back harder. "I think that when it's our time, it's just our time. It's hard, though. But you're holding up so well."

I want to talk more about it, but the house phone rings. I reluctantly get up to answer it.

"Whit? You left your phone here. How was Brady?" Delaney's excited voice comes through the phone so loud and clear that grandma hears her perfectly and smiles.

She elegantly walks from the room, apparently satisfied that I'm going to be busy with normal teenaged activity. I hope that it assuages her worry enough for now.

"Thanks, Laney. I must have set it down right before I left."

"Not a problem. I can bring it down. Is your grandma making dinner tonight?" The hope in her voice is apparent. Everyone loves my grandma's cooking.

"Delaney, I just had a great idea- why don't you join us for dinner?" I grin.

"I'd love to. I wish I'd thought of that." I can hear her smiling, too. She's so transparent. "Be down in a few."

I anticipate her estimated time of arrival to be around five minutes - exactly the amount of time it'd take for her to find a pair of flip-flops and inform her mother.

I walk into the kitchen and grandma looks up from chopping an onion. "So, Delaney is joining us for dinner?" She'd been listening. I nod.

"She loves your cooking, like everyone else." The tantalizing scent of green chiles waft over me. "What are you cooking?"

"Tamales. Does that sound good?" My grandma makes everything from scratch. And she knows that her homemade tamales baked in cornhusks is my favorite thing on the face of the planet. She must really want to cheer me up. I give her a tight hug.

"It sounds delicious. Thanks for talking to me, grandma. You made me feel better."

I hear the front door swing open and Delaney's nose leads her directly to the kitchen. She bursts through the door and stops beside me, her dark red hair tied back in a loose ponytail.

"Tamales!" She runs to my grandma and squeezes her. "You're a goddess, Grandma Ava!" Grandma smiles and shoos us out of the kitchen good-naturedly.

"If you girls want to eat at a decent time, I need to get to work. Why don't you go for a walk or something? Dinner will be ready in a couple of hours."

We've barely made it to the sidewalk before Delaney starts drilling me about Brady. I fill her in on the run-in between him and Carter. The look on her face is priceless.

"Holy crap, Brady grabbed Carter? Like, he literally got into his face?" I nod and can tell she's impressed.

"Wow. He's really into you."

"I know. But it actually made me feel weird. His temper... well, it wasn't good. He seemed... different." There's no way I can describe to her how quickly his anger had appeared and then disappeared, like a flash grease fire.

She contemplates that. "He's probably being protective. But too, he might have some unresolved issues about his own brother he was tapping into. You never know."

That makes total sense, and is actually pretty freaking wise, but I still can't help but be annoyed by the whole thing.

"What do you think about Carter? That was pretty brave of him to come to your house like that. I wouldn't have had the guts- not with the way you were screaming out on the lake."

She's right. I definitely have to give him credit for that.

"I'm not sure what I think about him right now. When he was here, I saw a side of him that I hadn't seen before- it sort of changed my opinion. He seemed sort of vulnerable. I didn't expect that and I didn't know that his mom died. Maybe he's the one who understands what I feel like better than anyone."

His face flashes in my memory...the expression he'd had when he mentioned his mother. That devastating ache was very apparent on his face. He hadn't tried to convince me, it was just there...on his face, in his voice. And when I think about him now, I don't feel angry.

"You know what, Whit?" Delaney nudges me. "So much has happened lately. You don't really need to sort it all out right this second. You can just let it ride and see what happens."

She's right. I know she's right.

For the minute, I'm going to let it ride.

We fall into silence as we stroll past the harbor. The lake is quiet and still today. All around us, sunburned tourists are swarming in and out of the local shops that line the sidewalk, carrying souvenir bags and ice cream cones.

I'm just smiling at a little boy with a huge stick of cotton candy when I notice Carter sitting at a table at the Sandwich Hut. I start to lift my hand to wave, when I notice that Courtney and Brandy are sitting across from him. I close my eyes and inhale slowly, drawing the air in over my teeth in a long pull.

I open them again and they're all three still there. My eyes hadn't been deceiving me.

A pit forms in my stomach. I guess I'd been wrong about him. Anyone who chooses the Mean Queens' company is not someone I want to know.

Delaney follows my stare and I hear her gasp.

"Maybe it's not what it looks like."

"How can it not be what it looks like? It is what it is. Carter's having dinner with Courtney and Brandy. He doesn't look like he's being held there against his will. I don't see any handcuffs." My voice is derisive as I watched him talking with Brandy.

We aren't close enough to hear what they're saying, but I can see Courtney tossing her hair over her shoulder as she flirts. Gross. I've seen enough.

Just as I make that determination, his intense dark eyes meet mine.

I turn away abruptly and begin walking in the other direction as fast as I can without plowing down tourists.

Delaney keeps pace with me, not saying anything for once. She doesn't have to. She knows what I'm fleeing from.

"Whitney!" A strong hand clutches my elbow. I turn to find Carter staring at me in confusion. "Are you all right?"

"Of course I am. Why do you ask?" I decide to play dumb. I can't quite make my tone match my nonchalant question, though. The acid that it contains makes him raise his eyebrows.

"What did I do? I thought we were ok. Maybe..." He trails off as he tries to make heads or tails of my glacially cold expression.

"Um, I think it just threw Whitney off because you're eating with Courtney and Brandy. We don't usually hang out with the same circle of friends as they do." Delaney tries to come to the rescue. Unfortunately, I don't want him to think that I care.

"Delaney, Carter's free to choose his own friends. It's none of my business who he hangs around with. If he wants to slither around with snakes, that's his prerogative, even if he *will* get bitten. Snakes have fangs."

He's staring at me now with a look of barely concealed amusement.

In my agitation, I'm trying very hard not to notice how well he fills out his black t-shirt. Wide shoulders, chiseled jawbone, straight nose, smoldering eyes. His eyes get me every time. And now, as I look into them again, I find them filled with humor.

He steps closer to me.

"Whitney... Are you jealous?" His voice is low, meant only for me. I hadn't noticed before how sexy the huskiness of his voice is. It's difficult to ignore.

"Of course not!" I snap. "I don't care what you do." I sound too much like a petulant child for my taste, but I can't recall the words. They're already out there, lingering in the air between us.

"Because..." And he steps even closer. "It sounds like you are."

Over his shoulder, Courtney and Brandy are watching us with unconcealed malice. They would gladly dance on my grave after running me over in cold blood if the opportunity ever presents itself to them.

"Carter, seriously. I wouldn't waste my time on someone who swims with sharks."

"I thought they were snakes?" His eyes twinkle. "Whitney, I honestly don't even know them. I'm new here, remember? I was sitting at that table minding my own business and they walked up, introduced themselves and sat down. I didn't invite them."

I study his face. With an inward sigh of relief, I decide he's probably telling the truth. Courtney had a radar for testosterone- and she'd definitely gravitate to a good-looking new guy.

Carter grasps my elbow as I consider. I glance at Delaney and I can tell from her face that she believes him, too. And honestly, truly, I guess it isn't my business. But it feels so good to know I was wrong.

"Whi—" Carter's words are cut short as what feels like a semi-truck plows into us.

I fly backwards, landing on my back on the planks of the boardwalk.

Luckily, I'd had enough time to break my fall with my hands because Brady had appeared out of nowhere.

The jolt of falling dazes me for a second and I shake my head to clear my vision. Brady and Carter are shoving each other down the length of the pier.

The look of rage on Brady's face is startling- and completely disproportionate with the situation. A bad temper is definitely his flaw.

"What did you not UNDERSTAND?" He yells directly into Carter's face. "Keep your hands off of her!"

A vein in Brady's temple pops out, making the sneer on his face even uglier.

"Holy crap," Delaney breaths, before she chases after them, yelling for them to stop. I jump up and follow her.

"Brady... Stop! This doesn't make sense. Leave him alone! Please!"

I catch up to him and pull at his arm, but it's was like trying to force a beam of steel to bend. It's not going to happen. I'm about as effective as a mosquito buzzing around him. He shakes me off hard enough that I slam into a wooden post.

Carter shoves him back, then glances at me.

"Whitney, are you ok?"

Brady uses his momentary distraction to his own advantage and grabs Carter's shirt, yanking him close enough to literally spit words into his face.

"If you ever, lay even one finger on her again, I'll rip it off for you." And he shoves Carter away from him as he utters the last word.

Carter flies backward off the edge of the pier, dropping the 20-odd feet to splash into the lake below. Delaney and I both scream and rush to peer over the edge. Within a couple of seconds, he emerges sputtering through the surface.

I spin around and race back down the pier, until Brady grabs my arm, stopping me in my tracks.

"Whitney, he's not worth it."

His face is calm and back to normal already, the flash fury of his temper already dissipated. It's incredible to witness- like a brief summer storm containing a tornado. I shake him off.

"Don't touch me right now. What's *wrong* with you?"

His blue eyes stare back at me in confusion, like I'm the one who's wrong, like I'm not seeing the situation clearly.

I don't wait for his answer. At the moment, I don't care what it is. I rush down to the water where Carter is surrounded by a group of by-standers on the beach. I push through and kneel beside him. He seems to be fine, just really wet.

"Are you okay?" My shaking voice betrays how unsettled I am.

He nods. "I'm fine. What's with that guy? Is he on drugs?" His t-shirt clings to him now, and his flip-flops are gone- probably floating in the waves.

"I don't know what his problem is. I'm so sorry." I glance back up at the pier to find that Brady's gone.

Laney skids to a halt next to me, leaning over to catch her breath.

"Carter," she huffs. "Do you need a doctor? Dr. Johnson is eating at the Sandwich Hut if you want me to get him."

He shakes his wet hair out of his face. "Thanks, anyway, Delaney, but I'm fine. All I hit was water. I'm good."

Delaney starts back up toward the pier, presumably to inform the doctor that his services weren't required. Carter stares at me inquisitively.

"What's with that guy... really? Are you seeing him?"

Am I? The question gives me pause.

"I seriously don't know what his problem is. I think he just has a temper." A really bad one. "And no. I'm not seeing him." Even if I had been before, I wouldn't be after today.

A red bump is very obviously forming along Carter's cheekbone. I reach up to touch it and he flinches as my fingers graze the skin there.

"Does that hurt? I thought you only hit water." I raise my eyebrows.

"I thought I did. Maybe there was a stick in the water or something? I don't know."

The bump swells even as we speak.

"You need some ice. My house is close-by. Let's go get an ice pack."

He nods quietly and we walk up to the boardwalk, where we ran into Delaney. She glances at him, his bare feet and then at me curiously.

"Carter's coming back to my house to get some ice," I explain. She nods and falls silently into step with us. Her silence lasts a record-breaking 24 seconds.

"I thought you were exaggerating when you told me about Brady this afternoon, Whit. He *does* have a temper. What's his issue with Carter? He wasn't even doing anything!"

"I was with Whitney. I think that was the issue. The guy is jealous. And he has a temper. A bad combination." Carter shakes his head.

"But there isn't anything to be jealous of." I protest. "We weren't doing anything."

"He doesn't know that." Carter answers in an off-hand tone. "All he knows is that two times in one day, he showed up and I was with you. He must have jumped to conclusions. But he needs to learn to control himself."

So much for thinking that Brady's perfect. That illusion had been crumpled up and tossed away like scribbled-on paper today. We lapsed into a silence that lasts until we reach my house. We're halfway across the porch when Ellie rushes out to meet us.

"Dinner's ready, Whit! It's time to eat!"

I turn to Carter.

"Would you like to stay for dinner? Apparently, it's time to eat."

He sniffs the air appreciatively. "You know, I think I'd better. I might be in shock from hitting my head- food might help."

He smiles widely and I can tell that fear of shock is the last thing on his mind. Fear of an empty belly, maybe.

He holds the door open for us as we walk inside. Grandma glances at us and doesn't miss a beat. She just heads back into the kitchen to get another place setting.

We slide into dining room chairs, Delaney and Carter each on one side of me. Grandpa Vin stares silently from the head of the table, before he raises halfway up and sticks his hand out toward Carter.

"I'm Vincent, young man. And you've got a nasty lump there."

I'd forgotten already. I can see a bluish outline forming around it. I jump up to get an ice pack from the kitchen while Carter and Delaney explain Carter's run-in with Brady.

As I'm filling a baggie with ice, my phone buzzes in my pocket. I pull it out to find a text from Brady.

I'm sorry. Are you mad? I ignore it. I'd better not respond right this second. He might not like the answer.

It buzzes again.

I just couldn't stand seeing his hand on you. I'm sorry. I'm protective.

If by protective, he means psychotic, ok.

Another buzz.

Forgive me. Please.

I leave my phone on the counter and carry the ice pack to Carter, interrupting one of my grandpa's stories of how men behaved when he was young. Being Venezuelan, he apparently applauds the passion that Brady exhibited, while he's also impressed with Carter's tenacity.

"Son, just by being here after two run-ins with this other guy- shows me that you have what it takes to be with my Whitney." Grandpa takes a drink of lemon tea while I want to crawl under my chair. Oh my gosh.

"We're not together, Grandpa." I feel the need to clarify, my cheeks burning. "We're friends."

I quickly glance over at Carter and he has the same amused look on his face that he had earlier. Delaney's hiding her face in her coke glass.

Grandpa stares at me studiously.

"Whitney, never close doors in life. Wait until they close on their own. Until that time, life is full of opportunity."

Oh, God. I want to die.

Grandma smiles gently and pats his hand.

"Leave her alone, Vin. She can make her own decisions." I stare at her gratefully as she changes the subject and we finish eating.

An hour later, I find myself alone on the porch with Carter. Delaney had reluctantly excused herself to return home. I know she was dying to stay, but her mom was expecting her.

I look up from watching her walk down the sidewalk to find Carter studying me.

My lips press together cautiously.

"What?" I murmurs. "Why are you staring?"

The corner of his mouth tilts up. "I was just wondering if we're friends. That's what you told your grandfather."

I smile and shake my head. "I'm sorry about that….about him. He's very blunt."

Carter laughs. "You think?"

I giggle but then we fall into silence.

The air is heavy tonight, the humidity clings to my skin like invisible wet clothing. It's so heavy that it's almost smothering. I lift my hair off my neck to let the breeze blow across my damp skin.

"Seriously though, how *is* that forgiveness thing coming along?" Carter's words are soft, like velvet, the husky edge to his voice ever-present.

I ponder that for a minute.

"I've come to the realization that I'd already forgiven you. I just didn't know it 'til now."

He stares at me for a long moment before he nods. "Thank you. You have no idea how much it means to me."

"Well, I won't lie to you and tell you that I can forget it. Because I can't. Every single detail of that day is frozen in my head. But I'm trying to move past it. I don't hold you responsible- I can honestly say that."

"So...where do we go from here?" His eyes are bottomless dark pools that I might tumble into, and I fight the urge to step closer to him.

"I don't know."

It's the truth.

Chapter Nineteen

The doorbell startles me from sleep.

My eyes flutter open to find Samuel standing guard by my bed, as usual.

I grab my robe and clatter down the stairs. I'm clumsy because I'm not fully awake yet. It'd taken a long time to get to sleep last night since I was trying to sort everything out- how I feel about Brady... how I feel about Carter... worrying about my mother... my topics to worry about are endless and I touched upon all of them last night.

It'd taken a while.

I throw open the door without even looking and Brady is suddenly in front of me.

His shirt is the same exact shade of his eyes, a brilliant, breathtaking blue. He's smiling and holding an iced-coffee.

I hold my hand out wordlessly for the coffee and he hands it to me- never losing his smile. I'm surprisingly unconcerned that my hair hasn't been combed and I haven't brushed my teeth yet.

"I've been texting you. You've been ignoring me."

His smile doesn't waver. He's trying to unnerve me with his charm, I can tell. Normally, it might work. Not today.

"I didn't know what I wanted to say."

"Do you now?" He raises an eyebrow.

"No."

His brow wrinkles briefly in agitation, but smoothes almost immediately back out. His eyes are understanding.

"I guess I understand that. I'm sorry I blew the situation out of proportion, Whitney. It's just... I was burned really badly by a girl in California and I guess I haven't forgotten it. I'll try to be better."

I study him. I suppose that being burned by someone would be enough to instill a sense of suspicion. But that doesn't explain the temper.

"Brady, your temper..." My voice trails off softly.

"I know. I take after my dad, believe it or not. I'm working on it."

I nod because I don't know what else to do.

"Are you coming to the clinic to visit your mom today?"

I nod again. "I think my grandparents are already gone. I'll take a shower and then go myself."

"I'll probably see you there. My dad has me cleaning up brush out behind the clinic." He wrinkles his nose slightly with distaste.

"Okay. I'll see you there, I guess. Thanks for the coffee."

"You're welcome." He flashes his brilliant grin at me and I suck a deep breath in. Yep, he's still gorgeous-temper or no temper.

I jog upstairs to take a shower. Samuel is still standing by the windows in my room, staring down at the yard.

"What do you think about Brady?" I ask. "I know you were there last night."

"Of course I was. How do you think you kept from hitting your head?" he snorts before he turns serious. "I can't offer you advice, Whitney. You know that. I don't know what's going to happen."

"I'm not asking you to foresee the future. I just want to know what your impression is. You're millions of years old, right? You've been around a lot of humans."

He nods wryly. "Yes, I have. And they- you- never cease to surprise me. I don't know how to advise you about Brady. It's clear he has a temper. You should use caution- just as you should in every situation."

Well, that's a vague, unhelpful answer if I ever heard one.

"Okay, thanks," I murmur as I dig through my dresser and get dressed.

My grandparents had taken my dad's Land Rover, so I grab my mom's keys off of a hook in the kitchen. She had chosen her little convertible because she thought it seemed happy. It also screams "Look at me!" which keeps with her Type A personality.

I idle slowly down the street, remembering how to drive a manual transmission smoothly. I put the top down and turn the radio up, letting the sun shine on my shoulders and my hair blow in the wind. I can see why my mom likes this car. Driving it really does make you happy- at least temporarily.

All too quickly, I turn onto the road that led to the clinic.

I have to be honest and admit that I'm looking forward to going. I've actually been avoiding it for a couple of days now. It seems kind of pointless to visit my mom when she's not even aware that I'm there. Plus, being in the same room with Malphas completely freaks me out.

But I can tell that my grandparents are starting to wonder why I'm not visiting her.

While I consider that, a large, black, almost transparent shape drifts quickly across the street right in front of my car. It doesn't run, walk or crawl. It flits, like a shadow.

I suck in my breath as my windshield immediately ices over, the frost forming twisted vines across the glass.

I slam on the brakes and stare breathlessly as the diaphanous black form slithers into the road, then floats into the air, hovering directly above my car.

Staring at it in horror, I can feel the cold air surrounding it, freezing my arms and shoulders.

A face begins to take shape in it, a face with red eyes. Huge bat-like wings start to expand, to stretch from its sides, filling my entire field of vision.

The horror I feel is overwhelming and I scream as loud and shrilly as I can.

I'm surprised when it drops from the sky onto the ground, disappearing behind Dr. Parker's clinic... dragging its tail behind it.

The shadow had a freaking tail.

"Whitney?" Brady's voice filters into my ear, but it sounds like he's speaking through water. That's how in shock I am.

I lean over the steering wheel, trying to breathe. What the hell was that? It wasn't a person or an animal. It was literally as though a shadow had lifted itself off a wall and became mobile.

Brady leans over me, his face filled with concern.

"Whitney? Are you okay?"

I breathe slowly, sucking the air in and out as evenly as I can make myself, while my heart thuds wildly out of control. I nod and Brady pulls me out of the car, puling me against his chest.

I let him because frankly, I'm still in too much shock to do anything else. Almost against my will, I feel safe here next to his solid chest.

He won't let anything get to me.

After a second, I backup a step. "Were you behind the clinic just now?"

He nods, confused by my question.

"Did you see anything strange?"

He looks even more confused as he shakes his head. "No. Was there something to see?"

He hadn't seen it. But I know that I did.

I feel the beginnings of hysteria welling up and I do my best to tamper it back down. It's over with. Whatever it had been, it's gone now.

"Whitney, what happened? What can I do?" He seems desperate to fix the situation for me as he strokes my back with his hand, trying to soothe me.

"I'm sorry, it was nothing. I thought I saw something, but I guess I didn't."

"What's wrong with your car?" He looks at it questioningly.

"I killed it." *Because when a giant shadow flies above you, you forget to push in the clutch.*

He grins widely.

"Remember me saying that I wouldn't believe everything I heard about women drivers? I take that back."

I roll my eyes. He hadn't seen what I did.

"Want me to park it for you?" He doesn't wait for me to answer, instead just slips into the driver's seat. The car roars right to life as he turns the ignition. I watch him slide the car easily into a parking space as I suspiciously watch the pond behind the clinic.

There's still nothing there.

We walk into the clinic together. Ellie is sitting at a little table just inside the door working on a puzzle with Eleanor. She's curled over it in extreme concentration, but glances up when she hears the door click shut.

"Whitney!" Her eyes sparkle as she jumps up and hugs me. "We didn't want to wake you up. Grandma said you haven't been sleeping well."

I didn't know that anyone else had noticed.

"It's okay, monster. How's mom?" *Still possessed by a demon?*

"She's still asleep. Dr. Parker said she needs to rest, but that he'll start wanting her to wake up soon."

"Are grandma and grandpa in with mom?" She nods before she skips back to her chair to continue working on her puzzle.

Eleanor smiles gently at me as I walk past.

Great, I can see it coming already. I'm no longer "Whitney Lane, the girl whose dad died in the drowning accident." Now I'm "Whitney Lane- the girl whose dad died in the drowning accident and then her mother went crazy."

Perfect.

I poke my head in my mom's room, as Brady waits behind me. Grandpa's dozing while grandma reads to my mother. She gets up to hug me as I walk through the door.

"Mija! I'm glad you're here. I didn't want to wake you when we left. Your mom is still resting comfortably."

My gaze shifts to my mom- she's motionless with a blue blanket pulled up to her waist and a needle still stuck in her arm with fluid dripping through it. Her hair is braided now, probably grandma's doing. I dutifully sit next to my mother for the next few minutes, but it's the shortest visit on the record books, I'm sure.

It's not even an hour before I start pleading off.

"I'm sorry, grandma. I still didn't sleep well last night and I have a headache. I'm going to go back home and take a nap, I think."

She's instantly concerned, of course, and puts her hand on my forehead.

"Do you feel okay, Whitney? Or are you just tired? You look a little pale."

"I'm fine. Just exhausted."

"Okay, sweet girl. Go get some rest. We should be back home by dinner time, okay?"

I nod as I bend to kiss my grandpa's cheek. He's still asleep in his chair. I can see from the window that Brady's out back, pulling dead shrubbery out of the landscaping and putting it into a big pile.

As I walk through the lobby, I bend down by my sister.

"Ellie, I'm going to go take a nap. Do you want to stay here with grandma and grandpa or come home with me?"

As if she'd want to take a nap. Her answer is immediate. "I'll stay here and finish my puzzle."

I have to smile. "Ok. I just thought I'd ask. I'll see you in a bit!"

She nods and I continue out the door. I quietly close my car door so that Brady won't hear me leave. For some reason, I just feel the need to be alone.

I fall immediately into bed when I get home and close my eyes.

Chapter Twenty

When I wake up from my nap three hours later, the house is still quiet.

My grandparents aren't home yet, so they're obviously having a long visit with my mom today. Samuel is nowhere around, either. I yawn and stretch in the sun on my bed. I glance at my phone on the nightstand. I don't even bother to check and see if anyone has called. I'm just reveling in my solitude.

Which, of course, is short-lived.

Samuel appears on the edge of my bed three minutes later. He sits stiffly, his fingers folded on his lap.

"How are you?" he questions, his aquamarine eyes taking in my mood.

"Great. How else?" I shrug my shoulders and try to be nonchalant, but it doesn't work. He looked at me doubtfully.

"Where have you been, anyway?" I ask him. I hadn't felt him at the clinic, which was unusual.

"Reconnaissance."

I can tell from his expression that I'm not going to get more than that, so I don't push it. Instead, I just sigh and grab a brush and ponytail holder from my dresser.

"Where have you been lately? You've been gone so much. Today at the clinic, I saw something really strange.

And I fell out of the boat on the lake the other day. I didn't feel you there, either. That's not like you."

Samuel levels a gaze at me.

"I was with you today- I just wasn't in your car. And I was out there on the water with you, too. You were never in any danger. I held you up until Carter got to you. He can really swim."

Yeah. Except for one significant day.

He observes my expression. "Remember what I told you, Whitney. Things aren't always what they seem."

"What does that mean? Why do you always speak in riddles?"

Today is so not the day for this. I'm not in the mood to decipher cryptic angel puzzles.

"I'm not always able to tell you what I want to. Sometimes, I just pray that you'll figure it out."

"Well, I'm not that smart, okay?"

My voice breaks and I collapse on my bed, hugging my pillow as hot tears run down my cheeks. I hadn't realized how on the edge I actually was.

I hadn't asked for this, I don't want this and I'm so freaking done trying to figure it out.

Except a vision of Ellie's little hand floating on the water keeps emerging into my head. And I know that I can't be done. I have to figure out how to keep her safe.

My tears keep streaming, for what seems to be hours before I finally pull myself together. I glance at the clock.

"I don't know what's taking my grandparents so long. It'll be dinner-time soon."

I grab my cell phone to call them. No signal. I stare at it. It's strange. I've always had a clear signal in my room before.

"It's me."

Samuel gestures to my phone. "When I'm in human form, I block your cell reception for some reason. I don't know why."

He shrugs, unconcerned. It might've been nice if he'd mentioned that little tidbit before. It would've cleared up the mystery of all my missed calls.

I'm just getting ready to point that out when Samuel's demeanor changes completely.

He visibly stiffens as he stands next to my bed, his face firming into a stone mask.

"Your plan is unfolding. I feel it."

His statement is as firm and quiet as it is sudden.

"What do you mean? Can you tell me? You can see more now, can't you?"

He nods silently and bounds over my bed so fast that I don't even see him moving. He's suddenly next to the door.

"You need to go back to the clinic. Now."

He doesn't have to tell me twice.

I jumped up, grabbed my cell phone and keys and sprint for the door.

I throw open my mom's car door and fling myself into the seat. As I ram the keys into the ignition, my cell phone beeps. I have a signal now.

An ominous feeling that I can't explain fills my heart and I dread reading the message. The icy tendrils of fear wrap around my heart as I push the 'read' button.

I gasp because I have four texts and they all say the same thing.

I have your sister.
I have your sister.
I have your sister.
I have your sister.

Chapter Twenty-One

"Slow down!" Samuel commands, as I gun my mom's little car and fly down my street.

I ram the gears into place, one after the other as the needle on the RPM gauge bounces into the red.

"Slow down!" Samuel repeats, more insistent this time as the car lurches through a dip in the road. "You aren't going to help anyone if you have a wreck or blow the engine. It'll just slow us down."

He's so calm. Eerily in control of himself.

"How can you be so relaxed?" I shrill. My voice has an element of hysteria in it. "Malphas has my sister. I know you say that dying isn't something to dread, but I know now that there are things worse than that."

Like being possessed by an evil presence.

My mom's eyes, filled with evil, flood my memory. I stomp on the accelerator. The engine roars in reaction and the little car races toward the clinic.

"Whitney, I'm calm because I can see your plan now. However it turns out, it will be for the good. Don't you understand? They can't win. Not in the end."

The end isn't what I'm concerned about.

I'm concerned with the *now*.

I'm concerned with making sure my sister isn't possessed or killed by a malevolent demon prince.

We drive the rest of the short way in charged silence as I try to envision the nightmare that might wait for me when we arrive.

The little car shrieks into the clinic's parking lot, lunging into a parking spot. I leap out, racing through the doors.

And stop.

Everything around me is completely still. Not a sound. No music, no shuffling of footsteps, no beeps from machines, no Eleanor rustling papers at her desk. Nothing.

The nothingness fills me with apprehension so thick that I can taste it in my mouth. Three hours earlier, this clinic had been bustling with life. I feel Samuel with me as I race toward my mom's room.

Her bed is empty and unmade. The IV lines hang limply, no longer attached to anything, but the pump hadn't been turned off. The clear liquid drips drop by drop onto the floor.

No one else is in the room. I whirl around and sprint toward Dr. Parker's office. All I can do is hope that Malphas hadn't hurt anyone.

I find myself holding my breath as I approach the partially open door. There's no noise coming from within. I'm a little hesitant to enter, afraid of what I might find. But as I shove through the door, I find his office empty, as well.

I half expected to find it torn apart- because it seems like something an angry demon might do. It *does* look like the doctor had left in a hurry, though.

His chair is pushed far back away from his desk and his trash can is knocked over. Maybe he'd needed to run. My feeling of apprehension grows wilder and wilder.

Perhaps Malphas had taken everyone with him, not just Ellie. Maybe *everyone* is in danger.

I feel dizzy as I glance around, noticing a pile of crumpled boxes spilling from the overturned wastebasket.

Out of curiosity, I take a step closer, bending down to pick one up. It's a contact lens box. Blue tinted. Confusion clouds my thoughts. Why had Dr. Parker needed so many pairs?

"Why do people wear colored contacts, Whitney?" Samuel suddenly murmurs into my ear, his strong hand gripping my elbow.

"To change the color of their eyes," I whisper. That's a stupid question.

"Or?" He waits for my human mind to find an alternate answer.

"Or to hide them?" I whisper, as icy cold fingers of dread curl around my stomach in cold realization.

As I turn to stare in horror at Samuel, he stares back pointedly, his aquamarine eyes shimmering. His words rush through my mind. *My eyes shimmer sometimes because they aren't really mine. It's just how my real eyes react when I take human form.*

The cold fingers tighten their grip around my stomach and work their way up to my throat until I can't breathe anymore.

They needed to hide their eyes.

I rapidly scan my memory for more and remember what Samuel had said about fallen angels. They can manipulate humans- confuse them, seduce them. Their rules are different. The realization that is slowly forming grows even colder as it solidifies into a conscious fact.

My heart beats so fast that it feels like a continuous fluttering of wings.

The phone on the desk rings loudly, ripping through the deafening silence and interrupting my thoughts.

Every cell in my body knows that the call is for me.

Without questioning how I know, my feet guide me numbly and I pick up the receiver. I don't say anything; I just raise it to my ear.

Brady's voice, stone-cold and disdainful, filters through the wire, confirming what my heart already knew.

"Hello, Whitney." Goose-bumps form on every surface of my body as his icy voice chills me to the core. "I see you got our message."

As he speaks, I feel like someone kicks me in the stomach, knocking the air out of me.

"That you have my sister?   Yes, I got it, all four times."

I try to make my voice as cold as his, as icily confident, but that's impossible.

He's a fallen angel.

Corruption courses through his veins. It's nothing to him that he'd manipulated me- that he'd played with my emotions, which had been fragile in the first place. It meant nothing to him because he doesn't have those same emotions himself.

The Brady that I knew doesn't exist. The relationship that I thought I'd been forming with a beautiful, almost perfect boy is a lie.

I try to make my brain accept that incomprehensible fact. I mean no more to him than a dead autumn leaf crunched under his shoe. My stomach clenches as tightly as a vise around the knowledge of his betrayal. But even in my overwhelming shock and anger, my heart reacts with pain. I can't help it. I'm human.

"I thought you were my friend."

I can't keep the words from coming out. I thought he was much more than my friend and his deception is too heavy to bear. My words sound pitiful, even to my ears. I regret them immediately.

"Stupid, stupid humans. It's almost too easy sometimes…" his hard voice trails off and I steel myself.

He's not my friend. But he isn't going to beat me.

"You can't win," I tell him simply. "You lost the second that you fell, but you still continue to try. Humans aren't the stupid ones."

He pauses for only a beat before he laughs derisively, each note dripping with hatred. It stabs my heart like a knife.

"You have no knowledge of what you speak. Do you want your sister back alive?" He pauses, but doesn't wait for an answer. "You need to meet us at the pier tonight at dusk. Step aboard the boat in slip number 12. We'll be there with your sister. You need to bring us a boat-warming gift. Ask your angel what you should bring."

The phone goes dead.

I remain stunned and unmoving; the phone hanging from my fingertips. Once again, I have a new reality tumbling down around me. I struggle to make my brain accept it.

My eyes flash up to meet Samuel's black ones. He takes the receiver from my hand and replaces it, then stands motionlessly at my side- in full guardian angel splendor and strength. His enormous bronzed muscular frame gleams in the light. He was made for this.

My question is simple.

"What do I need to do?"

Chapter Twenty-Two

There is only an hour remaining until dusk.

We quickly find my grandparents lying in separate beds in the clinic, hooked up to dripping IVs. Samuel sniffs at the IV bags and confirms that they were a harmless mixture of saline and sedatives. I start to yank the needles from their arms, but then leave them where they are.

They'd be safer in the empty clinic in blissful oblivion than they would be anywhere else for the time being. I don't want them to be in danger, too.

Samuel scoops me up in his arms and before I realize it, we're standing on my porch. Apparently, angels fly faster than humans can even blink. No wonder he hadn't left footprints at the beach. If I lived, I know I'll find that fascinating later.

For now, though, Samuel has a lot of explaining to do.

It turns out that he's been withholding quite a few details because of those vague angel rules that I don't quite understand. As he speaks now, the intricacies of the plan surrounding me, *my* plan, keep me enthralled.

My dad had been focused on a dig in Israel for the past two years, which is a fact that I'm already aware of. It just never really interested me before.

He and Josef had found quite a few important artifacts throughout those two years, but apparently, they found one of real interest- and they didn't even realize the true significance.

"The artifact holds seven demons inside of it," Samuel tells me calmly, speaking of the weird marble disc in my mother's closet. No wonder I'd felt so unsettled when I held it in my hands.

"You might not know this," Samuel tells me, "But Mary Magdalene herself had been possessed by demons- specifically, seven of them. The son of God cast them out. The bible doesn't mention, however, what had happened to them afterward.

"Josef came to believe that the seven demons cast from Mary had been displaced into the disc. The fact that they found the disc in Magdala, which was where Mary was from, in combination with the unexplained strange events that kept happening at the dig site, made it seem plausible to him. Josef felt an evil presence whenever he was around it, which was what finally convinced him. And he was right," Samuel explains.

As he speaks, I shiver. I know that feeling.

"Humans should learn to trust their instincts," Samuel lightly admonishes me. I look away. I don't blame Josef for not wanting to listen to his gut. I know from personal experience that it's hard to tell the difference between your instincts and pure craziness.

"Josef had several near-misses and started to believe that his life was in danger. He sent the disc, along with several other artifacts to your father, because he felt that the disc needed to be kept from dangerous hands.

"The next day, he was convinced that he was being chased by shadows- like the one you saw on the way to the clinic. And he was. He tried to run, but tripped and fell into a deep dig." Samuel stares past me, as though he's actually watching it all play out in his head. For all I know, he is.

Josef's death hadn't been an accident.

"Why did they kill him? He'd already sent the disc to my dad. He wasn't a threat anymore."

"Josef didn't send a note with the artifacts- he knew that your dad would think he was being ridiculous. He planned to call him and somehow make your father understand the importance of the disc. But he died before he had a chance." Samuel's voice is serious.

"They couldn't let it remain with your father, either. He would've taken it to the University where it would've ended up in a museum. They couldn't have that. They needed it."

"So my dad's drowning wasn't an accident, either?"

Shock slams into my chest like a Mack truck. Samuel shakes his head slowly.

"I don't understand. I thought that demons- and fallen angels- can't physically harm humans. I thought it was against the rules." I'd heard that in church once. Had that just been something that humans had made up to feel safe?

"That's correct. They cannot directly physically harm a human. But they can trick them into harming themselves." I'm more confused than ever.

"They can do things to overwhelm humans... like taunting them with visions or appearing to them, which is what happened to Josef. He saw shadows following him along the wall and thought he might be losing his mind. He was so flustered as he ran that he tripped and fell."

Poor Josef. I know exactly what that feels like.

"A group of them can surround someone with their undiluted evil presence, which causes the human to feel dazed and confused. We call it 'oppression'. It only lasts for a short while, but sometimes that is enough to manipulate a situation."

Samuel stares at me hard.

"Carter Kelly is a swimmer and a sailor. Don't you find it odd that he didn't know what to do in a rip current?"

I nod. That part had never made sense to me- how a competitive swimmer wouldn't have known.

"He was oppressed, wasn't he?" I murmur. "He didn't know what he was doing."

"Yes. They overwhelmed him with their presence and he fell out of the raft he was in. He was confused for a few minutes, during which time your dad was trying to help him. Carter wasn't in his right mind yet, and so he fought hard against your dad."

I'm beyond stunned. It really hadn't been Carter's fault. Samuel had basically told me as much when he said that things were not what they seemed to be. I just hadn't realized at the time what he was referring to.

"Whitney, they knew your dad would be there that day. Because of your dad's character, they knew that he wouldn't stand aside and let someone drown. They were also well aware of what their presence would do to Carter. They stacked the deck against your dad that day, and it came out in their favor."

I'm beginning to realize the vast scope of what dark angels could do for Helel. There's not anything they can't accomplish if we allow ourselves to be used like that. I'm overwhelmed when I think about how our human plans intersect with the behavior of the dark angels.

Dad had started his dig in Israel two years ago. Brady had come to our school two years ago. That couldn't have been a coincidence. They had put their whole scheme into action way back then. It's almost too difficult to comprehend.

"Why did Malphas possess my mother?" I ask Samuel softly. "It doesn't make sense to me."

"Think about it, Whitney. They need the disc. They couldn't just walk up and ask for it. They couldn't just physically come into your house without your knowledge - I would have fought them. The only way they could come in was to trick you into allowing it. I can't interfere in your free will. And they know it. They needed to have some sort of leverage over you...so they used your mom.

"And they took human form. One became Brady. He seduced you in your dreams, which made you feel closer to him in real life. And dreams are just one way that they manipulate you. He also tricked you into believing that he knew what you were going through- that he had been through it himself."

More realization settles in around me. He never had a brother who drowned. The pieces just keep falling together.

"He took what was personal to you and used it to get to you. Do you see now what they do?"

I nod. How can I not? The evidence is right in front of me.

"He wormed his way into your life so that he had access to the disc. I couldn't stop him when you had already given him permission to be around you. And I couldn't tell you, either."

"The night that I found Brady standing in my dad's study... was he searching for the disc?" I had felt an evil presence that night- and I thought I was imagining it.

Samuel nods. "Yes, he was. I know you thought you were safe because I wasn't with you, but the fact is, I wasn't with you because I was in the study with Brady."

I swallow hard. How is it possible for one person to be misled so completely?

"What are we supposed to do with the disc?" I murmur bleakly, my voice shaking.

"Well, we can't allow them to have it. If they get it, they'll release the demons which will be catastrophic on many other levels."

"Can we destroy it?" I'm only slightly hopeful. I know it can't be that easy.

"The only way it can be destroyed is by God himself, His Son... or Mary Magdalene, since it was she that the demons had been cast from in the first place."

So it's hopeless then. Mary Magdalene is long dead. And I don't see God himself interfering. It's why He had created an army of angels in the first place- to take care of issues like this.

"Is that everything? Or do you know more?" I desperately hope there's no more. I don't know how much more I can take.

"Well, there are two more things."

I brace myself.

"Brady has a personal interest in the disc. His son is a Rephaim and he is one of the demons being held in the disc. He wants him back."

"What's Brady's real name?" I whisper. I can't explain why I want to know, I just do. It's hard to think of him as anything but Brady. But Brady had been kind and gentle. And Brady doesn't exist.

"His name is Eligor. Dr. Parker's real name is Procel. And Eleanor's real name is Lillith. They all have specialties that were an asset on this assignment."

Assignment. Destroying my life has been an *assignment*. I feel even sicker. I wait expectantly and then raise my eyebrows, urging him to continue.

"Eligor's specialty is appearing as a white knight-a person that swoops in to take care of everything. He is very good at appearing that he is kind and understanding. He is adept at human insight. Procel's specialty is in hidden or secret things." Like the disc. Okay, both of those things make sense. And Brady was extremely good at his talents. He'd certainly fooled me.

"What's the second thing?" I'm afraid to know.

Samuel's voice is quiet. "They can't just command the demons to come out of the disc. They require a human to send them into."

I stare at him blankly, not comprehending, while he stares back.

After a minute, he says gently, "That's what he wants you for."

My blood turns to ice.

"But Whitney, I won't allow it. It won't happen."

His voice rings with the confidence of a warrior. Even still, I can't begin to imagine the scope of the danger that I'm in.

It suddenly occurs to me that Samuel had left out Lillith a moment ago.

"You never said what Lillith's talents are," I say hesitantly. Samuel doesn't even blink.

"Her specialty is in kidnapping and killing children."

No wonder he didn't mention her.

My breath freezes on my lips.

Chapter Twenty-Three

The sun goes down in glory over Lake Michigan.

The golden warmth of the sun dissipates into an explosion of warm colors- of amber, gold, saffron and orange hues reflecting off the water back toward Heaven.

I watch it today with trepidation and fear as I clutch the ugly marble disc to my chest.

Today, the dying light signals something that surely isn't going to end well for me.

The weakening rays of the sun gleam faintly off of the rows of boats tucked safely into their slips for the night. I gaze down the pier at slip number 21.

A large white and blue boat with an enclosed upper deck floats gently next to the pier. It's the largest boat here and there are no visible signs of life. I can read the words *The Crazy Fate* painted on its stern. Well, that's a sick joke.

I whisper to Samuel. "Are you ready?"

"Always." I can hear the grim smile in his voice even though I can't see him.

We quietly walk down the length of the pier and stop in front of the *Crazy Fate.* She bobs gently as the water laps against her bow, as innocuous as every other boat here. But she's anything but harmless. I know that. I take a deep, calming breath and climbed aboard.

Nothing happens.

I don't know what I expected... maybe the boat to burst into flame when I touched it?

It doesn't. Everything remains still and quiet. No one comes to meet us, so I walk around and descend a small flight of stairs into the belly of the boat. I feel a strange invisible compulsion guiding me in that direction.

I also feel as though I'm marching to my own crucifixion. It doesn't help to know that I probably am.

I open the door at the bottom of the stairs and feel Samuel looming closely behind me.

"Whittie!" Ellie's voice cries in relief from across the room.

As soon as my eyes adjust to the darkness within, I see Ellie seated with my mother on a small sofa against the back wall of the cabin. It's not my mother, of course. It's Malphas.

Three angels are perched like enormous predatory birds along a short banquette of cabinets against the other wall. They look similar to Samuel, but the aura surrounding them doesn't exude safety and peace as his does. The atmosphere here is full of fear and dread, and it is crushing. My breath seems to leave me in a whoosh, as the evil weight of their presence pushes against my chest.

I swallow hard.

"I'm here. And I have what you want." My voice doesn't shake.

"So you are...and so you do."

Brady's chilling voice comes from the angel on the left- the one closest to me.

He unfolds himself from his perch and bounds off the banquette to land a few feet from me, standing at his full height. He's enormous, like Samuel. His hair is dark blonde and curly. Like Samuel, his eyes are deadly black.

Soulless.

I shiver as I look at him. I can't believe that I'd put myself into such close and personal proximity with this... *thing* so many times- and had even enjoyed it.   It's incomprehensible.

He's a monster.

I'm suddenly aware that the boat is moving, gliding smoothly out of the dock by itself and towards the bay. I'm pretty sure that no one is at the helm.

"Are you afraid, *Whittie*?" Brady asks innocently, circling where I stand.

"Watch yourself, Angel," Samuel warns. He steps forward and places himself between Brady and me. I can't seem to make myself remember that his name is Eligor. His voice is still Brady's.

"What are you going to do, *Angel*?" Brady sneers, as he circles around us like a jungle cat observing his next meal.

I do the simple arithmetic.

There are three of them and one of Samuel. I feel dread develop like a sinking anchor in my stomach. I'd known this wasn't going to end well. But the thought of Samuel accompanying me had comforted me anyway. He's the strongest thing I've ever seen and in the back of my mind, I'd still believed that he could protect me.

But as I examine the situation now, I realize I'd been wrong.

Even Samuel can't win with these odds. These angels have the same strengths that he does, and he's outnumbered. My heart sinks quickly in my chest.

I'm going to fail.

Samuel studies me intently. "Whitney. What am I?"

What the heck?

"You're a guardian." I murmur.

"That's right." And he smiles his brilliant, dazzling smile, which fills the entire cabin with light.

Every recess of the room is now revealed to me- every corner, every crevice, every crack.

Two other gigantic warrior angels are hanging from the back corners of the ceiling.

They drop lightly to their feet and stand shoulder to shoulder with Samuel. They'd moved so quickly that I didn't even register it as they crossed the room.

"Your mom and Ellie have them, too."

He'd just leveled the playing field.   My breath whooshes out of my chest.

Samuel grins at me and then turns back to Brady.

As he faces him, his smile changes into something deadly. It reflects off the sword that he's suddenly holding in his hand.

 Brady unexpectedly lunges at Samuel. I gasp, but Samuel had been waiting for it.

He blocks Brady's advance smoothly and easily. Only the metallic sound of their heavy swords smashing together in deafening clangs reveal the lethal seriousness of the situation. Samuel's face is impassive and calm while Brady's is twisted with malice.

They back out of the room and up the stairs, their muscles straining as they lunge at each other- back and forth- as they go. Thrust and parry.

 I quickly shift my gaze to the other two guardians. Large and ominous, they each squarely face the two remaining fallen angels. I smile.

I like these odds.

They simultaneously charge at each other, crashing together in mid-air. Two of them fly up through the ceiling- throwing the top of the boat to the side like it's cardboard. The boat rocks perilously from side to side in response, and water pours in from the rip in the sidewall.

Water pouring in on me. This is my nightmare.

The sun is completely gone now and the moonlight casts an eerie blue light onto the hull, just like in my dream.

The bluish light covered everything, the night engulfing me. I've never liked being on the water at night... the darkness hides too much. And I hadn't known the half of it before.

The lake is black glass around us, the night even darker above us. Samuel's in the air- his sword ringing as it connects with Brady's. I can't even see the other four angels.

Ellie absorbs everything in horror as my mother's hand remains locked around her arm like a steel tentacle, holding her firmly in place on the couch. Malphas' eyes glitter from behind my mother's. I can see the evil there and I know it isn't my mother.

But Ellie doesn't.

"Ellie, this isn't mom. It only looks like her. You have to trust me."

I know that Malphas can't physically hold her there. It's against the rules. The only way they'd gotten Ellie to go with them was to trick her.

If she gets up to come to me, Malphas can't restrain her.

But she thinks 's with mom. I feel sick. If I can't convince her to abandon mom and come to me, it's over.

I look around. Water is flooding the bottom of the boat. It's past my ankles now.

"Ellie, I don't know what she means." My mother's normal voice comes from her lips, her eyes turned towards

Ellie, maternal and soft. "Your sister is confused. You've got to stay with me. I'll keep you safe."

I fully understand now what Samuel had meant when he tried to explain how demons could manipulate us into hurting ourselves. I feel like someone had just poured ice water down my back.

My mother turns her face slowly back toward me and Malphas' eyes glint sadistically in the moonlight. The hair raises on my neck.

I take a step toward them, not knowing what I'm going to do. Until I realize that I'm still holding the disc. It's the only leverage that I have. How can I use it?

My eyes flit around the vicinity, taking everything in as I try to formulate a plan.

"Whittie…" Ellie's voice is uncertain.

Of course it is. She's six years old. To her, a mother's directive is absolute, unarguable. And a mother is someone who would never, ever hurt her. She has no way of comprehending what's going on here. She's not not equipped to understand and frankly, I'm not sure I am, either.

"Ellie, please, it isn't safe here. You need to come to me. You know you can trust me. You know that I protect you. Whose bed do you sleep in?"

I watch her consider what I'm saying.

She takes a hesitant step toward me, until Malphas draws her back in with my mother's sweet voice.

"Ellie, the boat isn't safe. Look at the water pouring in! Stay with me. You can't cross the boat. Any movement might sink it. I'll keep you safe." As he blatantly lies, Malphas turns his face halfway toward me again, just enough for me to see my mother's familiar smile.

I quickly discard caution and rush across the boat, grabbing Ellie's arm. I tug her toward me. I knew Malphas can't stop me- his weapon is manipulation. He can't use physical force.

"Ellie, we have to go. Now!" She comes with me, but looks over her shoulder at mom with a look of pitiful despair on her face. I don't want to leave mom here, either. But I can't get through to her- I can't break Malphas' hold. My priority *has* to be saving my sister. I know mom would want that.

The water is above my knees now and getting higher by the second. The boat is sinking- I can feel it dropping in the water. I have a vision of Ellie's hand floating on top of the water.

No. Not today. Not ever.

I plow through the water and dig through a cabinet on the side of the room. I pull out a life-jacket and strap it on Ellie.

"We're going to swim. Okay?   You can doggie paddle if you have to, but we have to swim. You can do this, okay?" She nods but keeps looking past me to where my mom is standing in water almost to her waist.

The boat tilts as it sinks, just like in my dream. I fight to find traction as my feet slip and slide along the smooth, water-covered floor. Malphas pastes a terrified expression on mom's face.

"Girls, help me!" She cries as the water rushes around her. She reaches out to us with helpless arms.

Ellie unhesitatingly lunges out of my arms to get to her, with the unconditional love of a child. She can't see the evil glint that shines from mom's eyes as Malphas looks at me.

"No!" I scream, just as the floor beneath me trembles when Samuel and Brady's full weight drops from the sky onto the hull of the boat.

The force of their landing knocks me to into the side of the boat, slamming my head into the jagged remainder of a wall. My surroundings blur for a second as the impact stuns me. I lean into the wreckage as I fight to clear my vision. I can feel warm blood trickling down the side of my face.

"Whitney, get your sister and swim!" Samuel's deep voice commands my attention.

I stare up at him. He and Brady are balanced with perfect agility on the slippery fiberglass as they face each other like hungry, bloody gladiators.

Abruptly, Brady turns to me and straightens out of his predatory crouch. He grins widely at me, his teeth gleaming in the moonlight, as he very deliberately plunges his sword into the bow of the boat.

As he pulls it out, water immediately fills the gaping hole, causing the boat to sink at a faster pace. Samuel knocks him off the boat and they continue their battle in the water next to us- hovering just over the surface.

In the chaos, I hear my mother's voice.

"Ellie, take off your life jacket. It'll make it easier for Mommy to help you swim."

I scream again in horror as I watch Ellie's small fingers obeying Malphas... as they quickly unclasp the buckle holding her lifejacket in place as the water swirls around her. I fight my way through the waist-high water to get to her.

But she's gone.

Water rushes in from every direction and too many things from the cabin are floating all around me. Cushions, cups, stray life jackets... I can't see well enough in the dark, so I just start feeling around with my hands as I struggle to work my way through the wreckage.

On the fringes of my consciousness, I register the sound of a motor, but I can't focus on it. I can't imagine the need for a motor now- the boat's going down. It's not going to do any good. The only place the *Crazy Fate* is going is to the bottom of Lake Michigan.

I dive down and feel around on the floor of the boat for Ellie. She's nowhere to be found. As I sputter through the surface of the water, I see my mom perched on the tip of the bow watching me helplessly hunt for her daughter, her face twisted into a sadistic smile.

"Mom!" I scream. "I know you are in there. Help me... please!"

Malphas smiles maliciously and I know that I'm alone. His hold on her is too strong.

I continue diving, emerging empty handed time and time again. Ellie's here. I know she's here. She couldn't have drifted too far.

I push my way to the back of the boat and my foot kicks something. I stop moving.

I know from my dream what's going to happen next.

A small white hand floats to the surface.

I scream and grab it, yanking Ellie to the surface.

Her face is pale, her eyes are closed. I know without even checking that she's not breathing.

I push her against the side of the boat, trying to balance her on the edge while I give her CPR. It doesn't work well. She keeps slipping to the side and I have to keep hefting her weight back up. I breathe into her little mouth and give her five chest compressions, as best I can. Is it supposed to be ten? I can't think straight.

"Whitney!"

A familiar voice breaks through my frantic concentration with a shout.

I look up from my sister's lifeless form to find Carter steering a boat right up alongside the wreckage of the *Crazy Fate*. His boat bumps into ours, the sound of the motor loudly drowning out Malphas' shrieks of rage. It was his motor I'd heard.

"Give her to me!"

Carter leans toward me and holds out his arms. I hesitate. Samuel had told me that things aren't what they seem. How can I be certain that Carter isn't a part of this whole thing, too?

I hesitate another second.

"Whitney! Give her here! Your boat is sinking! I can help her better on this one!"

I know he's right. I can't give her CPR properly on the rail of a sinking boat. If she stays with me, she'll die for certain.

With Carter, at least she'll have a chance.

I hand over her limp body to his waiting arms. He immediately lays her flat on the floor of his boat and begins chest compressions. I scramble over the rail and into his boat, kneeling to breathe into her mouth.

"Please, please breathe. Ellie… please," I beg between each breath.

My panic and fear make my words practically incoherent. It sounds like I'm chanting instead. The blood from my head smears on my arms and drips down onto Ellie. I give her another breath and am startled to hear a small gurgling cough in response.

I pulled back quickly as Ellie's eyes flutter open.

She spits water out of her mouth as she sits up coughing.

Carter pounds on her back, and sits her upright. She turns her head and abruptly vomits what must be two gallons of water.

My sister is breathing.

Carter isn't one of them.

The realization of these things leave my knees weak with relief.

"Get the disc!" Samuel is suddenly directly over my head.

In my desperation to save my sister, I forgotten the battle raging around me.

"Whitney, get the disc and hand it to Carter. Now!"

Brady swings his heavy sword around once again, and Samuel lunges backward to avoid the impact.

I look in the direction that Samuel had gestured to... and find the disc wedged in the broken wall of the cabin. I jump overboard and swim toward it, pulling it loose. It's cold and heavy in my hands, so heavy that it's difficult to swim with it.

I manage to get close enough to Carter's boat to thrust it with all my strength over the side. I hear the heavy thunk that it makes as it falls to the floor. I cling to the side of the boat in relief.

Carter picks it up and stares upwards at Samuel in disbelief, as I climb in beside him.

I can only imagine what he's thinking as he witnesses firsthand the presence of a heavenly creature. Watching enormous angels battling in the sky above him is quite the initiation. My introduction to their world had been calm and tranquil compared to this.

"I have it!" he yells to Samuel. Of course, he has no idea what *it* was. He stands motionlessly waiting for further instruction. He seems to innately understand that Samuel is to be trusted.

Samuel heaves his sword like a javelin at the side of the Crazy Fate, which is only just visible under the surface of the water. It'll be just a couple more minutes before it drifts quickly toward the bottom of the lake to join the thousands of other shipwrecks that are hidden there.

Samuel's sword strikes its mark like an arrow in a bull's eye, the handle standing tall and straight through the surface of the water.

"Break it! Use the sword!" Samuel bellows from high above us, before he turns to defend himself against Brady with his bare hands. I inhale sharply. This isn't good. He's unarmed.

Carter leans over and extracts the enormous, heavy sword from the boat with a great deal of effort. I watch his muscles flex as he wrestles to free it. Malphas is in the lake now, treading water next to the sinking wreck.

"Samuel," he rasps loudly. "You can't destroy it. Only one person can do that- and she isn't here!" He cackles loudly in triumph. My mother's face is smug and confident as Malphas' eyes glint in the dark.

"You're right. She isn't." Samuel's voice is loud and clear, his own expression confident as he stares pointedly at Carter.

"But a member of her bloodline is."

I look in shock at Carter, who stands in confusion, clutching the sword in his hands.

He has no idea what that means. Or what it means to me… that the dark plot which had loomed around my life for the past two years has been intercepted by good.

Carter had been placed into my life for a reason- to protect me from evil. My plan is becoming visible for me to see and it astounded me with its intensity.

"DO IT NOW!" Samuel booms in a voice loud enough to be heard in Heaven itself.

Carter tosses the disc in the air and while it spins like a heavy coin, he impales it with Samuel's spear, groaning with the effort.

The marble breaks into seven separate pieces as light explodes all around us. Horrible keening screeches split the nigh, and I realize with a shudder that the terrifying screams are coming from the disc pieces.

I watch as they land one by one in the water, immediately sinking. I envision them drifting to the bottom of the lake floor and settling into the murky caliginous depths.

They're gone.

Carter drops the sword on the floor of his boat and limply stands in place, panting from exertion. Samuel lands abruptly beside me, as Eligor, Procel and Lillith remain frozen in the air, all wearing expressions of shock.

"This isn't over," Eligor growls at Samuel.

I find that I can think of him as Eligor now. But before I can think anything else, they're gone. All three of them had vanished into the night.

I immediately locate my mother's inert form floating in the water.

I see the tip of a slithering black tail disappear into the water behind her, like a crocodile diving into a river. Carter dives from the boat, rapidly swimming to reach her. He hauls her back to safety, his strong hands clasps under her arms. She offers no resistance- she isn't conscious.

Samuel leans over and lifts her into the boat, laying her beside Ellie. Ellie grabs her hand as Samuel looks at me. "She'll be fine now. Malphas is gone."

I feel the last pieces of my plan click into place.

Chapter Twenty-Four

We take my mother back to the clinic, where Samuel assumes the appearance of Dr. Parker, just for a while.

We tuck my mother back into her bed and wait while she resumes consciousness. It doesn't take long. She opens her eyes, gazing around in confusion. Samuel had been right. She has no recollection of anything.

"Where am I?" Her soft eyes are perplexed.

I whisper assurances and then squeeze her arm gently; leaving 'Dr. Parker' to explain that she had been deeply depressed and had required hospitalization. I can't bring myself to stay and hear the lies. As guilty as I feel about lying to her, we know it's better that she doesn't know the truth- that she had been overcome by a demon and had almost killed her daughters. Nothing good could come from that. She's suffered enough already.

I find Carter in the room next to my mother's, sitting next to Ellie's sleeping form. She'd fallen asleep on the way to the clinic, the trauma of everything sapping every bit of her energy. Carter's dark eyes meet mine as I softly enter the room.

"Thank you," I murmur, putting my hand lightly on his shoulder. "For everything. You saved all of us tonight."

He smiles lightly. "Well, I had to find some way to make you forgive me, didn't I?"

Warmth spreads through me, leaving my fingers feeling tingly. I'd been right - he really does have a nice smile. It feels nice to be on the receiving end of it.

His expression changes to a serious one.

"Whitney, I'm pretty sure I'm not crazy. Or at least, I didn't used to be."

This time I'm the one smiling. I clearly remember that feeling- of trying to talk myself into believing that I was sane.

"Can you tell me what the heck happened tonight?"

"I'll try. But first- can *you* tell me how you knew that I needed help?" I'm confused about that part. Apparently, so is he- because he looks at me bewilderedly.

"Um, because you told me?" He digs into his pocket and pulls out his phone.

A text from my phone reads, *I need help in the bay. Hurry!*

I know that the overwhelming shock that I feel is reflected on my face.

"You didn't send it?" He's even more confused. I shake my head. My phone isn't even with me. It's on the seat in my mom's car.

"Well, I went flying out there, just in time to see a 60 ft. boat drifting out to open water. I just somehow knew it was you. I can't even explain it."

Yep, I know that feeling, too.

I feel Samuel's sudden presence. I turn to face him and his appearance as Dr. Parker unnerves me, causing me to take a step backward.

"Can you--" I start, but before I can even finish my sentence, my normal Samuel is standing in front of us, staring at me with aquamarine eyes. They shimmer once and I can see Carter doing a double-take. I smile. It's entertaining to watch my reactions on someone else's face.

"Thanks."

Samuel flashes a grin at me. "I told you that you have a plan."

I roll my eyes. "And didn't I tell you that I'm sick of hearing about it?"

He laughs and once again I feel like everything good in the world is surrounding me. My chest vibrates with the resonance of his heavenly grace. I can't help but laugh too.

As I glance over at Carter, he has the most bewildered look on his face as he laughs right along with us. No one is immune to it, apparently.

"Your mom is asking for you, Whitney," Samuel says. "She doesn't remember a thing."

I nod. "Can you…" I glance at Carter.

"Yes. I'll explain. What I can, anyway." I roll my eyes again and leave while Samuel starts at the beginning for Carter's benefit.

My mom is watching the door anxiously. As I walk in, her face visibly relaxes and she reaches for me. I bend down and hug her, overwhelmingly grateful that she's back to herself.

"Honey… I'm so sorry. I don't know how I let myself become so depressed. I'm a doctor; I should have recognized the signs…." Her thin voice trails off. "Dr. Parker said that you took care of me like a protective mama bear." She smiles gently. "Thank you, Whit. I don't deserve you."

I feel another tug of guilt for not sharing the truth. But I know that it needs to remain hidden. If she knew everything, it'd only make her feel worse.

"Mom- it's okay. You don't need to apologize. Everything is going to be fine now. You're going to get better. In fact, Dr. Parker thinks that you can come home tomorrow morning after you get a good night's rest." Her face brightens and she tugs me down for another hug.

"Is your sister okay? Where is she?" My mom's voice is thick with concern. I take a deep breath. I can never tell my mother that she had tried to kill Ellie.

"She's fine. She's sleeping. I told her that your mind was hibernating like a bear so that you could get better." The relief on mom's face is as apparent as her concern. We'd definitely done the right thing in not revealing everything.

"Whitney, you're so grown up. Your dad would be so proud of you." She closes her eyes for a minute and I can see the weariness on her face. I bend down and gave her another hug.

"You've got to get some sleep and then tomorrow you can go home!"

She smiles and nods, already curling up onto ball. I pull her covers up and creep out, relief beginning to sink in.

It's really over. I had won.

I walk into Ellie's room just in time to hear Carter ask, "So I'm really a descendent of Mary Magdalene?" His voice is full of wonder and Samuel nods.

"When did you know, anyway?" I ask as I move to stand next to them.

"I knew as soon as I saw him on the beach that day."

"The day my dad drowned?"

He nods again. I gulp. It's mind-boggling. He had known way back then... he just hadn't known how it would all fit together. He had absolute faith that it would somehow fit together with all of the other pieces of my plan. The quiet dignity and faith of an angel presents itself to me again for perusal. I envy him for having that calm sense that everything would, in the end, work together for good.

Suddenly a thought enters my mind as clearly as if someone had dropped it there.

If my dad hadn't saved Carter, then Carter wouldn't have been able to save my family tonight. He would've drowned that day instead. Apparently, Carter is one of the only people on the face of planet able to destroy that disc.

And that had saved us all.

"Samuel? My dad had a plan, too, didn't he?" My voice is breathless. "Part of his plan was to save his family… by saving Carter." It's not really a question. I know it's true. I guess I just want a confirmation.

Samuel nods. I can see the satisfaction on his face that I'd put it together.

"Whitney, everyone has a plan. Every single soul alive on earth right now has a plan. Your dad's plan- the final parts of it- were put into motion the second that they unearthed that disc. Yes, he died so that you can live. But don't mourn that. It wasn't a sacrifice.

"Your dad knowingly went into the water to save a perfect stranger, because that is just the kind of man that your father was. If he had known that he needed to perform that one act in order to save his family, he would've been there waiting at the break of dawn to make sure he wasn't late. You, your mom and Ellie were everything to him." As I listen to Samuel's deep voice, I know he's right.

Strangely, I don't feel sad. My dad was more of a hero than anyone will ever know.

The way the pieces of our individual plans had all worked together was confounding. I can hardly wrap my mind around the intricacy of it all. It's like someone had simply braided separate strands of a tapestry together and everything had come together perfectly.

There was a reason for my dad's death. And that's infinitely comforting. For weeks after it happened, I had railed against fate for taking my dad for no good reason. But I can stop. There had been a reason. And I know that if he were given a choice, my dad would do it again and again and again in order to keep us safe.

And then I remember the text to Carter.

"Samuel, how did Carter get the text to help me? I didn't send it- my phone was in the car!" I wait for an answer. But Samuel's back to his old tricks. He just grins mysteriously.

I shake my head. "Don't you think that it's a small enough thing to explain?" Angel rules seriously get on my nerves.

"I'm just playing with you, Whitney."

A joke? He can't be serious. He never joked. He laughs again at my incredulous face.

"Angels have great senses of humor, Whitney," he announces grinning. Yeah, I bet. I can't help but grin back. I have the feeling that I'd lucked out in the angel department.

"The text?" I remind him.

"I block your cell signal when I'm in human form. I don't block it when I am in my natural state."

"Okay. But how did you send the text?" I stop speaking when I notice that he's already shaking his head.

"Just tricks of the trade."

So, apparently he can manipulate technology from remote locations. Interesting.

"I don't understand, though…what about Brady? He called me all of the time from a cell phone while he was human."

Samuel shakes his head again- as if he's marveling over my limited human brain power.

"Whitney, what makes you think that he was human when he was talking to you?"

Oh my gosh, he's right. I'd only pictured Brady as human because that was what I expected him to be- but obviously I'd been talking and texting with a fallen angel.

I shiver and a cold chill runs down my back.

Carter notices, and walks to my side, putting his arm around my shoulders.

His warmth soothes me. I feel comfortable here, in the crook of his arm, as though it's where I'm meant to be. And I have a strange feeling that's was exactly the case.

I smile at the turn of events. Yesterday Brady had been a near-perfect wonderful guy who I was content to spend every waking minute with.

Today, I know that Carter had been the one all along- the one who was meant to be in my life. The one who was meant to save it.

It's astonishing. And it feels so completely right in the way that only things that are meant to be do.

"What about my grandparents?"

"Take Ellie and run along back home. After your mother goes to sleep, I'll move them into her room and then 'Dr. Parker' will wake them up. They'll think that they just fell asleep while they were sitting with your mom."

"And Ellie?" My eyes are sharply inquisitive.

"I promise you that when Ellie wakes up tomorrow, she won't remember much of anything about tonight. If she remembers anything at all, she'll just attribute to a nightmare." I know that's right. She's accustomed to nightmares.

Carter helps me load Ellie into my mom's little car and then he rides with me to my house.

He carries her up to my room for me and stands in the doorway as I tuck her into my bed.

There's no way I'm putting her in her own room tonight. I need to feel her warm, safe body near me. I tuck the covers in around her and stand watching her sleep for a minute. Her little fingers are clutched into loose fists as she sleeps heavily already.

I join Carter in the doorway and then lead the way downstairs to my porch swing.

Carter sits next to me in silence. The quiet isn't tense- it's as comfortable as an old pair of jeans. I know he's going over everything in his head, so I don't interrupt.

I just listen to the crickets chirp from the side of the porch and enjoy the soft breeze lifting my hair back from my face as the wind kicks up. I study the stars twinkling in the sky.

"Your mom is still there, you know," I murmur to him as I gaze above us. "I don't know where Heaven is, but I know that it *is* there…somewhere. And your mom… and my dad… they're both there right now."

The overwhelming sadness that I've felt for weeks is gone and I want to share that peace with Carter. He looks at me with his dark gaze, nodding.

"I know. I feel it, too. Whitney, am I crazy to say that I was meant to meet you? That it feels like all of this was meant to happen?"

I shake my head.

"I know it was. Everything that happened tonight was in my plan. And your plan. Our plans are connected."

And tonight they had collided.

"Before I met you, I was so angry. I was angry at my mom, I was angry at my dad for letting her die, I was angry at God…and I was angry with myself."

Carter's voice trembles and I grip his arm gently. I definitely know how that feels.

"But that's gone now. I don't know why. It just is. I think it has something to do with you."

A sense of peace descends upon my porch that I can't quite explain. We're just two souls who had been shown a small glimpse of the truth. We'd been able to take a tiny peek at the mysteries that surround our world.

Carter puts his arm around my shoulders again, pulling me closer to him. He makes me feel safe and I rest my head on his shoulder.

I smile to myself as I inhale deeply. I feel Samuel's sudden invisible presence and I know that no matter what, everything is going to be all right.

My plan will continue to unfold and pieces will continue to click into place... just like they're meant to do. And now I know that Carter is part of my pieces.

It's a good feeling.

I close my eyes.

I have the rest of my life to discover what else my plan will bring.

In the meantime, I have Carter.

And Samuel.

I feel his presence hovering nearby, and his familiar peace settles around me.

My guardian.

Everybody has one.

I glance over to find mine smiling in the dark.

He'll protect me for all of my days.

It's a fact that makes me smile, too.

The End

About the Author

Courtney Cole is the New York Times Bestselling author of the Beautifully Broken series.

She was born and raised in Kansas, lived the next portion of her life near Lake Michigan, and now resides in sunny Florida. To learn more about her, please visit her blog at www.courtneycolewrites.com or her website, www.courtneycoleauthor.com